A GLIMPSE INTO THE BEYOND

Alan MacDougall crouched before the aperture he had just discovered in the inner wall of the ruined tower and looked through.

A spectacular auroral display met his eyes. Brilliant rays darted from a black zenith, lengthening and shortening, advancing and retreating, all in ceaseless motion. On the misty horizon he saw what looked like a city of white, tinged with icy green and glittering like a multi-faceted crystal.

He stepped through the opening and felt a momentary vertigo. He turned around—and the stone tower was now a ghost of its former solid structure. Then he swung back as he heard the distant sound of bells and the muffled beat of horses' hooves. Coming toward him around a steep slope was a caravan of robe-clad men on horseback—led by a woman in flowing white garments.

Mirage, Alan told himself—or madness!

The Land Beyond The Gate

Lloyd Arthur Eshbach

A Del Rey Book

BALLANTINE BOOKS • NEW YORK

Dedicated to the memory of
William W. Sharp,
who, writing as
Fiona MacLeod,
awakened my interest in
Celtic fantasy and, more
directly, inspired this tale.

CONTENTS

The Singing Blades

On still and starlit nights, when warm breezes whisper over Scottish moors, stroking the benty blue grass and caressing the heather, one can hear the singing blades. High and clear, yet faint as an elfin sound, their song rises from the shores of a woodland burn or a hidden loch— high and clear, like the chime of distant bells. Yet, oddly enough, the eerie melody is heard only by those who do not seek it. When one listens, it dies in the solitude of lonely hills.

At other times can the song of the blades be heard. When the wind blows cold and keen and shrill from the gray North Sea, moaning and whistling through the rocky heights, when gales buffet the wintry waves and tatters of surf scud across bleak, forbidding shores—then do the singing blades ring joyously in the Highlands.

And hearing it, the old Highlanders say: "D'ye hear? The little auld folk 'neath the heather bells are havin' their fill o' fechtin'!"

It was not always so. Once the song of the blades was stilled, and only the sound of the wind swept through the valleys and across the fens and marshes. Then Malcolm MacDougall came to Scotland seeking ancient things...

Malcolm MacDougall made his way through the utter quiet of the oak forest that fringed the blue expanse of the Highland loch. Perfume rose faintly to his nostrils from the water lilies in the marshy edge of the dark lochan. Now and again he heard the dim, plaintive cry of a distant curlew. But the thoughts of Malcolm MacDougall were not of the wood, the lilies, or the curlew; they were miles behind him in the castle where he had spent the night. He saw again the solemn-faced old caretaker and recalled his somber words of warning as they parted.

"Ye're thinkin' o' wanderin' through yon black hills— so I heard ye tell the laird. 'Tis yer ain business, but I'm thinkin' ye'll regret it." The man shook his silver head dolefully. "'Tis lonely there, laddie—unco' lonely. Na mortal mon will ye find, na beastie nor bird will ye hear, save only the cry o' hoot owls an' the chirpin' o' bats.

"Na, na laddie—stay awa' frae yon black hills. Ye'll find only heaps o' stone that the Pechties built, a bit o' bronze, the scattered bones o' a puir mon dead lang syne. An', perchance, ye'll meet some o' the little brown folk themsel', or the Sidhe, or a ghaist o' an auld Druid hauntin' the wood. Dinna ye go the way ye plan, laddie, for the deil is in yon hills, awaitin' fer sic as ye."

Malcolm MacDougall scanned the gloomy heights before him, the tree-cloaked mount that rose humplike from the southern shore of the loch. It was an ancient oak forest the like of which, he had been told, no longer existed in all of Scotland. He could well understand the superstitious fear that surrounded this ancient spot. Its solitude and the gloom of its heavily wooded slopes were designed to awaken dread in Celtic minds.

Even he could sense the subtle spell of the stillness about him, could feel a weight, vaguely sinister, in the very air of the place. Yet, paradoxically, there was something else—a feeling of familiarity and well-being, as one might feel upon returning to childhood scenes after long years of absence.

It was a strange feeling, for he knew definitely that never before had he seen the shores of the blue lake.

He, his older brother Alan, and their father before them had been born and bred in America. Even his mother, whom he barely remembered since she had died while he was quite young, though Scottish born, had grown up in the States. This was his first trip to Scotland. A love for ancient things had led him to study archaeology and ethnology. And his Scottish ancestry had urged him to peer behind the veil of Scotland's early life. A month of wandering had brought him to the foot of the Highland mountain.

Malcolm saw a narrow, stony path leading up the hillside under the trees and he followed it. It wound around moss-green boulders, into shadowed ravines, and through clumps of thickest woodland—like an ancient stream bed, he thought. Almost, it seemed, he was moving back into an older time.

Low-hanging branches caught at his curly black hair and whipped his slender frame, as if seeking to restrain him. As he penetrated deeper and deeper into the forest, Malcolm was thankful for the first time in his memory for his slight stature, which more than once had been the despair of his tall, raw-boned, sandy-haired father and his even more massive brother. It wasn't his fault that he resembled his fine-drawn, dark-haired mother.

He came at last to an ancient, mighty oak, greater than all its fellows, its trunk as thick as a dozen strong men, and he paused to rest beneath its wide, gnarled branches. Time had not been kind to the forest monarch. Storms and lightning blasts of uncounted centuries had shorn away its crown and splintered its upper trunk, yet it stood undaunted, as eternal, almost, as the mountain that gave it life.

While Malcolm stood there scanning the forest with dark and deep-set eyes, that strange feeling of familiarity returned with overwhelming force.

Once before he had stood in the shelter of this very tree, watching for savage, bearded men who crept stealthily through the forest. There had been fighting that day, joyous battle with sword and shield, arrow and bow . . .

Malcolm MacDougall shook his head impatiently. What nonsense was this! He'd been listening too long to senseless superstitions. Yet in spite of himself, the thought persisted.

Scowling, Malcolm started up the rocky path, then stopped short. About three hundred yards to his left, if his memory had not failed him, stood a fortress of stone . . . Memory! What had memory to do with an idea so absurd? He glared into the shadows that lay on every side. This persistent recurrence of pseudo-memories had become quite annoying. He had experienced *déjà vu* before, but never with such startling strength. He'd have to snap out of it.

He hesitated. After all, he had no definite course mapped out, no plan that he must pursue. It wouldn't matter if he did turn aside from this rocky path; and if he failed to find the fort, his mind would be freed of its wild imaginings. With a shrug, he cut across the hillside.

The ground rose gradually beneath him, climbing to form a little hump on the mountain slope. As he pushed through the final barrier of trees and underbrush, his eyes widened, and the short hairs stiffened on the nape of his neck. On the crest of the hillock lay a circular wall of stone, weathered and crumbling—the remains of an ancient fortress of a primitive people!

For an instant, Malcolm MacDougall stood stock still, his mind filled with a great wonder and a feeling of unreality. Coincidence? Impossible. This fort was exactly like the one he had—remembered, save that this was much older, marred by the touch of time.

Slowly he climbed over the rough stone barrier and stood in a round clearing on a carpet of peat moss, thickly spread by centuries of growth. This was not as he recalled it. There had been smooth, flat stones underfoot, roughly fitted together, with earth-filled spaces between them. He frowned as hidden cords tugged at forgotten memories...

At the foot of yonder wall he had—he had buried his sword! Wounded, he had lain there awaiting capture or death and had thrust his blade beneath a flat rock so that it might not fall into enemy hands...

Grimly Malcolm MacDougall stared around the fortress, his brain a seething battlefield for warring skepticism and unwilling belief. Then, abruptly, he dropped to his knees at the base of the wall and began to dig with his fingers in the layer of moss. It was deep—too deep for such digging.

He swung his pack from his back and brought out a little, pointed spade. He set to work with this and in moments heard it rasp against rock. Impatiently he dropped the tool and worked his fingertips into a narrow crevice. He felt them grip a rough edge of stone and he gave a sudden, sharp upward heave, wrenching back a great slab of weathered gray slate.

He crouched unmoving while for an instant his heart seemed to stop; then it thudded against his ribs, and a strange, wild exultation leaped up within him. For there, in a matrix of black earth, lay his sword!

He stared at it with mixed emotions, examining it simultaneously with the eye of an antiquarian and with the gaze of this strange throwback who recognized the blade as his own. Despite its green patina of age, the bronze sword was a thing of beauty, a perfect piece of workmanship, double-edged and small, almost like a toy. Nothing could be finer than its simple symmetry. It expanded from the hilt toward the center, then narrowed quickly to a long, sharp point. It resembled a leaf wrought in imperishable metal. But most unusual was its grip—a haft too short to be held with comfort.

Once before he had seen a weapon like this; it had lain on a plush bed in an Edinburgh museum. And even then, he recalled, he had sensed something vaguely familiar about the blade.

Malcolm grasped the bronze sword. As he straightened, his mind and his sight seemed to blur. An instant of complete blankness, then...

He spun to face the slope below the fort. A fog had risen—it had come up from the lake without hint or warning—and it would hide the accursed Goidel, creeping up the hillside, darting from tree to tree. Dimly he could see movement in the thick underbrush. Arrows sang past his ears, some speeding down the slope, others darting out of the mist and shadows and leaping toward the fort. He had lost his bow and shield, but none could pass his sword!

Now the Goidel charged! Out of the fog they came; he saw their faces, their great swinging blades. They were giants, mighty-thewed, brutish, twice the size of himself and his comrades. They must not pass the wall! Shouting, he sprang to the top of the barrier...

And as the blurring of his sight had come, so did it go. Malcolm MacDougall realized suddenly that he stood upright upon the wall, the ancient sword raised high above his head. The mist had vanished, and of savage foemen there was no trace.

Weakly, Malcolm dropped back within the fort. Lord— but that had seemed real! He felt his legs trembling with relaxing tension, and perspiration moistened the palms of his hands, his brows, and his upper lip. Striving to check the hammering of his pulse, he gazed out over the valley. Below him, as serene as a landscape on canvas, stretched the Highland wilderness. Beyond, the sun glinted on the placid expanse of the loch. All was peaceful, save his own mind.

Had he actually experienced these things, been in this very spot, in some former existence? Reincarnation—was that the answer? How else could he explain these—memories, the finding of the sword?

He thought of the Celtic bard Taliesin, who had written: "I have been a light in a lantern a year and a half, I have been a bridge for passing over threescore rivers, I have been a director in battle, I have been a sword in the hand, I have been the string of a harp. There is nothing in which I have not been." Nor was Taliesin alone among the Celts in his beliefs. As a people, they found spirits in trees, gods in stones, and mystery everywhere.

Absurd? How could he say so in the light of what had happened?

His gaze fixed itself on a huge boulder jutting from the slope below the fort, and a curious frown appeared on his face. In his vision, the—the Goidel had seemed to be giants, twice his size. Yet he had seen one passing that boulder, and his head had been lower than the top of the great stone—and the boulder stood no more than six feet high! How could Malcolm account for this contradiction in size? Was it the vagary of a dream—or something beyond his present knowledge?

Still puzzled, MacDougall turned away and continued up the side of the mountain, plunging deeper into the Highlands. The bronze sword, wiped clean of earth, was at his side, thrust within his belt. And, strangely, it gave him a feeling of security and confidence greater than he had ever known, as if it were a well of strength from which he could draw at will.

The sun hung low in the west when he decided to make camp for the night. He stopped in a little natural clearing on the bank of a nameless mountain stream, built a fire, and prepared a simple meal. After he had eaten, he sat with his back against a boulder and stared into the embers, his mind busy with the experiences of the day. Abruptly he realized that his hands, without conscious direction, were polishing his sword on the cloth of his jacket—

polishing with a practiced touch, as if they had done it countless times before!

He heard a faint rumble of sound in the north and looked up. Darkness had crept over the eastern sky, deepening the shadows under the great trees. And a deeper darkness was rising out of the North Sea.

After that initial roll of thunder, a tense, dead silence fell. Malcolm listened with all his senses, alive to the gathering of nature's forces. He heard the gentle splashing of the little stream; there was no other sound. No breath of air stirred on the mountainside; the leaves of the oaks hung limp and heavy; no slender blade of grass moved. Even his own breathing slowed under the weight of a mounting tension. Then again from the north rumbled the faint, dull booming of thunder.

He saw, at the limit of his vision, a low bush dip its head toward him, solemnly, like one announcing an honored guest. Then a wave of rustling and sighing swept through all the forest, and the lull and frozen stillness fled before a cool wind. He heard the faint murmur and moan of the breeze, searching, like a grieving mother, in deep ravines, rocky crags, and every dark and shadowed place.

Now a bank of clouds swept hugely out of the north. It was a monstrous thing of angry purple and black, a bulging, mushrooming, lumbering thing, heavy with storm. It rolled ponderously across the sky, as if all the power of every wind of earth were pushing and piling behind it.

A serpent's tongue of lightning lashed out of the black mass in a momentary flare of light. As it died, there broke upon the slopes a mighty rumble, a bursting blast of sound. It was like the sound of a gigantic boulder rolling and bounding down the mountainside, banging and booming from crag and rampart to vanish in the deeps of the distant valley.

Malcolm MacDougall leaped to his feet, aroused by the thunder from his sensuous enjoyment of the approaching storm. Once before he had weathered a Highland tempest without shelter, and it hadn't been pleasant.

He glanced around, seeking a possible refuge. As clearly as if he saw it with his physical eye, he pictured a great round tower higher on the mountain... *Home of the Goidel—place of sorceries*... Like a whisper, only half heard, the thought passed through his mind.

For an instant Malcolm hesitated. Should he trust these "memories"? Then a sudden recklessness swept over him, and he laughed joyously, without conscious reason. Why not? This knowledge of things that he could not know had not failed him thus far; he'd follow its guidance wherever it might lead!

Quickly he stamped out his little fire, made up his pack, and flung it over his shoulder. With his sword at his side, he started up the flank of the mountain.

A low roar rose all around him, and the oak leaves soughed in the rising wind. There came gusts of greater violence, and at shortening intervals he felt sudden whirling currents of air that gave promise of mightier blasts to follow. The clouds sped to engulf the horizon, rolling swiftly, bending the treetops, and twilight merged with the growing darkness. The last bit of blue sky yielded to the angry surf of cloud racing like a tide beyond the peak, and black night enfolded the world.

Guided only by instinct and that uncanny memory of his, Malcolm MacDougall made his way through the forest. And at last, even as the first drops of rain spattered around him, he saw a square of light glimmering through the trees and he came to the tower he had expected to find. A flash of lightning at that instant revealed it clearly, rising before him like a remnant of a Gothic castle.

It was circular, built on a broad base, and tapering upward with a graceful curve. Malcolm had seen others of these structures—called by the old Scots "Pictish towers"; *brochs* to the antiquarian—but this was by far the largest, all of thirty feet broad at the base. Shelter—yet its windowless walls looked somehow forbidding, awakening instinctive dread... It seemed that he had known it and shunned it in an earlier day.

With a shrug Malcolm darted to the low, square door-way from which wavering light streamed. He reached it and was crouching to enter before it occurred to him to wonder at that light. Someone either lived within or, like him, had sought shelter from the storm.

He passed through a tunnel about six feet in length; and as he straightened inside the tower, MacDougall's gaze fell upon a log fire burning brightly in a stone fire-place set in the opposite wall. Its flickering light glinted ruddily upon a long row of leaf-shaped swords exactly like his own and on a row of small, round shields, all of brightly polished bronze. He noted this in a single startled instant. Then he turned hastily as a faint footfall sounded on the smooth flagstone floor.

"Hello!" he exclaimed.

A slow-moving figure emerged from the shadows be-side the doorway, leaving a crude oaken table at which the man had been sitting. He was extraordinarily tall, towering head and shoulders above Malcolm, and he was thin, a menacing figure cowled in a robe of black. Fierce eyes, so bright as to seem burning, glared from a face of frosty pallor.

"Hello," MacDougall repeated. "Sorry to intrude, but I couldn't find any other shelter, so I dashed in here to get out of the storm."

He could hear the fury of the tempest outside, the infernal din of thunder, the keening, shrilling voice of the gale, muffled only by the thick stone wall. Then he re-alized that he had received no answer and that the tall man stood motionless, staring fixedly into his eyes with those fiery orbs.

For a long, uneasy moment MacDougall waited; then he said with an attempt at lightness, "Maybe you don't understand English, so if you'll just give me a hint, I'll try to talk your language."

Still those strange eyes stared unwaveringly, and the tall figure did not stir. Only his shadow, a grotesque, misshapen thing cast by the flickering flames, moved with

the rise and fall of the light. MacDougall's uneasiness gave
way to dread as the moments passed. The man must be
mad—and he wished now that he had remained out there
in the wind and rain under the oak trees! From the corner
of his eye he glimpsed a long sword on the wall above
the heavy table and he wondered what he'd do if the other
decided to use it.

At last the tall man spoke, his voice hoarse and throaty,
as if it had not been used for a long, long time; his words
were in a tongue that MacDougall had never heard. Or
had he? It had a strangely familiar ring, as if it were a
language he should remember.

"Sorry," he said, "but that's all Greek to me."

The tall man spoke again, and MacDougall started. The
words were in Latin, but a Latin that was a living tongue,
spoken as it must have been in ancient Rome, not stiff
and mechanical as his own Latin must be.

"Who are you who comes to disturb Caermarthen, the
last Druid? Know you not that men shun the gaze of a
Druid's eye?"

"I am Malcolm MacDougall and I'm sorry if I have
disturbed you. If I may, I would remain until the storm
has passed."

His thoughts raced. Caermarthen, the last Druid! He
had heard of a book, *The Black Book of Caermarthen*,
which reputedly had been written by a Druidic bard. But
that person lived thirteen centuries ago. Druidism itself
was dead...Fervently he wished he were miles away,
anywhere out of the reach of this madman.

He thought wryly of the old caretaker's words: "The
deil is in yon hills, awaitin' fer sic as ye." He had spoken
the truth.

"You must leave," the self-styled Druid said in a voice
as forbidding as the moan and rumble of the storm. "I
want no visitors. Go now, or—" He broke off abruptly
and thrust out a long, bony finger. His eyes glared redly.
"The sword! The sword! You have found it!"

Involuntarily MacDougall fell back, his fingers clutching the hilt of his weapon.

The white face thrust forward hungrily, and the strange eyes burned like living coals in shadowed sockets.

"For thirteen long centuries I have searched upon every hill and through every valley for that blade," he rasped triumphantly, "and now you have brought it to me!"

Malcolm's dark eyes narrowed. He felt a tide of resentment sweeping through his mind. *Who was this man who dared to claim his sword? One of the Goidel, he seemed...And was! He remembered him now—Caermarthen, chief of the blue-skinned marauders! Sorcerer was he, and enemy of the Sidhe—but never would he touch the sword of Cinel Loarn, save to feel its point!...*

MacDougall shook his head dazedly. Those were not his thoughts. But he kept his hand on the hilt of the little weapon.

"This is my sword," he said grimly, "and I plan to keep it."

The fiery eyes met his with savage intensity. There was Satanic wrath in their depths, a hint of something coldly calculating, a suggestion of furtive speculation.

"But I need it—it will complete my collection. Look!" He waved toward the wall above the fireplace.

Careful, Cinel Loarn, came the ghost of a warning thought.

Malcolm turned to examine the array of gleaming bronze he had barely glimpsed upon entering the tower. In perfect alignment the small swords hung from their hilts, thirty or more of them, like soldiers on parade. Above each hung a round bronze shield, only a foot across, and tooled with marvelous artistry into a thing of beauty. For every shield there was a sword—save one. Beneath the disk at the end of the long row gaped a vacant space.

He half turned again toward the cowled figure—and a pair of sinewy arms whipped around him, pinning his arms against his sides. Instinctively he dropped to one knee, reached up, and with a burst of sudden strength flung

Caermarthen over his head. He was on his feet instantly, sword in hand, every muscle tensed.

Hot resentment flared. He had been tricked! This was not to be borne! He watched the tall man crawl erect, and an eagerness, a heady recklessness, tingled within him. He heard a voice like the voice of another speaking within his own mind:

Awaken, Cinel Loarn. Long have you slept. Awaken— and smite this despoiler of the Sidhe!

With the voice, like a resistless tide, a personality swept up from the depths of his subconscious, thrusting back and still farther back the mind and consciousness of Malcolm MacDougall. And he was Cinel Loarn, whom Sidhe and Goidel alike called the Little Fox.

With calculating gaze he watched Caermarthen swaying, half-stunned, fury growing on his bony face. The Druid had slipped from his long robe and flung it aside, and he stood revealed in the loincloth, sandals, and blue tattooing of a Goidel chief. A lightning flash, intensely bright, reflected from a massive, gold, two-headed serpent coiled about his upper right arm, each of the four eyes a different colored gem.

Bellowing, Caermarthen charged across the flagstones to his great sword on the wall above the table. Not bronze, this blade, but shining steel. He wrenched it down and whirled toward the Little Fox.

"Now shall you die," he rasped. "And you and your sword shall hang upon yonder wall!" His tongue was the tongue of the Goidel. And Cinel Loarn answered in the same guttural speech.

"Not so, Blue-belly! Never have ten Goidel been equal to one of the Sidhe!"

His last words were lost in the clash of their swords and a ripping, crashing report that burst simultaneously in the world of storm outside. For moments he fought without hearing the sound of smiting blades, with only bedlam of wind and thunder filling his ears. Then came a lull, and the ringing of bronze against steel rose above the storm.

After the first moments of conflict, Cinel Loarn knew he would be fortunate indeed to conquer Caermarthen. The Goidel rushed in with sweeping cuts that would have shorn his head from his shoulders and with mighty lunges that had force enough to cut him in two. He leaped back, out of reach—but he realized that he would have need of all his skill to avoid that slashing edge. His own blade seemed pitifully small, little more than half the length of Caermarthen's weapon. Yet he smiled as he fought, leaping in, darting away, weaving a veil of singing bronze before the fiery eyes of the Goidel chief.

Back and forth Caermarthen moved, passing slowly to the right, circling about the Little Fox, seeking to penetrate his defense. Cinel Loarn gave ground steadily but kept out of reach of that slashing blade, deflecting thrusts and lunges, avoiding death by fractional inches. He watched every move of his opponent, seeking an opening.

And it came! A vicious swing carried the great blade far to the left, and before the Goidel could recover, Cinel Loarn leaped in. By a hair's breadth the tall man escaped the thrust as he reeled away, but the Little Fox followed so closely that he could not bring his longer weapon into play. Just inside the low doorway, where rain drove inward in slanting sheets, the Druid's sandals slipped on the wet stones, and the blade of Cinel Loarn bit into his shoulder. Caermarthen staggered and fell to the flagging.

Poised for the death thrust, the Little Fox heard a chorused sigh rising from the wall above the fireplace. It was a faint sound, like the whisper of oak leaves under a vagrant breeze, yet he heard it above the lashing of the wind and the drumming of the rain. He looked up at the swords and shields—and his blade sagged limp in his hand.

Where every sword hung was the shadowy form of a man of the Sidhe! And for every shield there was a wraith-like woman! On every face was a look of pleading, of eagerness and—hope—hope awakened by the shed blood!

Swords and men, shields and maids—they were as one. They had hung there for long centuries, bound within their weapons, imprisoned by some ancient wizardry. Red wrath welled within Cinel Loarn, the hot blood pulsing in his temples. They were his brothers, his sisters—these Sidhe whom the Goidel sorcerer had chained! The one there alone was Ethne the Fair—who had been his mate! And Caermarthen had planned to hang him and his blade upon the wall—to complete the collection!

He whirled at a sound, whipping up his weapon barely in time to turn aside a savage blow from the Goidel. Then he leaped far back, again on the defensive. A change had come over the tall man. His left arm dangled as blood ran down from his wounded shoulder, but his sword lashed out with even greater power, driven by a fury of desperation, as if he knew he must win quickly or not at all. Every stroke was a threat of sudden death. And those strokes came swiftly, surely, with a speed amazing for so long a blade.

By a miracle, it seemed, Cinel Loarn kept away from that menacing sword. His arm had lost some of its firmness, and his breath rasped in his throat. The greater strength and size of the Goidel began to tell. The Little Fox tried to close in, but the sweeping cuts drove him back, around and around the chamber.

Faintly now, Cinel Loarn became aware of the whispers of the Sidhe, waiting, dread-filled: *Courage, Little Fox! Slay—slay swiftly! Remember your cunning, Little Fox!*

He had no breath to answer.

Then he heard another voice, rising above the rest: *Slay for me, Little Fox! Long have I waited for your return—and now you have come. Slay for love, Little Fox!* It was the voice of Ethne the Fair. If he could but see her . . .

Leaping far back, he cast the briefest of glances toward the lone bronze shield; he saw a shadow with scarlet lips, long tresses spun of night clouds, and deep blue eyes, so well remembered. New strength flowed into his wearied limbs; new cunning awakened within his jaded mind.

There was a trick he had used in other fights with the Goidel—strange that he had forgotten it. Retreat—still must he retreat—weakly, barely escaping thrust and lunge. Retreat, leading Caermarthen across the room. He sensed the oaken table behind him and felt it brush his back. His sword wavered, leaving an opening for a downward stroke.

He saw the silver blade descend swiftly, but his lithe form was swifter, dropping toward the floor below the level of the tabletop. And the long sword, driven with all the strength of Caermarthen's arm, crashed against the heavy oak planks.

A guttural Goidel curse burst from back-drawn lips as the weapon slipped from Caermarthen's grasp—a curse that died in a cough. For the blade of Cinel Loarn had leaped into his breast!

The Little Fox stepped back, his weapon stained with Goidel blood, his eyes on Caermarthen's pallid face. A momentary silence fell within the tower. Even the rush and roar of the tempest seemed hushed by the silent footfalls of death.

The fire died in the eyes of the Goidel chief. He swayed drunkenly. He looked down at the blood gushing from the gaping hole in his chest, the crimson hiding the blue tattooing. He looked at Cinel Loarn, curiously, wonderingly, as if face to face with a great mystery.

Then he laughed. It was not a pleasant sound. It was without mirth, hollow, ironic, clattering through the unnatural silence.

"Thirteen centuries," he muttered hoarsely. "Thirteen long centuries do I seek that accursed blade—and on the night I find it—it drinks my—blood!"

He tottered like a tree about to crash. His eyes glazed, but he did not fall. Cinel Loarn watched in horrified fascination as a dreadful change took place in the long, lean form. It seemed to shrink, to melt before his eyes. He heard the dull clangor of the golden serpent striking the floor. The features blurred—became formless—a flicker of light touched an eyeless skull—and that which had been Caermarthen sank into a mound of dust and disjointed brown bones.

Momentary vertigo seized Cinel Loarn, and he pressed an arm across his eyes. Memory seemed to fade in a dulling of his senses. Then dimly he heard a chorus of clanging and ringing as shields and swords rained from the wall. He heard voices, familiar voices of the Sidhe, an excited, joyous babble. He felt strange, heavy garments pressing upon him loosely as if cast over him by a careless hand. He stepped free of them and opened his eyes.

Ethne the Fair stood before him, and there was a smile on her lips and a warm light in her eyes. Gently his arm went around her—and he thought how good was life, and how sweet was love...

So now again, where there had been solitude and silence, the singing blades can be heard in the Scottish Highlands. And, strangely, they can best be heard when the tips of the great oaks bend before a gale, when thunder drums roll sullenly over peak and valley, when lightning spears dart through lumbering cloud banks. It is almost as if they rejoice in storm, as if the tempest awakens them to new and joyous life.

CHAPTER 1

The Two-Headed Serpent

Alan MacDougall came fully awake, his senses sharply alert. Something had broken in on his slumbers. He lay unmoving, listening, his gaze circling the little natural clearing. He heard only the sounds of the narrow rivulet tumbling down the rocky hillside and the rustle of leaves high overhead in the towering oaks. The campfire had died to a few glowing embers; but since the faint rose tint of dawn was visible through the great trees in the eastern sky, that was of no concern. He was quite comfortable in his sleeping bag.

Then suddenly he heard it—the faint bell-like tones of metal striking metal rhythmically rising and falling in volume, suggesting, except for their high pitch, swords striking swords. The sound was a continuing thing; and faint though it was, almost eluding hearing, he gained the distinct impression that the source of the persistent chiming was close at hand. Finally Alan MacDougall crawled out of his sleeping bag, drew on his hiking boots, added some dry faggots to the embers, and prepared for the day.

As he leaned over a little pool in the mere gutter of crystalline water, he chuckled at what he saw reflected in the mirrorlike surface—a blond, bearded Norseman whose head and whiskers had gone unshorn for almost five months. Plunging his face into the stream, he came up snorting, shook his head, wrung the water from his beard, and stretched the kinks from his powerful six-foot frame.

During all this the faint chiming persisted; to his regret, it ended while he was eating breakfast. He had planned to investigate. There had been a suggestion of direction—deeper into the woods and higher on the mountainside. He'd still hike in that direction. As nearly as he could determine, this was the general area where his brother Malcolm—Little Mac—had last been seen. His fortuitous stop at the old castle outside the wood and his conversation with the wizened old caretaker had given him the first clue.

The Scottish Highlands covered a lot of territory, and four years had passed since Malcolm had begun his walking tour. Alan's own absence from the States—an engineering project in Australia that he could not leave—had prevented his doing anything about Mac's vanishment until just six months ago; now he was on the trail. There *had* to be an explanation.

He broke camp, doused the fire, made up his backpack, and started up the slope, winding his way through the great trees. As if at a signal, he heard again the faint metallic clangor, farther up the slope. It was insistent, peremptory, urging him on—tantalizingly close, but receding as he advanced.

The forest seemed to grow darker and more forbidding, and the terrain appeared wilder. Alan MacDougall stopped in his tracks and burst into laughter. This was really insane! Following a barely heard—perhaps imagined—and totally inexplicable sound through a pathless forest was the sort of thing Little Mac might have done.

Abruptly he sobered. Was it indeed something his brother had actually done four years ago? And had it led him into trouble? Certainly the sound was strange, and it seemed to be leading—somewhere. Alan shrugged. He'd be on his guard.

Deeper and higher—and suddenly looming up ahead he saw a massive, ancient stone tower. With his sighting of it, silence fell, as if whatever was behind the faint chiming had accomplished its purpose.

Warily Alan MacDougall approached the round, gray structure. In his wanderings he had seen others like it, perhaps none as large and few as well preserved, but it was certainly nothing to fear. There was no sign of life, not even the normal sound of birds; the very air about him was hushed, with not a leaf stirring.

Pah! He was letting his imagination run rampant. He expected nothing ahead, and there would *be* nothing except the ruins of an ancient stone tower.

"Halloo!" he called out as he approached the low, square doorway. No response, of course.

With the eye of an engineer, he examined the structure. It appeared safe to enter; it had stood there without crumbling for uncounted years. He crouched and looked in; it was too dark to distinguish anything.

He drew a flashlight from his pack and, with the powerful beam trained before him, he stooped and entered, passing through what appeared to be a tunnel. Once within the high-ceilinged chamber beyond, he stood erect.

His torch swept the room in one swift circle, then caught as if frozen on an object on the flagstone floor. MacDougall held his breath for a numbed, timeless moment. His heart seemed to stop, the color drained from his face, and, even as he stared incredulously at the skeletal cadaver, tears blurred his sight.

"Little Mac!" The exclamation was hardly more than a whisper. He knew without checking that these were the mortal remains of his brother. So this was the end of Malcolm's quest! Still—there was a bare chance that it might be someone else. After all, that parchmentlike skin drawn over the skull bore little resemblance to anyone living. He had to be sure. Reluctantly, he knelt and drew a wallet from a trouser pocket. A glance was enough. Identifying cards proved conclusively that this was indeed Malcolm MacDougall's body. Then his own picture came to light, and for several minutes he gave way to shock and grief.

Finally regaining his composure, Alan thrust the wallet into a pocket of his jacket, straightened, and swept the room with his beam. What had happened?

He had been half aware of a second body—body? well, hardly that—lying about six feet from Malcolm; now he stared at the disjointed, age-browned, and utterly fleshless bones that many centuries ago must have been a man. A loincloth circled the pelvic area; a gold armlet in the shape of a massive double-headed serpent lay nearby; and thonged sandals rested near what had once been feet. Then he saw the sword—a longsword of polished steel halfway under a huge wooden table that stood against the wall opposite the fireplace. At one side was a heap of black cloth that turned out to be a long, hooded robe. Under the table, lying on its side, was a sturdy, three-legged stool. There was a stack of wood beside the fireplace; leaning near it was a modern axe, somewhat rusted. There were ashes in the fireplace—nothing else.

He noticed two openings in the curved wall, equidistant from the fireplace. These led into two long, narrow rooms, one with a plaited mat and a heap of coarsely woven covers, evidently once used as sleeping quarters; the other contained a small table holding a candle stub and an ancient parchment scroll, the vellum rolled on what seemed to be an ivory spool. A small stool nestled under the table. In the corner of the room stood a belted scabbard, evidently the case for the sword. MacDougall's beam flashed brightly from its polished filagree of gold and silver—an intricate maze of interlocking coils and swirls. Beautiful work—but the detail that amazed Alan was the brilliant polish of the silver, which, logically, should have been blackened by the oxidation of centuries. Carrying the sheath, he returned to the central room.

What had happened? How had Malcolm died? By the sword? He picked it up, thrust it into the scabbard, and laid it on the table. Nothing had stained the brightness of the blade. If it had been the sword, how had it been wielded? Certainly not by those ancient bones. Distasteful though it was, he examined Malcolm's body, but found no indication of a wound. More likely, death had been caused by a heart attack.

He felt a need for a breath of fresh air and for time to decide on his next move. After leaving the stone tower, he sat on a nearby boulder and tried to relax. He had a lot of questions and no answers. One thing was certain: he couldn't leave Malcolm's body lying there. It hadn't been disturbed in four years—there were no animal depredations—but that just wouldn't do. It was also certain that he couldn't dig a grave in this rocky soil; even with a spade, it would have been impossible. There was only one thing left to do. He'd wrap the body in a cover from the bed and build a cairn of rocks over it; there were plenty available.

It seemed an endless task, hot and tiring; but at last it was done. He stood beside the mound, hesitating. Out of his childhood he recalled the Lord's Prayer. Solemnly and with bowed head, he repeated the barely remembered words. He felt better at their conclusion. He had done his best.

A marker? Perhaps with the axe blade he could scratch a few words on a flat sheet of slate. It worked; and crudely but effectively, he cut into the soft stone: "Malcolm

MacDougall, U.S.A. Born 1955—Died 1981." As best he could, he anchored the stone on the face of the cairn.

Somewhere nearby must be that mountain rivulet beside which he had spent the night. Without too much difficulty he found it, washed up, and ate lunch—more than he would normally have eaten, since he would soon be backtracking and leaving the wilderness. As he rested, one thought that had been gnawing at the edge of his consciousness thrust itself to the fore.

If it had not been for that impossible, ever-so-faint metallic clanging, there was no possibility that he would have discovered this old tower! There could be no denying it. He would never have attempted to scour the whole mountainside—and he had been *led*! No matter how strongly the practical twentieth-century Alan MacDougall denied it, facts were facts.

The answer? There was none.

He rose and headed back toward the tower. Before he left, there were three things he was taking with him—the sword and sheath, the vellum scroll, and that gold armlet. It was surprising that they hadn't been discovered before by someone else—but he certainly wasn't going to leave them for another chance passer-by.

With his electric torch lighting the way, MacDougall crouched to pass through the entrance to the tower. He paused just inside the outer wall, characteristically examining the stones on his right. There should be something to indicate a former door—and there was. He noticed two rusty pins projecting from between rocks; once they must have supported a wooden door.

Inside, he examined the circular chamber more carefully than he had done earlier, and now he detected something that before had passed unnoticed—a dust pattern above the fireplace. A curious thing—he counted thirty foot-wide circles, and below each a leaf-shaped something suggesting toy swords under toy shields. No—twenty-nine, a pattern short under the last disk. He saw another pattern in dust above the table to his right—evidently where the long steel blade had been suspended. A scan of the rest of the wall, ceiling, and floor revealed nothing else.

He focused on the gold armlet and picked it up gingerly, examining it with narrowed eyes. It was amazingly heavy and massive, a masterpiece of finely wrought red-yellow gold, four-coiled, tapered, every individual scale a thing of perfection. But the head—heads, rather—drew his eyes and held them. First the gaping jaws with back-laid fangs, a crimson forked tongue, apparently carved of ruby—then the eyes. All were oval gems of identical size, cut cabochon. One was a white moonstone with strong crossing lines like a four-rayed star; the opposite eye was an icy-blue sapphire or aquamarine. The second head had one eye of crimson ruby; the other eye was a flawless blue-green stone, probably an emerald.

As he examined the armlet, Alan MacDougall shook his head decisively. He was not an expert on such things, though he knew a bit about gemology; but he was positive that this was not the work of Celtic craftsmen—not even southern European of the early Christian era. Maybe it was Egyptian or Persian, though that didn't quite fit either—but unquestionably it was a superb specimen of the goldsmith's and lapidary's art.

Stripping off his jacket, he bared his muscular upper right arm and thrust his hand through the coils. Could he get it on? It hardly seemed large enough, and though gold was a soft metal, there didn't seem to be any flexibility in this coiled band. Strangely, his forearm offered no resistance, nor did his biceps and triceps as the armlet seemed to snuggle into place. There it clung—and that was the appropriate term—yet without discomfort.

MacDougall squinted, then blinked rapidly to clear a sudden blurring of his sight. Strange! His eyes were completely normal and never caused him trouble. His sight cleared and he looked again at the armlet—and gasped with consternation.

The jaws of the serpents gaped wider in sly grins, and

two red tongues flicked out and back. The gem eyes gleamed with a light almost living.

Alan cursed under his breath and blinked again. He shook his flashlight. It must be a trick of his eyes, a flicker of the torch, or his imagination gone wild. The quicker he got the scroll and the sword and left this place, the better.

He aimed the beam at the farther doorway, the one leading into the chamber containing the scroll—then flipped the light to the left. Ridiculous—but he thought he saw two bronze disks on the wall where moments before only rough stone had been! He held the beam on what had to be hallucination—but it refused to go away.

Grimly he stalked across the flagstones toward what more closely resembled bronze shields than anything else. They were about three feet in diameter, slightly cupped, and ornately decorated with cabalistic designs. He touched one of the objects, and his senses told him it was there! He saw what appeared to be handgrips around its edge and without thought took hold of them.

The disk moved in his grasp and swung toward him as if on well-oiled hinges.

A flood of light, frigid and pulsing, poured into the tower chamber, and with it a breath of cool, invigorating air.

Alan MacDougall, suppressing normal disbelief, restrained an impulse to seek the sanity and safety of flight, crouched before the aperture and looked through. A spectacular auroral display met his eyes. Brilliantly glowing rays darted from the zenith, lengthening, shortening, advancing, and retreating in ceaseless motion. In large part they were colorless, though there were occasional suggestions of rose at the base and pale green at the apex, with the lightest hint of yellow between. But there was no permanence—only constant change. Then, on the misty, unreal horizon, he thought he saw what appeared to be a white city tinged with icy green—turrets and towers, minarets and spires—glittering indeed like a city of ice.

Mirage—it must be a mirage!

On impulse Alan MacDougall stepped through the opening; he felt a sudden compression, a momentary vertigo—then stood erect on a yielding green-white turf.

He looked around, eyes wide with wonder. He was beginning to enjoy this waking dream—for it must be such! Nothing like this could exist outside his imagination.

There were trees in the near distance, but trees like none he had ever seen—unless perhaps for the distorted creations on Chinese pottery, and of the same anemic green of the grass, vegetation that looked as if it had never felt the warmth of sunlight. He saw a road not more than a hundred yards from where he stood, a broad road seemingly formed of white sand and pebbles, winding down a slope and up over a gradual rise, narrowing steadily as it meandered toward that distant crystalline city.

Alan had not moved since stepping out of the tower. Now he glanced over his shoulder—and for the first time since the inexplicable blurring of his sight, he felt a stab of near-fright. What should have had the solid permanence of the round stone tower was the mere ghost of a structure, discernible only because he knew it was there. Beyond it—*through* it—he saw an expanse of the pallid meadow and another clump of distorted trees.

Uncomfortable sort of dream, he thought. If he had walked away from the tower—in his dream—could he have found his way back? No way would he move from that spot!

People! A city and a road presupposed people—and as if to accommodate his thought, he heard a distant sound—the tinkling of little bells and the muffled beat of horses' hoofs. Coming toward him around a curve and up a steep slope was a caravan of scores of, perhaps a hundred, white horses and their riders!

Alan studied the scene with intense interest. Man! His imagination was exceeding anything of which he felt capable. Why, he wondered, were the horses so small? For they were that, suggesting Mongolian ponies. All were ornately saddled with harnesses of white leather, stirrups and all other metal of polished silver, and with brightly gleaming silver bells everywhere.

The men of the caravan were marked by the same unhealthy pallor as the landscape, the only variation in the prevalent white being the long, hooded robes they wore; those were every pastel tint of the spectrum—though none were good, solid colors. All the riders carried lances and had longswords in silver scabbards at their sides, worn over their robes. Their faces were not clearly visible at that distance, but what MacDougall saw made him think of Orientals.

Almost instantly his eyes were drawn to the rider at the head of the caravan. It was a woman, wearing a headdress of palely glittering gems and flowing garments of brilliant white. Her horse was larger than any of the others, and her harness was more ornate. There was something regal about her carriage.

Mac, he thought to himself with a mental grin, this is more like a MacDougall dream!

At that moment a crystal-clear cry, unmistakably feminine, came from the leader, and the caravan drew to a halt. The woman faced his way, then suddenly spurred her horse off the road and up the slope in his direction. Approvingly he noted that she rode sidesaddle, as one would expect. Two riders immediately followed, one on either side; in seconds they had halted about thirty feet away. The men were indeed Orientals, with yellowish skin, almond eyes, and straight black hair. Quite openly they were examining the strange man standing alone on the hilltop.

Alan MacDougall stared fixedly into the most beautiful face he had ever seen. He wasn't good at this sort of thing, he thought, but only one word did justice to her beauty—ethereal. There was no suggestion of the Orient here; her complexion was that of a Dresden doll, her hair platinum blond, her features perfection. When she spoke, her voice was in harmony with the rest of her.

"Who are you? Whence come you? From Falias?"

Strangely, he understood her. Not strange, really. After all, it was *his* dream. But there were limits; he refused to answer a girl of his imagination.

She frowned, her expression growing indignant, more imperious. "Bring him!"

She turned her horse and sped down the slope. Instantly the two men dismounted and moved toward Alan somewhat warily, it seemed, their lances at the ready.

MacDougall scowled. This was going a bit too far. Time for retreat. He spun around and darted through the barely seen opening. Again that momentary discomfort; then, turning, he peered out to watch the consternation of the two men. They had halted not more than five feet from where he had stood, fright on their faces.

"Sorcerer!" one exclaimed. They dashed back to their horses, mounted, and sped down the hillside after their mistress. MacDougall swiftly closed the bronze door.

His flashlight lay where he had unknowingly dropped it, and it still sent forth its welcome beam. MacDougall picked it up and stood there as if transfixed, the unnoticed minutes dragging by. He was like one awakened from a particularly vivid dream; only this one was incredibly real. His mind reenacted every detail.

Suddenly he reached out, drew back the metal Gate, and looked out. Far away, much smaller now, just reaching the crest of the distant hill, the caravan was on the verge of passing from sight. Again he closed the door.

He looked at the second bronze disk—then, with a sudden thought, swung his beam across the room to the opposite wall—and there were two more identical objects! He flashed his light around the chamber, but saw no others—only the four. Four Gateways into—what?

Resolutely, Alan MacDougall moved to the doorless exit of the tower. He must get out of this place for a while and do some heavy thinking, free of its unearthly influence. When he was seated on the convenient boulder near the tower, he tried to organize his thoughts.

Extraordinary things had started with the first faint clanging that awakened him so short a time before. The sounds had led him to the tower—and Malcolm. Nothing else abnormal had happened until he had put on the armlet; then things had begun with a vengeance. The blurring of his sight had evidently enabled him to see things that normally couldn't be seen. That was oversimplification, but he had discarded the thought of hallucination; there was too much that the term wouldn't cover. He looked distastefully at the armlet, at the glowing, unwinking eyes. Removing the band would solve everything, or at least bring him out of this uncanny spell. It was the only sensible thing to do.

He grasped the heads of the serpent, pulling out and down. Nothing moved. He tried to slide the coils around, but without success. His jaw set grimly as he headed for the little stream, where he immersed his arm almost to the shoulder—but the armlet was anchored more tightly than before, if that were possible. It clung like something living.

Alan cursed and stalked angrily back to his rock seat, his expression a study. He struggled with growing apprehension, then suddenly he laughed, though there wasn't much mirth in the sound. No matter what lay ahead, he was stuck!

Rising, he walked slowly around the tower, carefully examining the rough wall. It was just as he expected—an ancient stone structure with no possible openings other than the obvious doorway. Yet he had gone through an opening into—somewhere—and had returned. And he'd seen intriguing things, to say the least—including an incredibly beautiful, though haughty, woman.

He was a hard-headed Scot who had always been proud of his pragmatic view of life—but he'd stumbled on something so wildly improbable, so utterly impossible, that he was determined to stick with it, no matter what lay ahead. That included a prolonged trip back into the—other world.

Plans? There was little to plan. He thought of rations. There was nothing he could do about food; he wished now that he had been less free with his supplies earlier in the day. Oh, well—there were people, and people ate—and he'd have to live off the land. He decided against taking his sleeping bag and the rest of his bulky backpack, settling for his knapsack alone. His heavier equipment could remain in the tower until his return. He made a quick trip to the stream to fill his canteen and returned to the tower. He secured the ancient scroll, carefully packing the cylinder of vellum into his knapsack, then picked up the sheathed sword and strapped it around his waist. He hesitated over the thonged sandals, but decided against them.

The hooded black robe was another matter. Robes seemed to be the fashion where he was headed, and it certainly would make him less conspicuous. He examined it. It must be very old, but despite its musty smell, it seemed surprisingly sturdy, coarsely woven, probably of wool, like monk's cloth. He put it on over his jacket, noting with satisfaction that it reached almost to the floor. Remembering the robed riders, he took off the sword sheath and fastened the belt over the robe.

Then he stood there, mentally struggling. He was as ready as he'd ever be. He thrust aside a recurrence of doubt about the whole situation. He thought momentarily of the three other bronze Gates, but decided to investigate them later—if there was a later.

He drew a deep breath and swung wide the Gate, admitting a flood of cold and flickering light. Carefully he turned off his flashlight, putting it into a capacious jacket pocket—and stepped through the opening.

CHAPTER 2

Tartarus

For a third time Alan MacDougall was aware of a momentary instability, a dizziness; as before, it was gone in an instant. Intently he examined his surroundings, seeking sight of motion, hint of sound. There was none, not even the faintest birdsong. He was alone in an unnatural quiet. The aurora overhead was a thing of frigid beauty, a shimmering curtain of leaping light extending to the horizon on every side, pouring out of a black and starless sky.

He turned and faced the ghostly doorway. Almost touching the wraith of a tower, he drew his sword and thrust it into the heavy turf at the very center of the opening. He'd have to mark his return route so he'd be able to find it again.

He had seen boulders scattered over the hillside, water-rounded rocks thrusting above the thick, pale grass. He wouldn't use them; nothing must appear disturbed. But there certainly were others in the little copse of unnatural trees whose removal would not be noticed.

He worked with care, placing first a small rock against the sword, then a second, somewhat larger, two paces away; a third, larger still, four paces from the second; and so on in a straight line. The last was quite large; straining and puffing, he rolled it over the meadow, depending upon the resilience of the grass to erase the trail. After all, there was no trace of the horses' hoofmarks where the trio of riders had come up the hillside. Finally, at right angles to the largest boulder at the very edge of the road, he placed another large rock, then stood back and surveyed what he had done.

It was a clear indicator when one knew what to look for. He didn't think it was too obvious; it should appear natural to the casual glance. Finally, after retrieving his sword, he returned to the road and stood there memorizing the terrain. He noted a lone tree of considerable size standing near a clump of smaller ones. He had a good eye for such things; time alone would tell if it were good enough.

He started at a brisk pace up the white road toward the crystalline city on the horizon. After an indeterminate period of time during which he divided his attention between the passing scenery and the strangeness of his state, he thought of the plodding hours and glanced at the watch on his left wrist. It had stopped.

He shook it—wound it—there was no response. He shrugged. What importance was time in a world where there appeared to be neither sun nor moon—only the ceaseless auroral sheets and beams for light—where, apparently, there was no night or day, unless this was night and day was to follow. He removed his watch and slid it into a convenient pocket.

The road led down a gradual slope, to pass through an extensive stand of trees—not the artificial-appearing growths he had seen before, but literally a forest, a thicket several hundred feet in depth and continuing in a belt that vanished over the hills on both sides of the road. As he approached the trees, he thought he saw furtive movement in the shadows.

He slowed. He knew nothing of what might lie in wait. There could be beasts of prey and there could be hostile men, more likely the latter. There was no turning back now. His destination was the crystal city, and this was the only apparent route. Firmly he gripped the hilt of his sword and strode on, keeping to the center of the road—like a small boy, he thought, heading through a haunted wood.

He saw no further movement until he had passed the first set of trees. Then, without warning, six men leaped from concealment. The were a wild-looking bunch, unkempt, their dress varying from a mere loincloth to a coat of linked mail and tight breeches. He noted this in a single glance, but his attention fell immediately upon their long metal-tipped lances pointed fixedly in his direction. Instinctively he whipped out his sword, though he knew he had no chance in so uneven a contest; he was not even a skilled swordsman.

"Halt!" he shouted with all his strength in this strange tongue that somehow he knew. "One more step and you are dead men!"

This sounded silly, he knew, but it stopped them momentarily. As one, the six froze, holding their menacing position. MacDougall's thoughts raced. In seconds they'd attack. He'd try to sweep aside the points, close in, and slash at their throats. But he realized it looked hopeless, an early end to his adventure unless a miracle intervened.

Faintly to his ears came a sound, breaking the unnatural silence—the drumming of horses' hoofs on the road behind him! Miracle enough!

A caravan—too good to be true! But it was!

Half turning, waving at supposed help on the way but keeping his eyes on the wild men, he cried, *"Hai! Hai! You've come just in time!"*

At these words, the first horseman appeared over the crest of the hill, followed instantly by others. With a cry of frustration, the six attackers melted into the forest.

What an accommodating world, MacDougall thought. A few minutes' delay and he'd surely have been a dead man. It must be another caravan heading for—what had the lady called it—Falias? Their timing was perfect.

As the lead horseman reached Alan MacDougall, the rider reined in his mount and glared down at Alan with icy blue eyes, his visage stern. No Oriental this—rather, a blond, bearded Nordic.

"Why did you cry out? And where are your companions, the spearmen?"

"Not my companions!" MacDougall protested. "I was walking along the road and they attacked from the forest. Had you not arrived, they would have slain me. Your coming saved my life."

Doubt and suspicion intensified the glare. "You were walking along the road—alone? No one does that. Whence come you?"

MacDougall hesitated. He knew the name of only one city. "From the west," he ventured. "I'm bound for Falias. I—I live in the hills."

"The West? Impossible! From Murias, the City Under the Sea! And you say you live in the hills? An Outcast! Seize him!" He waved to three of the nearest horsemen. "You'll go to Falias indeed—but in chains."

Swiftly the three riders dismounted; like their leader, they were big, powerful, blue-eyed men with hair like Alan's own. Just as swiftly, two grasped his arms and the third drew his blade and held it in readiness. Momentarily Alan's muscles stiffened to resist; then he relaxed. It would be folly to fight; besides, he'd be taken to where he wanted to go. He started to protest when one of them removed his sword, but desisted. Maybe he'd get it back; he hoped so—though he had to admit that, for him, it might be more of a liability than an asset.

He was being led through the maze of horses when another voice was heard, deep, harsh, and arrogant.

"What is the reason for this delay? There are schedules to be kept!"

There was something about the voice that sent a stab of apprehension through the horsemen. Hastily the leader of the group explained. With only a few words uttered, his reference to "an Outcast" brought a burst of mirthless laughter from the inquirer.

"An Outcast! He is already judged. Chain him to the last horse and let him run. If he falls, let him be dragged."

The speaker came into Alan MacDougall's view, mounted on a great gray horse, his robe and garments beneath uniformly gray. Even his face, lean and cadaverous, with deep-set gray eyes, seemed of grayish hue, and his mass of shoulder-length hair was iron-gray. Alan caught a momentary glimpse of the rider beside him— short and fat, dressed in deep purple—but his eyes remained fixed on the gray rider. To him he spoke angrily.

"I know nothing about Outcasts. It is true, as I said, that I came out of the hills—but I reached there from another world." He spread wide his black robe to reveal his, to them, unusual garments. "I entered this world from another through a Gate—a round, bronze—"

The broad man interrupted, startled and suddenly alert. "Through a Gate, you say? You are strangely dressed, indeed. Have you any proof of what you say?"

Alan put his hand into a pocket and drew out his flashlight. The very thing—if only it would work in this strange place. His watch hadn't. He touched the switch. A bright beam flared, full into the eyes of the gray man. He held it a moment, strangely amber in the silvery light of the aurora, then flicked off the beam.

"Have you anything like this in your world?" he asked.

"Mere magic," the gray man snarled, though a bit uncertainly, reaching for it. "Let me try."

"Hold!" The single sharp word demanded obedience. To MacDougall's surprise, the gray rider's companion, the fat man in purple, took complete charge of the situation.

"I shall take control of him, Arias. I would learn more of this Gate, of this Other World." He turned to the Viking holding the sword. "Return his weapon and bring him one of the spare horses." He spoke with the full certainty that he would be obeyed.

Suppressed wrath simmered in the eyes of the gray man. "But, Taliesin," he protested, "I passed judgment— and you take his unsupported word—"

The man named Taliesin spoke soothingly. "If need be, your edict may still be executed. But the possibility of news of the Gate dare not be overlooked. If he were not as he said, how would he know about the Gate itself? Or should I consult the Great Mother—the goddess Danu? I still have her ear, as you know."

"No, no!" The words came reluctantly but hastily. "As you say, judgment has perhaps been deferred." But there was hatred and malevolence in the lingering gaze Arias fixed on MacDougall before he turned away, as well as promise of a day of reckoning for his humiliation.

That's my first enemy, Alan thought.

Within minutes MacDougall was astride a sturdy sorrel, grateful that he was a good horseman, thanks to his years in the saddle in Australia. His sword belt again circled his waist, and he rode beside his unexpected benefactor. Alan now noticed that the man and his gray companion wore no weapons. They rode for some minutes in silence, adapting the gait of the horses to a steady rhythm; then Alan spoke, smiling ruefully.

"Thank you, sir. I am not a particularly good runner." As he uttered the words, he appraised his companion. The man was short and broad—rounded—but not offensively fat. He was balding, with a fringe of thick, white hair over his ears. His eyebrows were also heavy and white, yet his skin was smooth and unwrinkled, with no indication of aging. His eyes were brown and seemed to carry a perpetual twinkle. He had an altogether pleasant face.

"And what think you of Taliesin, my friend—if you have completed your study—as I have studied you, and like what I see. And what do men call you?"

Feeling a slight discomfiture, Alan replied, "Alan MacDougall—and I think—I trust—I have found a friend. Your name, Taliesin—I have heard it before from my brother's lips. He quoted some of your sayings—if you are the same man, the Celtic bard Taliesin."

Obviously pleased, the other replied, "I know of only one Taliesin, Alan son of Dougall. Here they call me the Bard of Bards." He hesitated. "And how long has it been since this bard lived and wrote in your world?" He seemed to hang anxiously on the answer.

"A very long time," MacDougall said soberly, doubt in his tones. "I know it seems impossible—but he lived in the sixth century after the birth of Christ, as we reckon time. Mine is the twentieth!"

The eyes of Taliesin grew large with consternation; he stared full-face at Alan. "The twentieth *century*? Surely you jest. Fourteen hundred years since the Lord of Light brought us to this land—six thousand years since the Daughters of Lilith died, if the tales are true." Taliesin peered searchingly at MacDougall. "Is it truth you tell? But why should you lie!"

Alan was no less shocked at what ne heard than was the Bard, as the ideas began to penetrate his thinking. A man out of mythology alive and speaking, in a physical body! But then, by all that was reasonable, this land could not be here. A land he had seen and entered by the hocus-pocus of a fantastic two-headed snake of gold. An ensorcelled land.

Taliesin sounded subdued when next he spoke, groping for stability. "Tell me of this Other World, the land where once—Taliesin walked. Of the gods of this world. Of what has happened in the land I knew—to the Celts, the Sidhe, and the Goidel—in fourteen centuries."

It wasn't an easy undertaking—Malcolm would have done it so much better—but Alan MacDougall did his best to describe the modern British Isles and to cover the history of the Middle Ages and the development of the modern era from its agrarian beginnings to the shrinking of the world with twentieth century communications and transportation. When he finally paused, he felt he had been woefully inadequate in his attempt.

He took the flashlight apart and showed its components. He thought of his watch, bared its delicate workings, and tried to explain its operation. "Here," he concluded, "it does not work. Here where there seems to be no time."

"You have noticed that?" Taliesin's words seemed detached from his actual thoughts. "Time here behaves strangely. It has no constancy. It varies according to events or experiences—racing by in joy or pleasure, though we have little enough of either—dragging endlessly in pain and trouble. Since there is no day or night—no sun to cause change—we eat or sleep according to need. Here even the tides are forbidden. There is no rain—the dew waters the land—though we know of no law that controls the dewfall."

There was an interval of silence while both men adjusted their views to new and startling concepts. Taliesin was the first to resume conversation.

"Only great cities—unbelievable machines—"

"Oh, no!" MacDougall interrupted. "I see I have given you a false impression. There is much that has not changed. The ancient round tower—I've heard them called *brochs*—from which I entered this land stands in a great oak woods in a part of Scotland where there are farmlands and wilderness areas and roads not as good as this one. There are parts of Erin and Wales and Scotland where the old gods are still remembered—and, if truth be told, are still worshipped—though the following of Christ has publicly replaced the older faiths. There still are places where it is said that the *Shee* roam the hills, seen only by a favored few, but still there."

The round face brightened. "You say truth?" The twinkle returned to Taliesin's eyes. "If all the other be true, why not this?"

"This world," MacDougal asked in turn, "surely it must have a name?"

The Bard shook his head. "For us it is simply the World or the Island. The place from whence we came—your home—is the Other World. In the old days some would have called this *Tir Tairngire*, Land of Promise. Or *Tir-nan-og*, Land of the Gods and the Ever-Young. Others called it *Meg Mell*, Plain of Happiness. Still others referred to it as *Tir-nam-beo*, Land of the Living. I have also heard it called Land of the Dancing Men. Some in the old days called the aurora the *Fir-Chlisneach*, the Dancing Men—a not unlikely name, since the beams flash downward, shortening, lengthening, retreating, like male dancers.

"You might refer to it as Elysium—or even Tartarus." His face grew grim and his voice fell to an almost inaudible whisper. "I call it none of these. To me it is simply a place accursed."

Again there was an interval of silence, broken only by the normal sounds of the caravan; the drumming of hoofbeats, snatches of conversation, a raucous laugh, a curse. Alan MacDougall let his gaze wander about him, studying the men. All were of Nordic type, most of them fair-haired, some dark, a few ruddy, all similarly clad with horned helmets and short-sleeved shirts ending at midthigh; some wore linked chain armor, their legs wrapped to midcalf, and sturdy sandals. They were so different from the smaller yellow men of the other caravan.

And this was a far larger grouping than that one had been, fully three times its size. The horses here were big, powerful, and of mixed colors. Included in this caravan were scores of pack animals, burdened with massive mounds of cargo.

While talking, Alan noted that he and Taliesin had fallen far back in the line, their pace unconsciously slowing. He looked over his shoulder to stare into the narrowed eyes of Arias, the gray man.

How much had he heard? Perhaps most or all of it. Did it really matter? Fortunately, there had been no reference to the—Gate. That, Alan was sure, would come later. If Taliesin attached so much importance to it, his own secrecy was equally important. He would be wary, *very* wary.

He noticed that the horses were slowing; soon they came to a halt. The caravan was in a picturesque little valley through which wound a narrow brook that started from a spring high on the hill to their right, followed the road for about a mile, then flowed under a small stone bridge and vanished around a hillock far down the valley. A few clumps of the strange trees completed the picture.

"We eat," Taliesin commented. "Follow." He led his mount up the slope, well separated from the rest of the men. There he dismounted, removed his horse's bit, and watered the animal, bidding Alan to do the same. One of the men approached with a sack of oats and fed both mounts, then tethered them with enough freedom to graze.

Taliesin was watching the motions of one of the riders—Arias, MacDougall realized. "Here we can talk without an audience." So the Bard had known! "One of the men will bring us food. Afterward we will continue our conversation." By way of explanation he added, "These are the servitors of Falias. They do all the work. Bards are held in high esteem in this land. We have much authority, more even than the Druids—and the Bard of Bards has power second only to the gods." He smiled broadly. "You are very fortunate to have come upon this particular caravan."

Even as he spoke, another of the Norsemen brought them their lunch—dried fish, roasted grain, hard-crusted loaves, some dried fruit. Alan realized he was quite hungry; the food tasted good, washed down with icy water from the brook. When he had finished, he lay back on the turf, watching the incredible play of lights overhead. It was a constant spectacular display: waving curtains of light mingled with leaping beams in undulating rows truly suggesting dancers—the Dancing Men.

Taliesin seemed to be reading his thoughts. "Beautiful, is it not? So idyllic, peaceful. Yet to me it is an accursed place. I said you may wish to call the land Tartarus. Hardly your idea of the Christian Hell, eh, friend? Hear me!

"This world is totally the creation of Lucifer! Those here are here at his behest and under his control. Oh— we have much freedom, much power to act as we wish, within limits. Magic, the arts of our former life, works here—but it is so futile. One wearies of spell and counterspell. It is meaningless, so here it is little practiced. For there is always the Dark One's control.

"Except you, Alan son of Dougall, if I mistake not, for you are still part of the Other World—if you speak truth. You alone of all of us have not yet died!"

Alan MacDougall felt a tightening, a stricture in his throat; an icy touch darted up his spine. What had he ventured into? And where would it end?

Taliesin spoke with sudden intensity, his narrowed eyes boring into MacDougall's. "You *can* go back? The Gate had not closed behind you?"

Thoughtfully Alan stared at the Bard, fighting doubt. How far should he trust this man? To a point, he suddenly decided.

"I have already done so. I entered this world and returned to my own, so I know the way is open. It was then I saw a lovely woman at the head of a caravan. I would see her again. Perhaps—"

Taliesin seemed not to have heard. "Then I have one more question. Can you find the Gate?"

Again Alan hesitated. "I *think* I can." He paused, then repeated, "I'm not certain, but I think I can."

An expression of vast relief appeared on the ruddy face of Taliesin. "Then there is hope. For you, I think, are not part of the Shining One's plans." He rose, MacDougall following his example. "Time to move on."

As they secured their horses and prepared them for travel, the Bard added, "I will tell you the story of this world, of the Four Cities, of the Daughters of Lilith and the sons of God—but not now. We will defer that until we reach my quarters in Falias."

Again on the way, he commented with his usual twinkle, "Better to be here than nowhere—but better still to be somewhere else." He shook his head dolefully. "No wonder life has grown monotonous. Fourteen centuries!"

There was little conversation during the remainder of the ride. Alan MacDougall remained at the side of Taliesin; but the Bard seemed preoccupied, deep in thought, evidently considering what he had already learned. The caravan passed through two other bands of forest like the one in which Alan had been ambushed, a fact that he filed in his memory for future reference. These were landmarks that could hardly be forgotten.

From time to time he had caught glimpses of the city ahead—the impression of flashing crystal seen through the lattice of trees or screened in part by the broad backs of horsemen; but after topping a steep rise in the white road he saw Falias in all its incredible splendor, sharp against the auroral sky.

It was reality in contrast with a reflected and misty image as it had appeared from a distance. It was frozen beauty wrought in ice-green crystal. It was a gigantic gem, a diamond among cities, a creation out of a dream, dazzling the eye and quickening the pulse. It was truly a creation of the gods.

Falias lay on a flat, elevated plain, thickly covered with the ever-present lime-green turf, the white road ending at the great city gates, which were already swinging wide to admit the approaching caravan. Within he could see a broad plaza filled with milling masses of people wearing strangely varied dress. There were hints of graceful white bridges spanning the central thoroughfare with serrated arches.

But it was the exterior that caught and held his attention. Great glistening spires thrust lance-sharp points toward the black sky. Towers and arches and huge polished domes, rising level upon level, created a vision of frozen loveliness, a city of enchantment that men could not have conceived and most certainly could not have brought to consummation.

At the very crest and center of the crystalline creation rose a magnificent tower of six scimitarlike blades, meeting to support on their merged tips a great, flawless, many-pointed, three-dimensional star. Though the rest of Falias seemed tinted an icy green, the star alone was a pellucid water-white.

And all of it, every polished plane, every mirrorlike curve, picked up and cast back in multiplied brilliance the eternally changing, the never-to-be-predicted frozen auroral fires.

It was a spectacle that, once seen, could never be forgotten.

Still bedazzled by his first clear vision of Falias, Alan MacDougall rode ahead with the rest of the caravan which, with its destination in sight, had quickened its tempo. At last they passed through the wide gateway.

Since he had been riding near the rear of the procession, Alan was conscious of the commotion and screams that rose up ahead long before he saw their cause. On both sides of the plaza, burly guards, sandaled and clad only in short kiltlike garments, were wielding metal-tipped lashes, driving back any man or woman who came close to the course of the riders. And with the density of the mob, this was hard to avoid.

There came a scream, shrill and pain-filled; Alan caught a glimpse of a bloody female body writhing, then suddenly motionless under the steel-shod hoofs that continued inexorably on their course. In silent protest, Alan looked toward Taliesin. The Bard gestured his helplessness and shook his head. He leaned toward MacDougall.

"Tartarus, as I told you," he explained. "A place accursed. And nothing I can change."

The caravan moved on to a crossing street, turned into it, and halted at what were evidently stables. Beyond them lay a series of buildings that appeared to be of commercial use, perhaps warehouses; the pack animals were led to platforms.

MacDougall, about to dismount, felt Taliesin's restraining hand on his arm. "We ride to my home." They made their way through the press of horses and rode at a canter up the main thoroughfare. About twoscore riders followed them, evidently Taliesin's servants. The crowd had thinned, and men with whips were no longer in evidence.

Still shocked by the callous disregard for life, Alan exclaimed, "Surely that death was unnecessary! Are such things frequent?"

"All too frequent. Few have regard for any lives but their own; and they cling to that life tenaciously. All of us have died once and have been given new bodies. There is no assurance that there is a third existence."

"But this lovely city—its incredible beauty—"

"Created long ago by the Angel of Light for another race and another time, of which you will learn in due course. We are—an afterthought."

MacDougall tried to thrust the ugliness from his mind, but one thought persisted. Tartarus—Hell—inhabited by people who had died and had new bodies!

The nature of the city changed as they rode on; the green-white buildings became larger, more ornate, with more space between them, surrounded by pale green lawns. The city itself did not appear to be very large; many of the buildings were unusually tall for the small areas covered.

When Alan asked Taliesin about the anomaly, the Bard answered, "Once I suppose there was need. Now the

upper levels are shells, the haunt of thieves and predators—some of the Outcasts."

They reached their destination, turning into a broad
white walk that led to what had to be called a mansion.
The architecture was not like any Alan had ever seen;
perhaps it more nearly resembled the ancient Greek with
a Moorish influence. With their appearance, a servitor
came from nowhere to lead away the horses, and the two
passed through a wide doorway that another servant
opened to admit them. Candlelight was the only illumination besides that coming through spacious windows,
glazed, it seemed, with sheets of translucent crystal. Crystal candelabras were everywhere.

The interior was a contradiction, since it might be considered sumptuous austerity. There were wide spaces but
few furnishings, yet these few were the ultimate in luxury.
All of it was an icy green-white, constructed of material
that defied identification.

They were met by a silent servant who took Alan's
robe. Taliesin motioned toward a gracefully curving, lightly
padded chair which proved to be quite comfortable; he
seated himself on another, broader, more sturdy one. Beside it stood a narrow table with an alabaster top, holding
sheets of parchment and writing tools.

"Welcome, Alan son of Dougall," the Bard said heart-
ily. "What time you spend in Falias you will be the guest
of Taliesin."

Rather feebly, Alan protested. "Thank you, but—I feel
like an intruder—"

"Thank your gods, my friend, that we met! If you were
to wander unprotected among the people out there, you
would be stripped to the skin in less time than it takes to
tell. Only strength or guile is recognized as law. Now you
will have my protection; and if I mistake not, an even
more effective power will be your constant guard."

MacDougall looked questioningly at Taliesin, but the
Bard made no further comment on this. "A room is being
prepared for you. There you will find proper attire. Food

is also being prepared, and after we've eaten, I suggest you sleep, as I shall. Refreshed, perhaps I may be able to answer at least some of the questions you may ask." He chuckled slyly. "Even where you may find the lovely Darthula, the woman whom you seek."

Alan was ushered to his room, where he found a vessel filled with water for his bath and a change of clothing— a loincloth, long, loose breeches of deep blue, and a light blue, short-sleeved tunic of waist length with gold braid around the neck and fringing the garment. There were also flexible, moccasinlike shoes. After washing, he put these clothes on, admitting to himself that he felt a bit silly—though now his dress approximated that of his host.

In another room—all these rooms were on the same level, spare and yet luxurious—the two men were served their dinner by a silent blond woman. Several times Alan was aware of her lingering gaze. Again he ate fish, bread, and fruit, fresh in this instance, rather than dried as on the journey. In addition there was a choice of a potent fruit wine or a flat, warm, beerlike grain beverage that was not at all to Alan's liking.

He and the Bard concentrated on eating with almost no conversation; after the meal's completion and a short period of relaxation, both made their way to their respective chambers. Alan MacDougall stripped to his loincloth and literally dropped to his bed, which was close to the floor, very firm, and surprisingly comfortable.

It was only as he stretched out and drew a single cover over himself that he realized his utter weariness, and an overpowering lassitude swept over him. There came with startling force a sudden thought—it had been a long time, a *very* long time, since he had slept, if one measured time by events.

It had all begun with his waking under the great oaks on the mountainside, his slumbers disturbed by the faintest metallic clanging. One thing had followed another— finding Malcolm's body and burying it—the gold armlet— the four doors—his entry into this strange world—the caravan—Taliesin's coming to his rescue—his reaching the fantastic city, Falias. Then this! All in one day! *Was* it one day? How could he tell in a world where time was not?

A lovely face arose in his memory. So her name was Darthula. Assuming Taliesin knew. It was a lovely name, so suitable.

His drowsiness deepening, he tried to concentrate on some of the strange details of the happenings—and on the very fringe of his fading consciousness he seemed to hear voices—voices in his own mind, as out of a dream.

It seemed to be a conversation already begun. The speaker was obviously feminine, her voice calm, low-pitched, but sternly commanding.

"And why, Morrigu, when you learned of the possibilities, did you not share your knowledge with the rest of us?"

The one addressed as Morrigu, also female, replied in harsh, almost raucous tones; a suggestion of a sneer in her words was masked by an obviously false veneer of sincerity:

"The Druid Arias is not very trustworthy, though I find him useful on occasion, so I planned to verify his conclusions myself before bringing the news to your attention, Mother Danu."

"That is utter nonsense, Morrigu," a strongly masculine voice exclaimed, *"and you know it. You planned to keep the knowledge to yourself and, if possible, use it for your benefit alone!"*

"As would every one of you if you could!" The voice of Morrigu grew shrill. *"Yes, every one of you—including you, Nuada—if you dared."*

The one called Danu spoke quietly. *"A quarrel serves no purpose. The important fact remains that there now appears to have come to us one who may have passed through the Gate—and who, according to Taliesin, may be able to return—should he be able to find the Gate again. Our first hope for release in ages. Until that knowl-*

edge is verified, the fact—if it is fact—established, that one man is the most important individual in this world. Has anyone made mental contact?"

A brief silence fell, then Morrigu replied reluctantly, *"I tried, but with no success whatever."*

"How about you, Dagda?"

Another masculine voice, calm as that of Danu, answered quietly. *"After you asked me for counsel, I, too, tried and failed. There is no common ground."*

"This makes matters more difficult, our task of guarding him more complicated. We shall have to keep him under surveillance through those around him. Each of you, of course, will assist. Are there any questions?"

After a long pause, a deep, arrogant voice exclaimed: *"Why this coddling of one mortal? Why don't we simply seize him and compel him to show us the way out? Are we gods—or have we no powers? I say the direct course is always best."*

A reply came from the one named Nuada. *"That would be your view, Balor. But—if my memory serves me, it was the Fomorians under your leadership who were defeated by the Tuatha De Danann. You'll follow our lead whether you like it or not."*

Balor sneered. *"In that same battle you died, Silver Hand. Remember?"*

Again came the quiet voice of Danu. *"The plan of surveillance will be followed—and, perhaps I should add, he will be protected from bodily harm by every means at our disposal. His is the most valuable life on the Island, since he alone has the key we have sought so long."* Another pause followed. *"If there are no other questions—conference ended."*

Alan MacDougall groped through a mental mist, seeking to understand the strange dream—if it was a dream! Those unusual names—he had heard none of them before, except that of Danu; Taliesin had spoken to Arias about the Mother Goddess Danu. The references to Arias and Taliesin would be something for the Bard to clear up. All of it was just another piece in this fantastic puzzle in which he had involved himself.

For the moment, though, only one thing was important. Sleep!

CHAPTER 3

World of the Four Cities

The sound of angry voices penetrated Alan MacDougall's slumbers. His first reaction was one of annoyance at being disturbed; then he recognized the harsh tones of Arias the Druid and came suddenly awake.

"We are aware of your authority, Taliesin, but it doesn't give you the power to keep for yourself what belongs to all of us. We believe you have learned the location of the Gate and we insist on your sharing the knowledge."

"You speak nonsense!" The Bard's voice, though quietly restrained, expressed thorough annoyance. "After my guest has properly begun his day, you can ask him for yourself."

Alan heard a third voice, highly impatient. "Do you mean to say that you will make us wait until he has eaten before we may see him?"

"I mean precisely that! Though you may care nothing for the duties of a host, I do not share your lack. I shall return."

MacDougall sprang up quickly, a grin on his face. He liked the spirit of Taliesin. Briskly he washed and dressed, then joined the Bard, who was waiting in what Alan thought of as the dining room. After greetings, a substantial breakfast was served the two, during which there was casual conversation. Afterward, they joined the four grim-faced visitors, who glared at MacDougall with obvious dislike.

Smiling politely, Alan acknowledged the Bard's introductions:

"Alan son of Dougall, native of a nation which did not exist when we walked the Other World... Arias, Chief Druid of Findias, City of the South, you have already met. Seated next to him is Moirfhius, Chief Druid of this city, Falias, the City of the North. On his right is Erus, Chief Druid of Gorias in the East. And next to him is Semias, who is Chief Druid of Murias, City of the West. Together they represent the authority of the World—except for the Bard of Bards."

Taliesin continued speaking for a few moments longer, but Alan MacDougall heard nothing of what the Bard said. Seating himself, he made a rapid appraisal of each of the Druids. Moirfhius, eldest of the four, had evidently been old when Falias was peopled. The gloom of years lay upon him. His black garments were styled like Alan's, but his tunic was longer. He had long, thin, gray hair, straggling whiskers, and a dour expression. Erus was of medium height and had pale, somehow hungry, blue eyes. He wore a flowing green robe, heavy with gold braid, over white garments. His armlets were wrought of pale gold and he was greatly bejeweled. Semias was a very tall, most unpleasant-looking man with a big nose and a great, square jaw, but smoothly shaven. His long arms ended in gnarled hands studded with thick knuckles. He was very powerful in frame and demeanor. And last was Arias, the lean, gray, cadaverous Druid. None carried swords.

Semias had difficulty waiting for Taliesin to finish speaking before he barked at MacDougall, "Where is this Gate into the Other World?"

Alan burst into a laugh, genuinely amused. "You don't beat around the bush, do you? That's an expression we use in my world. At least, it appears you believe I've really come from another world. As for the way I came, it would be very difficult to attempt to tell you where this Gate lies—even if I wished to do so—and I do not so wish. I have *not* told Taliesin. At the moment, I will tell no one.

"I have just arrived in this very interesting place and, thanks to the fine hospitality of Bard Taliesin, I believe I shall enjoy my visit. Certainly I have no thought of leaving at present. However, since I do plan to return eventually, I want to be sure the Gate remains open. There is a possibility, you know, that another using it might inadvertently close it. Or even intentionally close it for reasons of his own."

"But according to Caermarthen," ancient Moirfhius commented in a querulous voice, "he left all four Gates open for long periods and no one seemed to notice. Though he could not pass through himself because of the spell—"

Erus of Gorias interrupted smoothly. "I'm sure our visitor cares nothing about what Caermarthen said. As for me, I feel we are wasting our time. Perhaps later our friend will be more reasonable."

He stood up, as did the other three Druids, all moving toward the door. Arias and Semias turned as one to glare venomously at MacDougall before Taliesin, with a polite smile and a perfunctory farewell, ushered them out.

"What a strange lot," Alan MacDougall exclaimed when the Bard returned.

Taliesin slowly shook his head, his expression somber. "I see trouble ahead for you from those four. Semias and

Arias especially do not give up easily. But come—it is time you understood a few things about—Tartarus." He led the way to the chairs they had occupied after their arrival, apparently a favorite spot.

"Instead of your asking questions, suppose I tell you the story of this world as I understand it. Some of it I saw. Part is out of the tales told in my youth, and part is my observations and conclusions since I—came here.

"Long and long ago, when the world was very young and men had not yet come upon the earth to mar its virginal beauty, there was a day when time began. Lucifer the Bright One had just been cast out of the highest heaven because in his pride he sought to be like God." Taliesin's eyes filled as if with a dream. "Oh, he was fair, lovely as the dawn, but he admired himself too much. In that day he came to this world which the Greatest had looked upon and had said was good, and here he set up his dwelling place.

"Lucifer had power, power befitting the son of the morning, the Archangel of archangels, and he used that power to create. Beyond the misty wastes of the ocean, where sun and moon never shone and where tides never rose and fell, he caused an Island to grow. It was the World—his World. There would be no night to darken his creation, nor the blinding glare of midday, only bright and eternal dawn, because the light of it would be the unmatched beauty of the auroral fires. So there came into being the Land of the Dancing Men.

"That was just the beginning. He designed and created Four Cities for his World, each to be surpassing fair in its own way, each unlike the others: Falias in the North, a diamond surrounded by a velvety, pale green turf, a frost-grown city of icy crystals crowned by a perpetually flashing star . . . Gorias in the East, a city of gems set amid the jagged peaks and purple crags of amethystine mountains where pale gold seemed to ooze from the cracks in the rocks . . . Findias in the South—dark Findias rising like Falias from a plain, but also very unlike, for nothing grows in the black sand of the Desert of Gloom; torchlighted Findias, flaming against a sky of jet, where even the aurora appears but rarely, and then in timid waves that wax and wane, the Dancing Men never; Findias of the White Spear . . . and Murias in the West, the sunken city hidden forever in the caverns of the deep, where malachite walls cast back the chimes of carillons of jade and where faintly heard echoes in the hollows sound like sea-wolves growling and howling in endless fighting in the distant, shadowed dark."

Taliesin's voice ceased for a few moments, but Alan MacDougall made no sound, his mind painting pictures awakened by the imagery of the Bard. When Taliesin resumed speaking, his words were almost an intrusion.

"And then Lucifer created Lilith and gave her the breath of life. The Angel of Light surpassed all of his creations in giving beauty to the woman he had made. Hers was an unearthly loveliness. I have seen her, as I have seen her creator—whether in the body or no, who can say?

"Words are not equal to the task of describing Lilith. Her great eyes were blue as the sky over the Highland hills of my childhood, or tinged with the purple of the sea before a storm. Creamy white was her skin, with the faintest blush in her cheeks, and rowan-red were her lips; her hair was a cloud of shining, golden light, and she had a voice that was music to the ear.

"And there was none to hear its harmonies except her creator, for Lilith was alone. It is told that Lucifer fathered her first children—twin girls of great beauty. They grew up in that land where time was not, and the angels who had been cast out with Lucifer were their lovers. And all their offspring were daughters, for so had the Shining One decreed.

"So laughter rang through the Four Cities and on the plains and amid the hills, and the World of Lucifer became peopled by the Daughters of Lilith, and they were very lovely. They lived like flowers, thoughtless as summer blooms, alive for joy alone. For they had no souls.

"And the deathless clan of the sky loved the Daughters of Lilith.

"Then God made Adam of the dust of the earth and gave him Eve. And in the World of the Four Cities there rose a sighing. As flowers fade, so faded the Daughters of Lilith, for the angel lovers came no more; the sound of their wings was heard no more over Falias and Gorias and Findias and Murias. It came to pass that silence fell upon the Island Lucifer had made. And the glory of the Dancing Men was displayed where no eyes watched.

"In the world of Adam, the centuries followed their slow and plodding course. Lucifer, who had nurtured his enmity toward the Almighty One who had cast him out, had become Satan; as the sons and daughters of Adam multiplied, he tried to strike his Enemy through his creatures. Misery grew great among men; and Satan and his angels became very busy. Lucifer had forgotten the toy of his first creation.

"Forgotten—but not forever!

"To an island in the North Sea came a people called the Nemedians. They found already living there a race of sorcerers named Fomorians whose spells were too strong for them. They finally withdrew to the Northland, the place whence later came the servitors of Falias. And there the Nemedians became expert in all the arts of divination, Druidism, and all the abilities that were to make the more adept of them gods.

"The first of these—and the most gifted—was called Danu, and she became the mother of the gods, the *Tuatha De Danann*. With their new knowledge, they returned to the islands from which they had been driven. They were as gods of light compared with the Fomorians, who were evil and malformed and who practiced dark and gruesome sorceries. They fought a continuing war which was finally won by the *Tuatha De Danann* at the bloody Battle of Moytura. I was there and I could tell you tales—but not now. There is still much that must be told."

Taliesin stared into emptiness. "I have thought much

during the centuries since I left the Other World, and I see things now that I did not see then. I see now that the gods are not born—they are made! Oh—the gods of the Gaels were born of women, but none were gods until men worshiped them. With worship came their godhood; with belief came power.

"I know whereof I speak—for I was born of a goddess, yet I chose to be a bard. I chose to live by thought and word—by the tales and runes wrought by the mind rather than by the spells of magic. So men thought of me as Bard Taliesin—and none worshiped me—and no god's estate was mine.

"The goddess Ceridwen was my mother. It came about that, as she brewed a draught of poetic inspiration in her magical cauldron, three scalding drops fell on the fingers of the mortal who was helping, one Gwion. To ease the pain he thrust his fingers into his mouth, thereby suddenly acquiring knowledge of all things. The goddess, realizing what had happened, was furious and would have destroyed Gwion, but he fled. She pursued—but in his sudden knowledge was included shape-changing; hence in his flight he became various things. Ceridwen, in turn, became the appropriate predator to attack each form he adopted, forcing another change. He last became a grain of wheat, upon which she became a hen and swallowed the unfortunate Gwion. Later she bore him as an infant son whom she cast upon the sea. But the son survived to grow and become Taliesin the Bard."

Taliesin smiled slyly at Alan MacDougall. "This, at any rate, is the tale that men told in the olden times—and who am I to gainsay them! After all, I was not yet born when these things happened.

"But there came a day when men turned to a new god, a god who had died yet lived—whose priests claimed that he was the only Son of the One who had made all things—and men no longer worshiped the *Tuatha De Danann*. In time, the gods, even as mortals, forsook their flesh.

"It was then that Lucifer remembered his first creation.

Or so I think, and so I am certain it must be. For in new bodies we awakened in the Land of the Four Cities. Again the Dancing Men had those to watch in wonder as they leaped and cavorted between the glowing veils of light against the black velvet of the sky that had no stars.

"At first we were few—but many died, especially in time of war; and though many dwellers of the Isles had turned to the new god, many others still clung to the old way. Soon this world was peopled by those who once had lived and were still in the power of the Dark One. The four Druids you have met were given charge over the Four Cities. And I was set over all.

"It was then that Lucifer began his colossal jest—or so I believe. The servants, the warriors, the ones whose labors must keep this small world functioning, were not people from the Celts and Gaels! To Falias came the Northmen, the sea marauders, the Vikings. To Gorias were brought yellow men with different eyes, the Ch'in. To Findias came the Trolls, the workers of metal, who love to tunnel in the earth and who prefer the dark places. And to Murias, finally and most appropriately, came the Fomorians, the very ones whom the *Tuatha De Danann* had driven out. I say appropriately, for they had been prowlers of the sea who had driven the sea-wolves through the dark ocean deeps.

"There came, too, the god of the Fomorians—one-eyed Balor, they called him, or Balor of the Evil Eye; for though he had two eyes, one was always hidden because sight of it brought instant death. With him came others of his kind, like Fea the Hateful, Nemon the Venomous, and, worst of all, Morrigu.

"All the gods were worshiped and regained the powers they once had in the Other World. But one thing they had learned. Life could end. And perchance there would not be a third world with new bodies where they might awaken."

Taliesin shook his head ruefully and smiled. "Bear with a garrulous old one just a little longer, Alan son of Dougall.

Memories long repressed have been awakened—and long has it been since I found one to listen to the tale I tell. Almost I have finished. I must tell of the final jest of Lucifer.

"The gods met in conclave at a certain place, there at the behest of the Shining One. I, too, was there, though not in the flesh. Then he appeared in their midst in all his splendor, with a brightness on which none could look; he was surrounded by a host of lesser angels. There he told us he had caused four Gates to form—one, perhaps all, a way between this world and the one whence they had come, and through it we could return to the other life, if we could find the Gates—or perchance the right Gate. He said he had placed a guard upon the other side, bound by a spell, and that on both sides the key to success lay in a quest."

Taliesin sighed wearily. "Through endless, timeless centuries, the gods and Druids and any others who learned of the Gates have searched for them, but always in vain." Bitterness grew in the voice of the Bard. "And that is Lucifer's jest. The Gates are there—but we are never intended to find them, though we seek forever!

"And then you came! And you are not part of the Luciferean plan, of that I am certain. So now you can see why there is—interest—in Alan MacDougall."

Silence followed the Bard's long recital. Alan's thoughts were in turmoil. He had heard so much that was beyond his imagination, so much that his pragmatic mind wanted to reject as wild fantasy. Yet—he was here, in a land that simply couldn't exist—by the logic of his engineer's mind—yet *was*! There was so much for his near-eidetic memory to dwell upon, but which, for the moment, insisted on acceptance.

He thought of the strange dream he'd had, just before—or after—going to sleep.

"Any comment I might make at this point on what you've told me would be ill-timed. There is so much that is so new . . . I must think . . . But perhaps you can explain this unusual dream of mine." Then he repeated, almost verbatim, the strange conversation during which he had seemed to be an audience of one.

Taliesin's eyes grew wide with surprise as he listened. When MacDougall concluded, the Bard laughed in amusement, to Alan's surprise.

"I find it amusing," Taliesin explained, "because the gods were trying vainly to make direct contact with your mind—yet somehow *you*, who have no such skill, heard all they said in conclave. This I cannot explain—but I can understand their frustration.

"I have some small skill at perceiving thoughts myself, but I find all your thinking is your own; none of it is open to my reading... There were five gods you heard speak. First Danu, whom I have mentioned before, the Mother Goddess and most respected of the *De Danann*. Then you heard Morrigu, generally thought of as the war goddess, a very unpleasant individual, not one of the Family. Nuada of the silver hand, the third speaker, twice was King of the *Tuatha De Danann*. He lost one hand in battle; and Diancecht, physician of the gods, made him an artificial hand of silver, so skillfully constructed that it was as useful as his own had been. But of course it was a blemish, so he could no longer sit upon the throne. Later his original hand was restored and he regained the Kingship. Then you heard Dagda, the 'good god.' A harper of rare ability, he has little cause for harping here. He is a god of simple tastes, but a formidable fighter. And the last speaker was Balor of the Fomorians, Balor of the Evil Eye.

"These gods—and all of the others—can meet in a sort of conference without being physically present; you must somehow have heard such a meeting. What you heard verifies what I said about the importance the gods place upon your being here and of their protecting you.

"As for the mention of Arias and me—of course we reported so important an event as your coming; though, in fact, Danu and Morrigu would have known without our

informing them." Taliesin smiled slyly. "Not everything
does Danu read in my mind; only what I choose. I am of
her blood—and I can block intrusion as I wish—as I am
doing now." He looked keenly at MacDougall. "Have I
made things clear?"

"Just one more question. You named the young
woman—Darthula—in whom I expressed interest. How
could you be so sure?"

Taliesin laughed in quiet amusement. "No problem at
all. She was on her way to see me! I will be sending an
escort to accompany her here after we have decided what
your and my immediate activities will be."

"She came here to see you?" MacDougall was puzzled.
"But you were not here—"

"I suppose I should explain it all," Taliesin said resignedly. "A special messenger came from Gorias recently as emissary of Darthula, asking for an audience.
She wants me to act in her behalf in a dispute with Erus
of Gorias. She planned to come when Erus also would be
here to attend the School for Druids, where he would be
teaching. Though I knew I might not be here when she
arrived, I told her to go ahead with her plans and I arranged for her to stay in a dwelling I reserve for guests.

"My trip to Findias in the South had already been
planned, a conceit of mine since others could have han-
dled the details of the trading trip just as well. But I enjoy
the change of scene and welcome any excuse to bring it
about. We went with a cargo of food and returned with
the copper, brass, and bronze metalwork we needed. On
the return, Arias of Findias came with us to attend the
Druid's seminary. They have, I understand, a large class
of applicants for training."

"A Druid's seminary? I thought no children were born
in this land. Whence come these applicants?"

Taliesin hesitated. "True, there are no children or youth,
nor can there be; but there are—replacements—for those
who die. And among them are some who seek to learn
the craft." He stood up as though eager to end the con-

versation. "Is it your wish to meet Darthula when she arrives here for our meeting, or would you prefer to call on her yourself before I send for her?"

Alan also rose. "Oh, I'd rather call on her myself. Where do I find her?"

Taliesin gave him the simple directions: a walk northward along the same street to a pillared white mansion with large, barrackslike buildings and extensive stables behind it, these to house the guards and their mounts. It was the only structure of its kind.

"You will want your sword," the Bard concluded, "though you'll hardly need it."

MacDougall grimaced. "I'm not a swordsman—"

"To go unarmed is to invite trouble."

"Yet you and the other Druids carry no weapons."

"We have other—powers—and at need we command the swords around us."

With a shrug, Alan went to his room and returned with his weapon strapped about his waist.

Taliesin examined the scabbard in fascination. "I noticed it on the way, but not carefully. Beautiful work. Once the property of someone important—" He looked intently at MacDougall. "Tell me before you go: How did you find the Gate to—Tartarus?"

MacDougall, making a sudden decision, bared his right arm to display the serpent armlet. "I found this on the floor of the tower in which the four Gates appeared. Until I put it on, I could see nothing unusual; afterward, it played tricks with my eyes, and in the walls I saw the bronze disks, one of which I opened to enter this land. The armlet clings as if it were part of me. I simply cannot remove it.

"I found also that I know the language spoken here, though I have no idea what tongue I speak. Certainly nothing I've ever studied."

Intently Taliesin examined the two-headed serpent, making no attempt to hide his excitement. "I have never seen its like, but I have heard of it—and that quite recently. It once was worn by Caermarthen the Druid, as I think was the sword you bear. He recently joined us."

"But how—?"

"He was of the olden times, but Lucifer's arts kept him trapped in the other life. He was the Guard of the Gates. Something released him, and now he is here."

MacDougall thought of the age-browned bones on the flagstones where the armlet had lain. The remains of a man recently dead? He shut out the thought.

"I'll be on my way," he said, "unless there is something else I should know."

Taliesin smiled and bowed. "May good fortune attend you."

As Alan started briskly along the sidewalk, the ever-present aurora forced itself on his consciousness. How could anyone ever become accustomed to the spectacular display? Brighter by far than the Northern Lights of the Arctic, it was also far more changeable, going from sheet to curtain to vertical beams and a blend of all three with kaleidoscopic rapidity.

There was a flow of pedestrians moving in both directions, and MacDougall became aware of their frank stares. He supposed it was his dress, probably marking him as someone important. In the white pebble street, an occasional horseman rode by; but MacDougall paid little attention to these.

Now that he was on the way to see the beautiful Darthula, he felt like a fool. After all, what justification did he have for making the call? They had seen each other under strange circumstances—but what made him assume she'd want to see him again? He chuckled faintly. She couldn't do worse than slam the door in his face, or, if he got inside, have him thrown out. He'd soon find out what his reception would be, for he had almost reached the mansion Taliesin had described. As he approached the walk, he heard a sudden exclamation at his side.

"My sword! That is my sword!" A long, bony hand grasped his arm and spun him around.

Startled, MacDougall stared into the deep-sunken eyes of a tall, black-robed, bony-faced man. At the same instant the hand shifted to his upper arm, tightening convulsively about the two-headed serpent armlet. Fury blazed on the cadaverous face.

"My armlet too!" The hand swooped down and tore the weapon from its scabbard hanging at MacDougall's side, the man leaping back with the point at Alan's breast.

All this had happened so unexpectedly and with such speed that MacDougall was momentarily frozen. But when the steel point touched his skin, he reacted instantly, reflexes responding without conscious direction. A powerful sweep of his arm thrust the blade aside, and he sprang at his assailant, his hands closing on the scrawny neck. The force of his effort bore the other off his feet, the sword clanging free.

They crashed to the walk with the attacker underneath, gasping and tearing at the constricting fingers, his tongue protruding, his face turning purple. MacDougall eased the pressure, his anger fading. He didn't want to kill the man.

"Are you crazy?" he ground through clenched teeth. The other tried to answer, but only wheezing sounds came from the gaping mouth. Aware of the growing crowd ringing them, MacDougall released his grip, retrieved his sword, and rose, holding the blade in readiness.

As the man lay gasping, slowly recovering, Alan thought of the words of Taliesin concerning the former owner of the sword and armlet—Caermarthen the Druid; and at that moment he noticed that the man bore no weapon. This most certainly was the Druid who had recently arrived in Tartarus. But, he thought stubbornly, he wouldn't give up the sword—and more emphatically the armlet—without a struggle. He doubted that he could surrender the armlet at all.

"You must be Caermarthen," Alan exclaimed, "but when you died you left these in the Other World. I found them; and you lost all claim to sword and armlet." His expression grew grim. "You almost died a second time."

Sudden fear appeared on the still-flushed face, and the Druid struggled to his feet. He looked wildly around, his eyes suddenly lighting, then gasped out, "Erik, Sven, Ingolf—seize him!"

At these words, three stalwart Norsemen, drawing swords, sprang from the ranks of the watchers and darted toward MacDougall. Instinctively he flung up his sword. He was no swordsman and he knew it, but he'd fight until he was cut down.

All three Vikings swept in as one, with the tallest a step ahead of the others. He came rushing in on Alan's left with a broad sidesweep of his longsword at the very moment that the second Viking lunged. No one could have parried those blows, certainly not the unskilled MacDougall. He made no effort to do so, but with a precise timing that he knew was not his own, he slid underneath that double flash of steel and leaped out again. His sword blade, no longer shimmering steel, now gleamed redly for half its length.

One Northman hurled his sword aside and flung both arms around his waist, then slowly sank to his knees and fell forward on his face, legs twitching and quivering.

The other two came charging, one wielding a slashing edge, the second a darting point—but the blade of MacDougall, as though with a life of its own, sent the strokes slithering away harmlessly. With furious effort the attackers drove in with thrust and lunge and sweep, causing MacDougall to marvel as he flicked away flashing blades or matched body speed with swift counterstroke, evading death by a hairsbreadth. For this was not his skill. Verily it seemed as if he were possessed by an unmatched master of the sword. And even as his darting blade found the hollow of a Norse throat, there flashed through his mind what Taliesin had said concerning the protection he would receive from the gods.

As frothy blood spouted from the great gash and the man dropped like a felled tree, the lone survivor leaped in, engaging Alan's blade—and suddenly the Norseman's sword flew through the air to land in the middle of the street, point buried in the white sand.

The blond warrior crossed his arms and glared into the victor's eyes. "Strike, and may Loki damn you forever!" he rasped. "How can we slay a warlock?"

MacDougall shook his head. "Get your sword. A brave man deserves to live." The Viking's eyes widened in surprise as he circled the victor, moving to retrieve his weapon. Alan wiped his own blade clean on the tunic of one of the fallen men.

He faced the Druid, more interested in his own strange reaction than in Caermarthen. He should feel sick, nauseated. He had just killed two men! Yet he was aware only of a feeling of unreality, of utter detachment. Actually, *he* had killed no one. It was the work of whichever god had controlled his sword, his legs and arms, his entire body.

"Mercy! Mercy!" the terrified Druid cried. "I relinquish all claim—" He faced the silent crowd. "Protect me!" he bleated.

The watching Norsemen moved slowly forward, their expressions menacing though wary. There was no way, MacDougall thought, that he could escape a concerted rush.

"I'll not touch you," he said, "if you'll just answer some questions—" He halted as an interruption came from an unexpected quarter.

With a great shout, scores of strangely clad Oriental warriors began pouring out of the buildings behind the home where he expected to meet Darthula. These were the Ch'in—the guards from Gorias! No longer robed, they wore the waist-length, quilt-type armor plate of the ancient Chinese warrior and carried long, gleaming lances. The greatly outnumbered Norsemen melted away, and the Ch'in ringed Alan MacDougall protectingly.

He turned to Caermarthen, who stood trembling. "There were some brown bones in the tower where I found this sword—and near them the body of my brother, a slight man with black hair. If you indeed came from the Other World and from the tower, tell me what happened."

"By all the gods of the *Tuatha De Danann*, I have no knowledge about your brother's death. He—slew *me*! He appeared out of the storm with a sword for which I had searched for thirteen centuries, since it was part of the spell that bound me to that endless exile and the key to my release. We fought, and that accursed blade drank my blood. It gave me release, but not as I had expected. I suppose I should be grateful."

"You wore the serpent armlet; why couldn't you pass through the Gate as I did?"

"The curse. I could see beyond the Gates, but there was an invisible barrier that prevented my entry."

Alan MacDougall frowned in thought. "One more question. The scroll I found—what does it say?"

Caermarthen answered with obvious sincerity. "In truth, I have no idea. It was in the tower when I was put on guard, and I studied it repeatedly, but could never determine its meaning."

MacDougall motioned to the men of the Ch'in. "Let him pass." A way opened and the Druid scurried through.

One of the Gorias guards bowed and spoke in the universal language of this land. "The Princess would speak with you. Your name?"

Returning the bow, Alan gave his name and followed the yellow man into the pillared dwelling. He was ushered into a room very like that of Taliesin, even to the exquisitely spare furnishings. He caught a glimpse of a female servant disappearing through a doorway, but his gaze was held by the lovely face he had expected to see. Darthula! The name had been created just for her. She was seated at the far end of the room in almost theatrical staging, her hair piled high in a platinum halo, her diaphanous garments of palest blue. Her expression was aloof, disdainful.

"Princess Darthula," the guard announced, "this is Alan

MacDougall." With one hand she gestured faintly, and the man swiftly withdrew.

Alan bowed deeply, then straightened and looked fully into her face. Subservience, he had decided, was not for him. He spoke in an assured tone. "I thank the Princess for sending her guard to my rescue—though I seemed to be doing quite well before they came."

Darthula's color deepened. She was not accustomed to being addressed in that fashion. She ignored his words and said, "Tell me—are you not the man in strange apparel I saw standing alone near the road to Falias; and when I approached and spoke, your tongue was dumb? And when my men sought to obey my orders, you vanished?"

Again MacDougall bowed, but there was faint mockery in his answer. "In truth, I first beheld your beauty under the circumstances you cite; and I could not answer because I was stricken speechless by your loveliness."

The blue eyes flashed and her color heightened even more, though her tones remained restrained. "But—how could you disappear? Are you a god? Or a weaver of magic spells?"

"I had come from another world," MacDougall answered quietly, "and when your servants greeted me so royally—with pointed lances—I stepped back through the Gate."

The hauteur and stiffness were gone as Darthula half rose in her excitement. "The Gate! Tell me more!" She clapped her hands, and when the Chinese servant reappeared, she ordered, "Feiyen, a chair for my guest." She had it placed at her side.

MacDougall seated himself and held back a grin. What a difference that magic word "Gate" had made! She must know about the way to escape. But somehow her sudden new interest gave him little of the satisfaction he had thought it would. Her interest was not in him, but in his knowledge.

Now she was all eagerness, pressing her guest for information. He told her even less than he had told Taliesin, saying nothing about the gold armlet. He learned to his relief that she had no real idea about where she had seen him. When he finally rose to leave, she urged him to visit again, even to come to Gorias, where he would be treated as a very welcome guest. She extended her hand and, as he bowed over it and kissed it, she gave no indication of displeasure.

Outside, he started retracing his steps southward, his thoughts in a strange state. On the one hand, he dwelt on the unquestioned beauty of Darthula, whose loveliness was greater than he had ever seen in a woman. On the other hand, the feeling of unreality again asserted itself, as if he had entered some Lewis Carroll Wonderland. He almost expected a white rabbit to appear, or a grinning Cheshire cat.

Instead he became conscious of the muted sound of horses' hoofs charging along the sandy street at his rear, coming from the north. As the sound changed suddenly to a louder clatter, he half turned to see at least a score of horsemen bearing down on him in two columns. In a flash, he realized they intended to grab him from both sides!

Seconds away from contact, he darted into the street, where a slow-moving horse was being driven northward. To the rider's utter surprise, MacDougall caught his right foot and, with a single powerful heave, flipped him off his mount. Leaping into the saddle, he kicked the frightened horse into action, almost touching the oncoming chargers as they passed. By the time the attackers had slowed their mounts and swung around, MacDougall had already gained a substantial lead. The confiscated animal, he realized in moments, was an unusually fleet runner.

Knowing nothing about the streets of Falias, Alan was at a disadvantage. If he turned off what was evidently the main thoroughfare, he might get into a dead end—assuming there were dead ends—and be trapped. Since he was steadily increasing the distance between him and his pursuers, he continued straight ahead.

After a time he noticed that the houses were more widely spaced; eventually, they ceased to appear altogether, the white street alone continuing. Turf had reappeared, covering the plain with a smooth, pale green carpet. Some distance ahead, a mile or more he judged, he could see the bulk of a great white building unlike anything else he had seen in Falias. Indeed, it seemed entirely out of harmony with the original design of the city.

He glanced back. The pursuers had slowed to a walk; several had actually halted. This was puzzling—then he thought of his "protection." The *Tuatha De Danann* must somehow be responsible. But there was no point in his stopping. He sped on toward the great white building.

It was a walled block about six storeys in height and at least a mile in length. No windows or doors marred the vast expanse. The road led into a broad, rectangular opening beyond which Alan glimpsed flashes of green. As he approached it, slowing his pace, a backward glance revealed the horsemen growing small in the distance, heading back into the city. Strange! They'd given up or had been called off. MacDougall shrugged. That gave him time to investigate this curious building.

He rode through the entranceway into what appeared to be a small park, but a park with only one path, leading to a normal-size doorway that was barely visible, flush with the wall. There was no sign of knob or handle. The usual smooth turf was broken only by some of the strange picture-book trees that were typical of this land. There was no indication of life.

MacDougall slid off the horse, tethered it to one of the trees, and removed the bit from its mouth. The animal began to graze as Alan walked up the path to the door. He pressed hard on the smooth white panel, but nothing happened. It seemed as solid as the wall.

He doubled a fist to knock—and the door opened outward. Two of the Norsemen, in typical dress, complete with horned helmets and swords, walked out. Startled, Alan MacDougall stepped out of their way, grasping the hilt of his weapon. They brushed past him as if he were not there, moving stiffly down the path. They were blinking like men awakened from a deep sleep, exposed to sudden light, and there was something almost mechanical in their stride.

The door was nearly shut when MacDougall caught it, swung it wide, and stepped inside. It closed softly behind him.

Momentarily he stood motionless, his heartbeat suddenly accelerating. The place was cold—like that of a house in midwinter after it had been vacant for a long time. There was complete silence. He held his breath. A faint blue glow illuminated the room, seeming to emanate from the floor, walls, and ceiling. Directly before him, hanging from invisible supports, was a great metal dome, like a huge reflector, all of twenty feet wide. Its base stood about eight feet from the floor. From beneath it came an intense blue light, warmer than the surrounding air.

MacDougall looked about wonderingly and with a strange eerie feeling. What *was* this place?

To the left and right of the dome, resting on sturdy supports about three feet tall, were endless rows of long, narrow boxes, suggesting—Alan gasped—suggesting coffins! He stepped to the box nearest him, and a chill tripped up his spine.

In the receptacle, under a transparent cover, lay the naked body of a man, eyes closed, utterly still. In the pale blue light, the form looked ghastly. As he glanced into the first box in the next row, which held the cadaver of a woman, the truth struck Alan MacDougall.

Taliesin had said they had replacements for those who died. This was the house of bodies, the Hall of the Dead—waiting to be given life!

The two who had walked out before he entered were replacements for the Norsemen who had died in the fight! Restored to life, clothed, and sent back into the city!

He had enough of this place! He sprang to the door, flung himself against it, and came to a jarring halt.

The door was locked.

CHAPTER 4

Balor Strikes

The silence seemed to deepen, to become more absolute, if that were possible, as Alan MacDougall stood motionless just inside the refractory door. He fought an impulse to hold his breath; even his breathing seemed out of place. The cold started penetrating through his thin garments, chilling him to the core.

MacDougall, he thought, now you've done it! The rows upon endless rows of boxes were suddenly uncomfortably suggestive. Calming himself with conscious effort, he examined the door with utmost care, looking for a way to open it. No luck. Although he could see where the door met the wall, the jointure was so perfect that they seemed to merge. There was no knob, no handle, no apparent hinges; without tools, there was no way out!

But someone must be here—surely those men coming

out had had help in their resurrection! He took a deep breath and shouted at the top of his voice. "Hallooo!"

The word echoed hollowly through the great hall, slowly fading into silence. He was alone.

Taliesin and the gods! The protection he was to receive—surely they'd find him. But—no! They kept track of him through the people around him, and here there was no one.

He caught himself yawning. Damn! He was getting drowsy—it must be the cold, or perhaps the strange blue light—and that really could be bad for him. A long aisle stretched between the wall and the—coffins. Might as well call them by their proper names, he thought. He began jogging in place, then started walking briskly toward the distant end of the building, a half mile away at least. If he stayed with the wall, he couldn't get lost.

There had to be a way out—and of course there was, he thought with sudden relief. He had entered when the door had opened to permit two Norsemen to leave. It would open again when another was restored to life.

He simply had to wait until someone out there died.

But what if he was a half mile away when the door opened? No problem. There had to be some sort of warning, some time involved. That green dome must be the means of restoration; and certainly a body that had been cold for centuries, no matter how sustained—even by Luciferean spell—would require time for recovery. Somewhat reassured, he continued his brisk walk, then began to jog.

He reached the far wall, retraced his steps, and started another round. Again he became aware of a growing drowsiness, despite his quickening pace. Then, as he had done when on the verge of sleep the previous—night?—he heard voices, within his mind, obviously. He recognized the one he recalled as Danu's:

"I have called you because of Balor. He has blocked all communication with Semias, Druid of Murias. I can sense his touch. He himself will answer no call. This can

only mean that he is taking some kind of action which he wants hidden from the rest of us. Has any of you information?"

There was no immediate response, then Nuada growled, *"Why he was included among us never made sense to me. Always trouble, and he's at its root!"*

"Ours is not to question," Danu chided, *"but we can be grateful that he is not one of the Family. There is another matter—the whereabouts of our visitor from the Other World. He is alone, so we have no line of observation. From the serfs who pursued him, we know he was fleeing toward the Forbidden Area. When they became aware of this, of course they stopped. His flight, as you know, was caused by an attempt to seize him, a plan directed by Arias of the South."*

MacDougall could sense the steely note that entered her thought. *"Were you behind the effort, Morrigu?"*

The goddess' raucous voice replied in mock indignation. *"Whatever made you think so unkind a thought? You must know that I have great difficulty in controlling Arias. I shall chide him for his failure; his failure, that is, to cooperate fully with me."*

There was more conversation within the *Tuatha De Danann*, none of it of significance to Alan MacDougall. He was more concerned with fighting his drowsiness. To sleep under these conditions would be fatal. Once more in his jogging he had reached the wall, and now he decided, since he had to keep moving, that perhaps seeing something of the place might help him stay awake. Besides, the voices had ceased.

He examined his surroundings.

For the first time, he noticed that the coffins seemed to be on a sort of endless belt, made up of wide, overlapping disks. At the end of the first row he observed a U-track leading to the second row; disks similarly united the third and fourth rows; and so on. He also noticed a ramp going to the next level and he followed it. The floor above was an exact replica of the main one below, at least with regard to the caskets, as were the next two levels.

The fifth level was strikingly different. There were no coffins here, only a vast, empty chamber that stretched into the distance in the mist of pale blue. He noticed the lines of the conveyor system, and the picture became clear. Once this floor, too, had been filled with waiting bodies, but they had found release—if that was the term. Correction. That many had been revived, probably the cadavers on this level moving to lower floors.

He started estimating the number of bodies, but as the figure began to take shape, he desisted, revolted. There were thousands upon thousands!

Another ramp led to what appeared to be the top level, much narrower than the others; as MacDougall peered upward, he saw a difference in the illumination. This was not pale, misty blue, but the flickering white radiance of the aurora! Anticipating a welcome change, he climbed the slope, blinking in the comparatively brilliant light.

The ceiling, the roof of the great building, was formed of sheets of pellucid crystal. The spectacle was fantastic, the entire sky the ever-marvelous aurora. Then his gaze fell on the contents of the upper chamber, and all thought of the veils, curtains, and rods of restless light vanished.

Drowsiness gone, he stood frozen, staring intently through the bright interior. Had he actually seen what he thought he saw? He'd had a spectral impression of floating wraiths. Not wraiths, but bodies, as transparent as figures of glass—and all, he now realized, were women unclothed. He sensed crystal casings, coffins like angular bubbles, blocking no light, packed tightly together and heaped three high, one upon another.

This, he thought wildly, was the most insane thing he had seen thus far in this insane world. By contrast, the contents of the lower floors were the most logical thing in the world. Unless—and in a flash he saw the solution, out of the tale Taliesin had told him.

These must be the Daughters of Lilith, who had faded

from the Land of the Four Cities when God placed Adam in the beautiful garden and the deathless sons of the sky had ceased to call. Their bodies were here, reserved for the day when Lucifer, again in power, would restore them to life for the visits of his minions! Whence so wild a thought? Certainly not Alan's. Did he actually *believe* such an answer? Refusing further speculation, MacDougall turned his back on the incredible scene and strode down the ramp.

As he reached the fourth level, he became aware of a faint, barely discernible sound, one not his own. Its cause quickly became evident. The rows of coffins were moving! He saw now that one row and part of a second had been emptied—and all the cases on this level were slowly, so slowly, moving. It was an eerie sight in this cold and quiet place. Fascinated, he watched—then was suddenly struck by its significance.

A body or bodies moving under the dome! And all of the others moving up a spot or two or three!

Swiftly he raced down the ramps to the first level, panting, catching his breath. He came to the dome in time to see four of the boxes move into place under the blue light now growing in intensity. That which followed was like something seen in a dream. MacDougall knew there was movement only because of the changes that occurred; the pace was so slow as to be undetectable. How long he watched he could not tell. He only knew that he stood transfixed for an endless period, his front warmed by the radiance fanning out from beneath the dome, his back chilled.

First the substance and the cover of the caskets became wraithlike, dissolving, finally disappearing, exposing four nude bodies, three men and a woman, all in the prime of life. They lay in a sort of matrix that perfectly fitted the contours of their bodies. In the blue radiance, they had a ghastly, waxen, artificial look. With the passing of time, the intensity of the light increased until MacDougall had to shield his eyes from the glare. Looking through the cracks between his fingers, he saw the first apparent movement as the four sat up slowly, like automatons; then, with the tilting of their supports, they slid erect and stood motionless in the full glare. Turning, they walked stiffly toward the rear to pass through a wide opening. All of it suggested the slowest of slow motion on a movie screen. And as the upper parts of the caskets had dissolved, so did their bases.

Alan MacDougall moved for the first time since the fantastic spectacle had begun, stretching to ease his stiffness. The brilliance of the light abated, though warmth still emanated from beneath the dome. He turned to warm his back, from time to time glancing over his shoulder.

The four finally reappeared, fully dressed in garments appropriate to the Viking period, the men armed. Moving directly toward the doorway, their eyes fixed straight ahead, they passed within a few feet of MacDougall and ignored him completely. They walked as if under compulsion, as a robot might walk. When they paused before the door, MacDougall sensed movement behind him as four more caskets began inching into position.

The door swung open and, one after another, the Norse passed through, Alan close at their heels.

He inhaled deeply as the bright aurora flared overhead; the closing door shut in the faint blue glow. It was good to be out!

He followed the group as they marched stiffly down the white walk through the little park to the exit. His horse was grazing peacefully where he had left it. Halting, he watched until the newly restored people reached the area near where his pursuers had turned and retreated. There they were stopped by a small body of waiting horsemen. As nearly as MacDougall could count, there were eight men in the group. After what appeared to be a brief conversation, the four Vikings continued toward the city, conversing in a natural fashion.

Alan MacDougall grimaced. Those blasted horsemen

didn't give up easily! Then one of them stood erect in his stirrups and waved—and MacDougall's heart leaped.

Taliesin! Certainly there wasn't another in this land who looked like the Bard of Bards! Then why didn't he approach? Alan realized the answer as he recalled the phrase "the Forbidden Area," from the conversation of the *Tuatha De Danann*. The taboo included everyone, even Taliesin.

Quickly he caught his horse, replaced the bit, and rode toward the waiting group without a backward glance. He'd seen all he ever wanted to see of the macabre Hall of the Dead.

Taliesin greeted MacDougall with obvious distress on his round face. "Are you unharmed?"

"Unharmed? As far as I know—yes. But it's not an experience I want to repeat. I had no warning—those thousands of bodies—even the Daughters of Lilith—"

Hastily the Bard interrupted, sounding almost frightened. "I do not wish to know! All this is Forbidden."

"By whom?" Alan asked curiously, then suppressed a half chuckle. "Lucifer?"

Taliesin's eyes narrowed. "It is not humorous. The area and everything about it are prohibited. There is a barrier in all of us—even the *Tuatha De Danann*—forbidding knowledge of the place."

They were riding toward the city as they talked and soon passed the four whose departure from the great white building had permitted MacDougall's escape. The Norse now were engaged in animated conversation.

"Just one question, Taliesin," Alan persisted, "and I won't mention the matter again. It's about the replacement procedure; are just enough men or women sent out to make up for those who died?"

The Bard responded with evident distaste. "I have no answer—except that there are a great number of disposal units in each of the Four Cities, covered openings leading underground—and the number of bodies dropped into the openings is always replaced in kind. Each city has its own replacement center; and though six of the Ch'in, nine of the Northmen, and one woman passer-by were killed, those six yellow men will be replaced in Gorias."

MacDougall weighed what the Bard had said. No burial, but simply dropping the dead, as he visualized it, down a manhole; then some underground system automatically transmitted news of arrivals to the proper replacement centers in the Four Cities, even distinguishing between male and female, Norsemen and Chinese, Trolls and Fomorians. That system had worked unattended for fourteen centuries—or for who knew how long in this timeless land.

He thought of Taliesin's remark that six of the Ch'in had been killed. Obviously Darthula had to be involved—

He caught up with the Bard. "Fifteen warriors killed—six of them Ch'in. What happened?"

"The attempt to seize you failed." Taliesin's voice and expression were grim. "With Darthula they succeeded. The Ch'in fought well, but they were greatly outnumbered. It happened after she left me and was returning—"

"Darthula kidnapped! By whom? And why?"

"It must be the work of Semias, since he has left the city and the other Druids are still here. And I am sure he did not act without the full support—no, the urging and prompting—of Balor of the Evil Eye, the god of the Fomorians. As to why, I see two possible answers, perhaps truth in both." Taliesin slowed their pace.

"Either they assume Darthula knows something about the location of the Gate, since you visited her—and you told me she had seen you when you first entered our land. Or—and this is more likely—they are using her as bait to trap you, figuring you would follow her, again because you expressed interest in her. Arias certainly supplied information which he gained during the ride into Falias; and Balor and Semias are efficient watchers, so we may be sure they know of these matters. There is little that is secret here, except whatever goes on in your mind."

They rode on in silence, entering the heart of Falias

where pedestrians appeared more frequently, as did other horsemen. They did not resume their conversation until they had settled into chairs in Taliesin's home. The Bard called a servitor and gave instructions for dinner to be prepared.

"Surely you must be famished," he said to Mac-Dougall. "You were—away—for three sleeps."

"Three sleeps!" Alan exclaimed. "Impossible! I'm hungry, but not unusually so. But of course—it's the insane time in this place." He changed the subject, saying matter-of-factly, "It's my fault that Darthula was seized, so of course I'll have to follow. That is, if I can count on your help—"

"But that is exactly what Balor wishes," Taliesin objected. "You can't realize all that is entailed. The step Balor has taken, if he is pursued as you plan, could lead to great trouble, perhaps even to warfare between the Four Cities and, worse, between the gods. Balor must be aware of this and, it appears, is willing to take the risk."

"Surely you exaggerate," MacDougall protested. "Why war?"

"Because almost certainly you will be captured by the Fomorians if you attempt to rescue Darthula. And they would find ways to make you lead them to the Gate." As Alan began to protest further, the Bard added, "Would you sit idly by and watch Darthula being tortured? You don't know Balor—nor Semias—nor the Fomorians. And this at the very least they would do."

MacDougall stood up and began pacing the floor. "You mean I wouldn't have a chance? Even if all the other gods were to help? Where are the magic powers they are supposed to possess?"

"True, the *Tuatha De Danann* probably would help; but even among them, there are those who would seek to gain an advantage for themselves."

"What are the alternatives?"

Taliesin hesitated. "There are two. One—you show the way to Danu and let her decide who should pass through. The other—" Alan saw that it took an effort on the part of the Bard to complete the statement. "—you elude me and go back whence you came and close the Gate."

MacDougall looked with surprise at his host, then grinned. "I appreciate that, but I am aware that you also have a desire to return to the Other World. From now on, you'll stick closer to me than a brother." Alan's jaw set stubbornly and he scowled. "No, my friend, I really have no choice. Unless you somehow prevent it, I'll do my damnedest to get Darthula out of the mess I've gotten her into. And I hope I can count on your help."

Taliesin shrugged resignedly. "I was afraid that would be your answer. And of course I'll help all I can. We shall eat and sleep so that you are well rested. Then, with a retinue of my best men, we'll start. Darthula, of course, has been taken to Murias, and that will be our destination."

MacDougall had some difficulty in getting to sleep, his mind seething with all that had filled his life since the last sleep and with what lay ahead, but finally slumber came. He awakened refreshed, with no idea how long he had slept. He decided to put on his own garments; certainly he would leave nothing of his behind, for he had no intention of ever returning to Falias.

With or without Darthula, he'd get out of this place! Thought of the lovely girl caught him up short, raising questions. Sure, she was beautiful and physically alluring; during their brief contact she'd appeared to be intelligent as well—but he was thinking about her like a dreamy-eyed adolescent. He, a staid bachelor of thirty-three—whatever made him harbor romantic ideas about her? Why did he assume that she'd want to go with him? Oh—she, like everyone else who learned of his knowledge of the Gateway out of this land, wanted to leave. But that didn't mean she was interested in him as a person, a man. However, the fact remained that he'd gotten her into her present difficulty and would have to try to get her out of it. That much was clear.

As he clipped his canteen to his belt and slipped the strap of his knapsack over his head, he thought of the scroll. Maybe he should show it to Taliesin. He groped for the cylinder.

It was gone! Someone had removed it!

"Taliesin!" he exclaimed, then regretted his outcry. He certainly wasn't going to accuse the Bard of filching the scroll.

Taliesin appeared instantly. "You called me?"

"I spoke your name involuntarily," MacDougall answered. "I've just found out something is missing from my knapsack." He described the vellum cylinder. "It was here when I left to visit Darthula, and now there's no sign of it."

The usually jolly face became serious. "And you think that perhaps I removed it?"

"No!" Alan shook his head emphatically. "Perhaps a servant."

"That can be answered quickly."

The Bard called out sharply and, when the maid appeared, he sent her to gather all the domestic staff. In moments they assembled, standing quietly waiting. Taliesin questioned them bluntly, describing what was missing. All promptly denied having any knowledge of the scroll and were dismissed.

"I can vouch for their innocence," Taliesin said. "I read their thoughts as they answered. Did anyone in Falias know of the existence of the scroll? Did you refer to it in conversation?"

He means Darthula, MacDougall thought. Then he remembered—he had questioned Caermarthen about it not at all secretly. He so informed Taliesin.

"Then there is our answer. It was the work of one of the Druids. Or even one of the gods. What Caermarthen knows, the rest know. And if one of the gods—Balor, for instance—decided to do so, he could appear in this room while the household slept, take what he wanted, and reappear wherever he wished."

"They have that ability?" MacDougall demanded.

"They have that ability; in concert they can even take others with them."

Alan grimaced. "I don't suppose the scroll is of any importance—except that it was in the tower, according to the Druid's statement, when he was bound there. I wish now I had shown it to you."

"It may be very important," Taliesin disagreed. "Yes, if only I had seen it. I have skill in such matters. Great skill." He frowned ruefully. "Perhaps we shall find it." For the first time, he noticed that MacDougall wore his own clothing.

"I suppose it is prudent for you to dress thus—though eventually you and I shall have to be disguised as Fomorians. Their garments are such that they will easily hide what we are wearing. Time enough to don them just before we enter Murias. To put them on now not only would be uncomfortable during the ride but would indicate our destination to any watching Druids.

"But come—we will break fast."

They sat down to the usual breakfast of Falias, varied this time by an oatmeal porridge, served with honey and a thick milk that MacDougall decided must come from mares; he ate without question, believing he'd enjoy it more in ignorance.

They had almost finished eating when they heard a knock on the door. A male servitor entered and, at the Bard's nod, announced, "Calling is Yen K'ang, captain of Princess Darthula's guard."

"He may enter."

The yellow-skinned man came through the doorway, only then relinquishing his lance to the servant. He bowed deeply, revealing an ornately braided headdress and shoulder armor made up of two-inch squares of silver, wired together and suspended from a loosely fitting silver collar. As he straightened, Alan noted similar armor fully covering him to the waist, below which a pale yellow skirt reached to the knees. Knee-length boots of canvaslike fabric completed his costume.

"Welcome, Captain K'ang. What is the purpose of your coming here?"

"Respectfully, I speak for my men. There are almost one hundred of us. We are leaving for Gorias without Princess Darthula. We are greatly shamed, for we failed to protect her. Because she came to see you, we are wondering if you have plans to pursue her abductors. If so, we would go with you, if we may."

Taliesin nodded thoughtfully. "As you surmised, we have such plans. We will be leaving very soon. And—yes—you may go with us. You may prove to be very useful. I respect your loyalty to your mistress. I should add that I am certain she will not be harmed. That is not the purpose of her abductors. Where are your men?"

"We are mounted and waiting outside." The Ch'in smiled. "We have not blocked the street; we are a long line, one horse behind another."

"Are your men well supplied with provisions? This may not be a rapid operation."

"Indeed. Well supplied, each man with his own ration."

Taliesin stood up and bowed. "We shall join you soon." The servitor appeared and ushered the visitor from the room.

The Bard resumed eating. "That provides a partial answer to what I thought might be a problem. I have thirty men whom I trust, but I had expected to add others to our forces who might not prove as dependable. These Ch'in are good fighters and loyal to their Princess. My plan is now simplified."

Breakfast finished, Taliesin issued orders; shortly thereafter, a mixed caravan of Norsemen and Ch'in moved along the white street toward the southern gate, Taliesin and MacDougall leading the way. The Ch'in rode their white Mongolian horses, but had put aside the pastel robes MacDougall had seen when he first stepped through the

Gate. Taliesin, Alan noted with silent wonder, had a sword belt and sword about his thick waist.

Guards with whips appeared as if by magic, but because the horsemen remained strung out in a single line, there was no need for their services. The great gates swung open, and they left Falias behind them.

As they reached the crest of the first hill, MacDougall drew rein and turned for one last look at the crystal city.

Half apologetically, he said to Taliesin, "Incredibly beautiful, from the outside. Since I may never see it again, I want to remember it thus."

For much of the ride, which retraced his journey into Falias, MacDougall saw little of the landscape through which they moved. He was mentally reliving the happenings which, to him, seemed to have filled two very hectic days, but which—who knew—might have taken a week—or an hour—of his own time! Certainly for him, time had not lagged in the Land of the Dancing Men!

As they approached the area where MacDougall thought he would find the memorized landmarks, he turned to Taliesin and asked, "Tell me, where *are* the gods and goddesses—Danu and Morrigu, Dagda and the rest? I've been wanting to ask, but never thought of it before when we were together."

The Bard nodded. "A natural question, and not a difficult one to answer. The *Tuatha De Danann* and the gods not of the Family have bodies of flesh and blood, since they were born of women; but they have powers far beyond those of the Druids, let us say, though here that power has lessened. They live in the Four Cities according to their own desires. They assume any shape they wish and move about as they wish. Balor and Morrigu usually stay in Murias by choice, though they are not limited to the sunken city. Danu and Dagda are most often associated with Falias—but they are not strangers in Gorias. Dalua the Dark King and Nuada, despite their being so different, seem to prefer Findias, among the Trolls—for reasons totally unlike. The metalworking of Findias fascinates Nuada. His famous invincible sword was forged there. And Dalua feels more comfortable in the shadows of the gloomy tunnels.

"Dalua, the *Amadan Dhu*, whom men call the Dark Fool, the Witless One, is the strangest of the gods. He is the one who laughs when there is no reason for mirth, whose touch is supposed to impart madness or, some say, death. He is not as witless as men believe. As for his touch, I cannot say.

"Then there are Camulus and Lugh and Orchil..."

Taliesin's voice droned on with the pantheon of the gods; and though Alan MacDougall seemed to be listening intently, looking steadily at the Bard, his gaze went past him, searching. He saw the first indicator, a tree standing out from a nearby copse—then a long slope, the rock by the roadside—and finally the graduated stones pointing to the Gate! It required iron control to keep his expression unchanged, but he succeeded. Now he knew he *could* find the way out!

At a slight break in Taliesin's recital, he asked casually, "How many gods are there in Tartarus?"

The Bard frowned. "I have never counted. Probably twenty—perhaps more—but most are never heard from, apparently satisfied to lead quiet, undisturbed lives. Like all of us, they are doubtless wearied by an existence where little or nothing changes."

Conversation died and the miles crept by. Then an idea occurred to MacDougall. He watched the roadside for a logical spot, quite different from the actual location of the Gate. He found what he wanted; then suddenly, turning his horse, he kicked the heels of his hiking boots into the animal's ribs and sent it racing across the pale meadow toward the space between a pair of large trees.

Instantly two of the Norsemen who had been riding directly behind him were in hot pursuit, catching up with him in moments; as he flung himself off his mount, they did likewise, grasping and pinioning his arms. Within moments Taliesin had joined them.

"You see," MacDougall said, smiling broadly, "I knew it wouldn't work—though of course the Gate is far from here. But I had to make such a test."

The Bard's eyes twinkled. "I thought as much. But obviously I could not take the chance—though my impulse was to let you appear to succeed."

At Taliesin's word, Alan and the Norsemen caught their horses, mounted, and resumed the ride as if nothing had happened. They reached another stretch of woods and, in its midst, a crossroads where they turned to the right. Alan noticed a slight upgrade, gradual but continuous.

Taliesin commented, "The left arm leads east to Gorias, straight ahead is the way to Findias, and westward lies Murias. There are no other roads on the Island."

After a time the topography changed to a rather sudden ascent, going higher and higher into steeper hills, passing through a long stretch of pallid grass. They came to a stream and stopped to eat and to feed and water the horses. After a short rest they went on, finally reaching the highest hilltop, crossing a wide plateau covered with heavy woodlands, then starting downward. The descent was more rapid than the climb, bringing them to a rolling flatland with fields of oats and rye and barley; scattered farmhouses nestled among trim, tidy orchards.

Their course led close to one of the orchards, a peach orchard, and Alan noted another anomaly of this time-mad world. There were trees in full bloom, trees with small green fruit, and others with red and yellow peaches bursting with ripeness. Now he saw the possible source of the honey he had enjoyed for breakfast: countless bees noisily reaping the harvest of nectar in the sweet-smelling blossoms.

"This is where much of our grain and fruit comes from," Taliesin commented, "though there are other farming areas, one of them south of Gorias and one nearer to Findias, but far from the black plain. About half of the fish we eat comes from the fishermen near Murias and the rest from the north shore above Falias. The farmers and fishermen are of any of our races, and none live in the cities. They are solitaries who want it that way."

They passed through the farmlands and reached a thick wood of honest evergreens, some of great size, indicating centuries of growth; beyond lay the sea. Before they had passed completely through the woods, Taliesin brought the caravan to a halt and spoke to the group.

"There is no chance of our rescuing Princess Darthula by force. The Fomorians are fighters; they are not fond of the other peoples of the Island; and, of course, we are greatly outnumbered. Success can come only through stealth and the work of a few.

"You Ch'in, you men of Gorias, will remain here in the woods, divided by the road into two groups, out of sight but guarding the way to or from Murias. There are others interested in controlling the Princess and even more interested in MacDougall. If either or both are brought out, it will be your job to rescue them. If we succeed, we may come running with the Fomorians after us and will need your help.

"As for you men of Falias—you will have a different role to play. Svend Olafsson, you will be in charge. All of you will enter Murias, and you, Svend, will ask the guard at the gate to direct you to Semias the Druid, as you have a message for him from me. He has quarters in the Hall of Games. You will be carrying two messages— one for Semias and one for Darthula, which you will insist on delivering in person. The message to the Princess first— this is imperative—and then the message to Semias."

From somewhere in his voluminous garments, the Bard produced two small scrolls, one white, the other gray, and handed them to Olaffson. "The white one is for Darthula—make no mistake." He watched as the Norseman stowed them carefully in an inner pocket.

"I think you will be free after delivering the messages, but I could be mistaken. If you are imprisoned, which I don't foresee, offer no resistance. If not, remain at the

Hall of Games, ready for a possible call from me. You will join the Fomorians as spectators at the arena—a logical place for you to wait. If things go wrong, you will have to make your own decisions. And should the operation end successfully without need of you, I shall let you know. Questions?"

There were none.

"Meanwhile," Taliesin concluded, "MacDougall and I will enter the city undetected and be about our own tasks. On your way—and may the gods be with you!"

The thirty Norsemen left the partial concealment of the woods and started toward Murias. Taliesin and MacDougall watched them go. The Ch'in, after dismounting and leading their horses, dispersed quickly into the deep woods. Captain K'ang took half his men into the thicket across the road; the rest vanished into the nearer shadows.

Strange, Alan MacDougall thought. They were heading for a city, but no city was in sight. From the various casual references to Murias—"the sunken city, the City Under the Sea"—he had not expected to see one, but it still seemed strange. For the first time, he really looked at the scene ahead.

Up to this moment, and during their entire trip, they had not seen another living soul. Perhaps this was not surprising, with people confined mainly to the Four Cities. But now he saw signs of life. The shore was about a half mile away, the deep blue of the sea meeting the white sand of the narrow beach, the azure waters vanishing into, almost merging with, the aurora-lighted sky, the dancing lights reflected on the placid, barely moving surface. The spectacle of the two auroras, one the mirror image of the other, was startlingly, breathtakingly beautiful.

Placid! Never had MacDougall seen such peaceful waters. The faintest breeze blew in from the west, just enough to cause a slight ripple on the millpond smoothness. There were boats out there, oar-propelled, with no provision for a sail; some were fairly large, with crews of six or eight men busily netting fish. To the north, not far from the water's edge, was a cluster of houses and low buildings, a small fishing village with wharfs and docks and other boats lying at anchor.

But the object that caught and held his attention was a narrow island, two miles or more in length, pointing like a hand straight out from shore. A gray stone causeway, roughly twenty feet wide, was the arm, extending from the white road onto the island for perhaps a half mile. Besides the island itself, Alan stared at a familiar, blocklike, white building at its far end—an exact duplicate of the replacement center—the Hall of the Dead—in which he had been a prisoner.

The Norsemen had reached the island, and suddenly they seemed to be riding down a steep hill, first the horses and then the riders disappearing rapidly. They were descending a declivity—a ramp, MacDougall realized. In a few moments all were gone.

"Into the sunken city," Taliesin commented, aware of MacDougall's watching. "It lies deep beneath the sea."

About to respond, Alan stopped short as the Bard's arms shot stiffly above his head, his face looking skyward; then his fingers stretched out and his rigid arms moved downward, describing a slow arc, held at shoulder level for a moment before descending slowly to his sides. He lowered his head and stared directly forward. His lips were moving, but no sound came forth. A ritualistic gesture, Alan thought.

He saw rising out of the sea a tenuous gray cloud. He could see it growing, thickening, sweeping shoreward. There was the faintest of sounds, a whispering of a rising wind, bearing ahead of it what had become a dense wall of fog. MacDougall saw the fishermen rowing frantically toward shore. They vanished as the tempo of the wind increased; in moments it reached the little island, first blotting out the replacement center, then sweeping over the ramp, moving on to the causeway, and creeping up the road toward the two watchers. He felt the first touch of the unnatural wind, chill and sodden.

"Dismount," Taliesin directed, doing so himself, "and tie your horse to a tree. There's a long rope behind the saddle. Leave bridle and saddle in place; we might need the mounts in a hurry." From his saddlebag the Bard drew black garments, loose and flowing trousers and jackets; he gave a set to MacDougall and began to put on the other set himself. "Put these on over your clothes—and the cloak over your backpack. Among the Fomorians, the hump will appear natural. Fasten your sword over the garments. I've brought a weapon myself, not to use it, but because the lack of it would appear conspicuous."

With only half his thoughts on what he was doing, MacDougall continued to watch the thickening fog. "Impossible—a fog in a world without sun or clouds!"

He must have muttered the words; as if in response, he heard Taliesin say, "This is a common spell, once much used by the Druids for concealment, but never used in this place to my knowledge." The Bard added deprecatingly, "In a world without clouds, I anticipated difficulty—though there is the moisture that causes the dewfall—so I secured the help of Mother Danu. The fog will hold until she dispels it."

He inspected MacDougall critically, then shook his head. "Those yellow whiskers and hair are too noticeable. No Fomorian looks like that. We'll have to change you. I think my powers are equal to it."

Alan stared narrowly at the Bard as his lips moved with silent words and his short fingers formed cabalistic designs in the air. Alan didn't think he cared for this magic hocus-pocus. Thoughts of rebellion formed, but were never completed; he was aware of a strange, creeping sensation moving through the muscles of his face, a flowing, a thickening. Involuntarily MacDougall's fingers went to his chin. His beard was gone! He felt thick, wrinkled folds of flesh, a sharp, angular jaw, a huge nose, heavy, pendulous lips, and thick brows over deep-set eyes.

"I needed a shave," he growled, "but this is ridiculous!"

Taliesin chuckled with satisfaction. "A perfect Fomorian! I'll join you." And with the words Alan saw the Bard's familiar face flow into a grotesque caricature, the chin receding, a small, red, buttonlike nose replacing the ample member, the eyes protruding and moving together. Alan gasped.

"I don't like any part of this—" he began, but Taliesin interrupted.

"Don't be alarmed. Trust me. It's very elementary shape-changing. The effect is only temporary—and quite necessary. Now we're ready. Let us enter Murias."

Taking MacDougall by the arm, Taliesin led the way with sure steps into a velvety fog almost tangible in its density, their footsteps muffled by the veil of gray mist.

CHAPTER 5

The City Under the Sea

The fog thickened with each step. MacDougall had to resist an impulse to slow down, to grope his way; but the Bard, apparently with some inner sense to guide him, maintained their brisk pace. They left the flat stone walk, entering upon a steep ramp, and it became necessary to hold back. The descent seemed interminable.

At last they reached a level stretch of walkway that ended in a great bronze barrier. It was a double door, all of thirty feet wide and more than that in height, green with the patina of age. There was a suggestion of intricate design in bas relief ornamenting the surface, but the fog hid all details.

Taliesin moved to one side, grasped a huge bronze ring, and pulled. It hardly moved, but from beyond the door they heard, faint and muffled, a single, deep bell note. Within moments the door opened, moving ponderously inward. MacDougall caught a brief, clouded glimpse of two bulky figures pulling the doors—they vanished in a great insurge of fog of unparalleled density. And behind it, enveloped and concealed by it, Taliesin and MacDougall walked unchallenged into Murias, the City Under the Sea.

Alan felt the Bard's firm grip on his arm, steering him to one side and through a narrow doorway. They were in a small room furnished with two chairs and a small table, hazy in fog. Behind them, they heard a heavy, querulous voice:

"Fog! May Nemon curse the one who formed it. Come in—whoever you are!"

At Taliesin's urging, they hurried through the chamber and out through a second doorway. Horses! MacDougall became aware of the strong smell of horse flesh. They were in a great corral crowded with hundreds of horses, most of them at feed boxes. The two smoothly moved through their ranks, causing little stir among the docile animals. There seemed to be no one in attendance; evidently their care fell to the gatekeepers.

They reached a retaining wall, gracefully wrought of uniform blocks of polished malachite; Taliesin halted and closed his eyes, frowning in concentration. MacDougall, after a single glance at his companion, seized the opportunity to inspect his surroundings.

He gazed upward into a vast curving dome, like the roof of a tremendous amphitheater, all of a thousand feet high at its center. He thought of the interior of the Hall of the Dead, for this ceiling also glowed. It was an anomalous thing, an unbroken sheet of soft, white radiance with no impression of glare, yet the source of a brilliance that lighted all the city! Where he stood, evidently near the edge of Murias, appeared to be an elevation with everything sloping downward toward the center, then rising gradually to a point in the distance at his own level. Somehow he thought of himself as being inside a great, circular, double-convex lens. And there were no streets—at least nothing that he could recognize as such. There seemed to be no order in the positioning of the buildings, nor any uniformity of design, except that all were built of green stones—what seemed to be jade or serpentine or malachite, a blend of rough and polished blocks and plates—and all were beautiful. Each dwelling stood alone, narrow lanes forming zigzag or rectangular walks around them, suggesting more than anything else a vast maze.

MacDougall was recalled from his wondering survey by Taliesin's voice.

"Olafsson has just delivered my message to Darthula. Semias the Druid is there; after the Princess read the scroll, he took it—as I knew he would—as well as his own. My men were dismissed. She's under guard, of course; but now I know where she is. I might have known—the most logical place in Murias—the Place of Games. There is no other large building, and that has many rooms."

He led the way along the wall to a gate; they passed through and joined the pedestrians in the area. "What I wrote to her is not important, simply the assurance that the gods have not forgotten her and will act. I warned him to be certain no harm befalls her."

MacDougall was barely aware of the words, his attention arrested by his first glimpse of Fomorians. One word sprang unbidden into his mind:

Hideous!

They were twisted, misshapen, distorted; none really resembled another. Taliesin's—and he supposed his own—malformed features were handsome by comparison. They were equine, vulpine, goatlike, porcine. Some had protruding fangs, pointed downward; others had upward curving tusks. Some were almost chinless; others had great prognathous lower jaws. Skins were scaly or thickly warted, leathery or crossed and recrossed with deeply scored wrinkles. One hopped past on a single central limb;

another dragged a useless extra leg; a third had goatlike hoofs suggesting a satyr. In short, every possible malformation existed in every possible combination.

Only in one characteristic was there resemblance—without exception, their expressions were of gloom and savage hatred personified. And little wonder, appearing as they did.

Under his breath, MacDougall muttered, "How in hell could creatures like this exist? What kind of diabolic mind could create such monstrosities?"

Taliesin heard him and laughed faintly, though his features remained grimly set. "Your questions are well expressed. In Hell indeed—and creations of a diabolic mind. None but Lucifer."

"But these buildings!" Alan protested, momentarily forgetting to hold his voice down. "They are beautiful. In its own way, Murias is as lovely as Falias—and to be peopled by such as these!"

Taliesin's hand fell on his arm. "Calm yourself. You forget that this land was not made for us, but for the Daughters of Lilith. When the Dark One repopulated the empty city, it must have appealed to his sense of humor to combine beauty and grotesquery."

They were making their way through the twisting maze of lanes as they spoke, utterly ignored by the Fomorians they passed. MacDougall followed Taliesin's leading, without an idea of course or destination. The Bard apparently knew where they were headed, and that was enough. They were descending a gradual downward slope toward the center of Murias.

Suddenly noticing, Alan commented, "No horsemen here. Everybody walks."

"For obvious reasons. This place was not planned for any other means of travel. And since most Fomorians never go outside their own city, walking suffices. That accounts for the enclosure for the horses just inside the city gates." Taliesin, Alan noticed, seemed preoccupied, his thoughts elsewhere.

As they walked, MacDougall became aware of a pervasive background sound. Just barely audible, it was a faint but lovely chiming, as of countless carillons, unpredictable melodies, high and sweet, always there, never obtrusive. He listened intently, marveling at the strangeness of this added note of beauty in the midst of all this ugliness...

Then, deep in the lower register of his hearing, came another sound, as subdued, barely there; but this was a grating, jarring growl—a rumble as disturbing as the carillons were soothing.

What had Taliesin said? "The chimes of carillons of jade...echoes in the hollows like sea-wolves growling."

What a place of contradictions!

Without warning, extraneous words formed in MacDougall's mind—Taliesin's.

"Don't speak. If you are receiving my thought, simply slow down and drop back a few paces." Wonderingly, but without hesitation, Alan followed directions. The thought continued. *"I cannot perceive your thoughts; I believe you are able to receive my direct communication. I am being observed—I can feel it. Probably not physical watching, nor is it Semias. I fear it is Balor. And it has just begun, of that I am certain, for I am very sensitive to such spying. I know, too, that none of the gods can perceive my thoughts when I wish to prevent it, so I am fairly sure you have not been identified."* After a short pause, the thought continued.

"If you have understood all this, gradually increase your pace and pass me. Keep going in the direction of the dome which you can see rising above all the other buildings. We still have some distance to go. I will direct you."

Trying to make his actions appear natural, MacDougall slowly drew abreast of and passed the Bard, continuing for another twenty steps or so, then maintaining what he judged had been their pace. Taliesin kept up the strange one-way communication, effectively guiding him. After a

time, their destination resolved itself into a towering octagonal structure of green stone, ornately carved, to a
degree suggesting a cross between an Oriental mosque
and a Grecian temple. Alan noticed that most of the pedestrians seemed headed for the same building.

Taliesin's thoughts betrayed tension. *"I am becoming
disturbed. This was a stupid thing to do; but what has
been done cannot be undone. If I can convince Balor that
I entered Murias alone, that you are still outside the city,
we may be able to arrange for you to get to Darthula. It
is asking much; but if you two can somehow be isolated,
together and unobserved, with some shape-changing there
are possibilities of your getting away.*

*"You keep going and circle to the entrance on the other
side of the building, which is the one generally used by
spectators. I'll go in on this side, but I'll continue to direct
you. In any event, go to the central arena. There will be
some sort of contest in progress. My men are in the Games
Building, most of them at the arena, available if we need
them."*

Taliesin's flow of thoughts halted briefly, then continued somewhat hesitantly.

*"I believe I can deal with anything Balor can bring
into play—and Balor will be our main problem. But there
is always the possibility that you may be left to your own
resources, so I think I should tell you that your armlet
has powers of which you have no knowledge. Shape-
changing is one of them. In time of need, simply think
into the serpent—I know of no other way to describe it—
and visualize what you wish to be. Similarly, it will enable
you to discern the true appearance of others employing
shape-changing. There are other powers, but I hardly
think you could use them without special instructions."*

The flow of thoughts ended, and MacDougall grinned
wryly. The Bard certainly would have withheld this last
bit of information if he had not felt it important for
MacDougall's actual survival. He wondered what those
other powers might be...He concentrated on his im-

mediate actions, growing more tense. He was on his own—and this was no game.

On the heels of the Fomorians, he entered the Place of Games. A soft, white glow illuminated the curving corridor in which he found himself, the walls and ceiling shedding internal light. He followed the caricatures of men who apparently knew where they were going, noting occasional ornate bronze doors in the left wall. One of these, standing ajar, revealed silent Fomorians seated about a large table, intent on a game involving blocks of polished green jade which they moved around on lined boards. Finally, ahead lay a wide-open doorway in the right wall, providing entrance to the upper levels of a great arena that was his destination. The others entered, moving down a long steep ramp, past row upon row of seats, about half of them empty, finding places closer to the arena floor.

MacDougall paused just outside the entrance and looked around. The corridor evidently circled the amphitheater. Just ahead on his left was an intersecting hallway. He walked casually toward it and found a broad passageway, half of it a ramp leading to the next level above and the rest a way to another parallel, circular corridor. Retracing his steps, he seated himself in the top row and took in the scene.

The glowing ceiling, ten feet above him, was ornamented by a delicate tracery of mingled flowers, vines, and formless concepts that were somehow ethereal. The place was designed, obviously, for a different audience from that which it now held. Below and opposite him were the Norsemen, shunned, it appeared, by the Fomorians, the nearest sitting at least a dozen feet away from the visitors.

At the moment, six Fomorians were completing mopping the floor and now carried pails of red-tinted liquid through exits in the ten-foot-high wall rimming the arena. As they disappeared, ten others came out of another doorway—tall Fomorians wearing chain-mail vests over loose garments, longswords at their sides. As they appeared, a change came over the audience. There was no loud reception, but rather a low growl, a hungry sound, its savagery intensified by its very quiet.

All of it seemed incongruous in this place. Who, he wondered, had been the performers to appear before an audience half celestial; what was the entertainment? Ethereal dancers? Angelic musicians? Certainly not anything resembling the grotesque gladiators now in the center of the arena.

These, as if at drill, formed a wide circle, standing about five feet apart, facing the watchers. As one, they drew their swords, thrust them aloft, and with a shout turned to engage a foeman. It was an extraordinary spectacle—but it had barely begun when a sharply sent thought came from Taliesin:

"I have found them—Darthula, Semias, and Balor. Come to the second level—" There was a break in the thought, then a hasty resumption: *"Balor is attacking mentally, but I can . . . Oh, no! Morrigu and Dalua have joined—"* Sharply cut off, the communication ended.

MacDougall stood up instantly and stepped out into the corridor, halting just outside the exit. He felt a strange shifting of his facial muscles; as the grotesque features went, so his blond whiskers and hair returned. He looked swiftly about, but saw no one. The change had not been observed. He strode toward the ramp leading to the floor above.

Clearly, Taliesin had met more than he expected. Not only Balor, but two other gods—Morrigu, the goddess with the voice of a crow, and Dalua, a god the Bard had called the Dark King—had joined forces against him. Taliesin's powers had been blocked, immobilized.

MacDougall was completely on his own.

He moved up the ramp, slowing as he neared the top, crouching, looking warily about. His eyes widened. Certainly he hadn't expected a parklike vista of fountains and flowering bushes. Through the mist of jetting water, he saw, fortunately some distance away, a group of Fomorians gathered about a familiar figure, Semias the Druid.

Alan crouched behind the foliage, attempted to spread the branches, then drew back, startled. These weren't plants at all—they were hundreds of incredibly beautiful replicas of bushes carved in jade with flowers formed of varicolored gemstones. But they afforded concealment and permitted his scanning the nearer end of the great chamber. He saw no one. He looked back at Semias, who seemed to be giving directions to the dozen or so Fomorians. He looked around for shelter and saw a wide doorway screened by cloth-of-silver draperies. Nothing else offered. He certainly couldn't remain where he was, nor could he make a direct approach to the Druid. Better to cross the open space. He could run or crawl; he did neither, but walked purposefully toward the opening, hoping he was not observed and that no one was in the room. Holding his breath, he parted the drapes and entered. The room was empty.

Turning, he spread the curtain a mere crack and peered toward the group. There was no indication that his movements had been noticed. With a glance, he took in the chamber. It was a bedroom with a very large, low-lying bed set against the wall opposite the door, its cover a black, silky material, smooth and wrinkle-free. He stood on a rug of purest white with a soft, deep pile. Beside the bed was what appeared to be a dresser of white metal, probably silver. A low, backless stool before the dresser, formed of the same metal with a white pile seat, completed the furnishings.

In the walls to the right and left were narrow bronze doors, closed but with no sign of knob or handle. He saw an opening in the wall close to the low bedstead. Warily he investigated. It was a bathroom with strange but recognizable facilities. The walls, he noticed, were gently curved, and the light coming from walls and ceiling was subdued and restful.

Quickly MacDougall crossed to the door to his right

and gently pushed it open. It moved soundlessly on hidden hinges and, after he stepped through, moved back into place. This room was an exact replica of the one he had left. He crossed to the third, which was precisely the same. And all were alike in showing no sign of recent occupancy. He thought he knew the answer.

These were the rooms once used by the Daughters of Lilith and their lovers from the sky! Untouched—for how long? In this timeless land, in rooms where nothing happened, perhaps no time at all. No matter. What mattered was what he would do.

One fact was clear. Unseen, he could now approach Semias, perhaps overhear what was being said. Probably the Fomorians were being put on his trail, but there was a slim chance he might get a clue to the whereabouts of Taliesin and Darthula. At any rate, he'd better move.

But he hesitated.

He should really obey that inner voice—*now that you're alone, get out of Murias—back to the Gate and your own world.* This would solve all the problems his arrival had created. Maybe if he could do his own shape-changing... For the moment, he'd try to learn what Semias was up to. Four more rooms, he estimated, should bring him on a level with the Druid. He passed quickly through number four, entered five, then stood stock-still, staring.

This room was occupied! Incredibly occupied! Impossibly occupied!

On the black-covered bed lay a sleeping woman, as beautiful in a very different way as Darthula, her only garment a diaphanous, knee-length, pale blue gown that revealed more than it concealed. Her long auburn hair, gently curling, formed a ruddy frame for a face of rose-tinted ivory, several graceful strands draped artlessly across full breasts. But most startling were broad gold bands that circled wrists and ankles. From all four circlets flowed yards of sturdy gold chain, joining at the head of the bed with small rings free to slide about on a single massive ring anchored to the metal bedstead.

MacDougall saw all this in a single startled glance. Though he was not aware that he had made the slightest sound, the girl moved, stretching, and her eyelids parted slightly. After an uncomprehending moment, her eyes, deep blue-green, met the man's, came into focus, and, startled, opened wide. She sat swiftly erect, her full lips forming a soundless "O."

"Please," MacDougall entreated hastily, "don't scream! I had no idea anyone was here. I'll leave at once."

"Oh, no—don't go!" Her voice, low and sultry, harmonized with the rest of her. "I never see anyone. Only Balor—and the woman who brings me food...But who are you—and how dare you come here? All men fear the god Balor."

"You are being kept here by *Balor*?" MacDougall demanded incredulously.

The woman grimaced distastefully. "You find it hard to believe? You think I am not one to attract—a god? Even a god with one eye?"

"Oh, no! You are beautiful. Only the idea that the gods—and women—"

Impatiently the girl stood up, waving her chained arms. "That is not important! It *is* important that we leave. I have had enough of chains. Take me out of this."

"Of course!" MacDougall replied apologetically, though he had not yet fully recovered from the shock of his discovery. Almost mechanically, he stepped to the dresser, upended the metal stool, and drew his sword. "Put an arm chain here," he said, pointing to the bottom of the metal leg. It took only two blows of the steel blade to cut through the soft gold. The other chains followed, and the girl was free.

Impulsively she flung her arms around him, pressing tightly against him, and kissed him warmly. "Thank you—and what is your name?"

MacDougall drew a deep breath as the girl stepped back. "I am Alan MacDougall. And you?"

She stood proudly erect. "I am Macha Mongruay. In

the old life I was Queen of the City of Emania. They called me Macha of the Ruddy Hair. Here, I lived in Findias until Balor saw me and desired me." She laughed, and there was genuine amusement in the sound. "The Evil Eye is old—and though he still desires me—he *merely* desires me!... And which is your city? Falias, I wager. And why have I not seen you before?"

MacDougall decided to evade. "Falias indeed. And I have only recently joined the living. We should be going— but have you no other garments?"

Macha looked down at herself and smiled. "Oh, yes." She moved quickly into the bathroom and emerged in delicate sandals and a long robe, only slightly less transparent than her sleeping gown. Together they entered the next room, crossed it, and continued into the one beyond it.

"Do you know this building?" Alan asked. "A way to leave unseen?"

"Yes, indeed. Through Balor's apartment. The way I was brought here. He spends little time there, being busy elsewhere." They continued moving as they talked; when they had passed through two additional rooms, Macha halted and peered between the curtains.

"Almost there. One more room, then we have to cross the hallway; but since few dare to come into this area unless summoned, we should meet no one." As she had not mentioned Semias and the Fomorians, they must have dispersed.

She led the way and Alan followed, beginning to wonder about this entire impossible episode. Such things didn't happen, not even in Tartarus. And this Macha—she must have hypnotized him. To think of taking her from Balor— he must be mad.

They had entered a sumptuous apartment, with massive furnishings of gold and silver and a deep, dark green rug. There was no sign of Balor. Then, on a long table, MacDougall saw his scroll! With a triumphant exclamation, he seized it and thrust it into a pocket in his black Fomorian cloak.

"This is mine. It was stolen from me."

"Don't waste time," Macha said impatiently. "Balor could return, and then you would be in great trouble." She hooked an arm into his and led him toward a bedroom. "We leave by a stairway in a room beyond this. Hurry!"

"But," Alan objected, "you can't walk outside without wearing more clothes! You would stand out like— like—" He groped for words. "Besides, though I am as anxious as you to get out of here, two friends of mine are here, held prisoner by Balor and Morrigu and a god named Dalua. I won't leave without making an attempt to find them."

Macha of the Ruddy Hair drew back a step and looked at MacDougall with a mocking smile. She laughed, not a pleasant sound.

"From Balor, I know a way out of Murias that two of us can follow; but not four. And certain it is that you have not been in this place very long if you think to outwit the gods you mention—Balor, who can slay with a look, Morrigu the Great Queen, the war goddess, and Dalua the Dark King, the Laughing One, whose touch brings madness." Again the strange laugh, utterly foreign to the sultry tones of the seductive redhead.

She stepped back, drew apart the folds of her robe, and looked at MacDougall with her most alluring smile.

"Am I not lovely? Am I not—woman? Lovelier than that pale puppet Darthula? And yours—if we escape." She moved closer and seized his arm. "We must hasten!"

"I—let me think." MacDougall's voice was strained as he turned away, concealing his face lest he betray his thoughts. There was a sinking feeling in the pit of his stomach. He had been an utter fool! He had *not* mentioned Darthula! He knew it. The deception had almost been perfect—and he had accepted it without question. He would have noticed nothing except for that single slip . . . What had Taliesin said? "Think into the armlet—power to show the true form of shape-changers."

With eyes narrowed, concentrating with all his faculties, he fixed his thoughts on the two-headed serpent coiled about his arm. He became aware of an—opening—a widening—of his perception. He felt the woman press against him and was conscious of a sudden chilling that made his flesh crawl.

He looked at her and, in one fleeting instant, saw a wrinkled crone with corded, masculine muscles and distended veins, beaklike nose, coarse gray hair, powerful, pointed chin, red-rimmed black eyes under craggy gray brows, and clawlike talons of fingers gripping his arm. With utter revulsion and with all his strength, he flung her away.

Morrigu! It could be no other. And she had kissed him!

She spun across the room, lost her balance, pitched head first against the corner of a metal chest, then dropped heavily. A brief twitch, and she lay still, blood welling from a long gash in her scalp.

Momentarily shaken, Alan MacDougall stood unmoving. What an idiot he had been! He saw now what had really happened. Morrigu, chancing to see him, perhaps in the amphitheater, then seeing his entry into the bedrooms, had changed into the alluring Macha, complete with chains and transparent garments, and waited for the fool's arrival. And he had thought he could pit his wits and abilities against the powers of such as—that! Now he had only one hope—somehow to get out of Murias.

And, as if echoing his own thought, there came a silent communication from Taliesin, seemingly distant, weak, but clearly understandable:

"I feel a weakening of their control. I hope, Alan, I can get through to you. Get out of Murias—your only hope. Try for invisibility. Invisibility, understand. Visualize it and think into the armlet. Together they are too strong for us. Don't concern yourself with Darthula and me. Get out!"

A new voice entered the picture, this one audible, deep, and vibrant, coming from outside the apartment—the voice of Balor, as MacDougall recalled it from the dream-detected conference of the gods.

"Something has happened to Morrigu—I sense it. Her own fault—working alone for her own gain, I vow. Serves her as she deserves."

A second voice, that of Semias, muttered a reply, low and unclear.

They were close—he must find a hiding place. Invisibility? He hoped it would work—but he'd need time to try, if only a few moments. He dashed into the bedroom. Maybe the bathroom? No—if they treated the hag's wound, they'd want water. The bed was too low to slide under, but there was a great chair in the corner! He sprang behind it, crouching down with no time to spare.

He heard Balor's voice. "Morrigu, unconscious! And look how she's dressed!"

"She's fallen—or was struck," a strangely eerie voice, probably that of Dalua, said.

Semias cried out. "That scroll is gone!"

"Then that accursed MacDougall has been here!" Balor said. "Semias—out the back way. That's a fresh wound—he can't have gone far." Sounds of scurrying and more conversation followed, evidently attempts at reviving Morrigu.

But MacDougall had his hand on the gold armlet. He thought of invisibility, of light passing through or around him, of crystalline transparency. He thrust all doubt from his mind. Here in this world, strange powers *worked*! And suddenly he knew they *had* worked.

He opened his eyes, held a hand before them, and saw the back of the chair with nothing to hide it. He looked down and saw the green of the rug, with two indentations where his shoes pressed into the fibers.

Strange exhilaration surged through him. What a power! He stood erect, secure in the certainty that he could not be seen. His belief was confirmed by his being ignored by the two working on the unconscious Morrigu. She now lay on the nearby bed. A vessel had been filled with water, and they were bathing the gash.

The three gods were no more than ten feet away. Gods? MacDougall had difficulty in thinking of them as deities, they were so completely human. There could be no mistaking Balor, a veritable giant, little short of seven feet tall and proportionately broad. His garb was coarsely woven green breeches and jacket. Two swords, one long, one short, were suspended from a broad gold belt of meshing plates. He had grim, craggy, savage features, a short black beard, and thick, shoulder-length hair. Slanting across his forehead was a narrow gold band from which depended a hinged golden eye patch, hiding what must be his lethal eye.

The other god, Dalua—MacDougall heard Balor so address him—was greatly different. He was a small, thin, swarthy man. His most striking feature was a pair of unusually large, deepset black eyes that seemed to burn like live coals buried in black pits. Backswept, straight black hair, somewhat unkempt, dropped well below his shoulders. Tightly fitting black garments accented his cadaverous frame.

Even as he surveyed the two, MacDougall's thoughts were chaotic. He seemed in an enviable position—unseen, with a sharp sword and his enemies open to attack. But it was an idea to be discarded immediately. Even if he wanted to strike—and he didn't—he knew it wouldn't work. While he struck at one, the other might undo his invisibility, guessing at the truth.

He thought of his original purpose, the rescue of Darthula, perhaps now within reach because he could not be seen. This idea, too, he discarded with the same dispatch. First, Taliesin had advised him—no, ordered him, to get out of Murias, and the Bard should know what was best. Then, too, after his experience with Morrigu—and he shuddered at the thought of that gross creature appearing in so seductive and beautiful a form—did he want anything to do with any of the women of what he had come to call Tartarus?

After all—and he had dwelt on this before—every one of these beings, men, women, gods—serf or ruler—had died! All that was left of their original bodies were brown and crumbling bones. And their new bodies were supplied—he now accepted the idea—by Lucifer! But Darthula was so very lovely!

He had only one purpose now—to get out of Murias, find the Gate, and get back to the stone tower in the Scottish Highlands—alone! No more playing hero, rescuing fair damsels in distress, no matter how beautiful or alluring. No more meddling in the affairs of a land that, humanly speaking, had no right to exist.

A sudden raucous cry from the bed checked his thoughts. Morrigu had awakened. By sheer force, Balor held her down, trying to quiet her ranting. MacDougall heard himself berated in terms, familiar and unfamiliar, that made him grateful the goddess was not aware of his nearness.

With the commotion at its height, he decided the time had come for him to move. Any slight sound he might make would be concealed by Morrigu's antics.

With utmost care, MacDougall moved across the bedroom toward the exit he knew, deciding against the way out leading he knew not where. He held his breath and gripped his sword rigidly against his side to prevent its brushing against furniture or the doorway. He reached the door to the corridor, heard a footfall outside, and stepped back hastily.

The door swung in to admit the returning Semias. He passed within a foot of the invisible MacDougall, moving briskly into the bedroom.

"No sign of him anywhere. We've lost track of him."

This brought a fresh tirade from Morrigu. During the flood of words, MacDougall slid through the doorway and let the door close gently behind him. He had already decided to go through the bedrooms; in the corridor, sounds of footfalls on the hard mosaic could raise questions. He counted rooms. The gold chains dangled from the bed where he had found Morrigu, not an illusion, but inexplicable solidity. Four rooms beyond this, he looked through the silver curtain, saw no one, carefully slid through, and quietly descended the ramp. Several Fomorians were moving through the hallway toward the exit; he followed, needing only to avoid actual contact with anyone. He safely reached the lane outside the Hall of Games.

The return trip to the entrance of Murias took Alan MacDougall at least three times as long as the walk guided by Taliesin; but eventually he reached the edge of the city. There he paused, uncertain. Right or left? A faint smell of horseflesh helped him to decide.

Arriving at the great gate at last, he searched for the gong, hoping it was not mounted above the gate and out of reach. He found it to the left of the gate, about ten feet above the pavement. Drawing his sword, he struck the gong a single sharp blow, then waited.

Eventually the gatekeepers appeared from their little room, removed a heavy bronze pin that locked the gates together, and slowly drew them aside.

MacDougall stepped through into the thick wall of fog still holding that part of Tartarus in its velvety grasp. So Balor's suppression of Taliesin's powers had not terminated the fog. But of course—Mother Danu had aided in bringing it into being, and it was in her, not Taliesin's, control. Moving steadily up the ramp, he heard, muffled and faint, his last sounds from Murias:

"Come in, come in, whoever you are."

Alan chuckled into the thick cloud that engulfed him. He was out of the sunken city and he planned to stay out. At last he was really alone.

CHAPTER 6

In the Fog

Slowly but steadily, Alan MacDougall mounted the ramp. He could see nothing, only fog. He stretched out his arms to either side, held them shoulder high, and moved gradually to his right until as he had hoped, he felt a rough stone wall. He continued up the ramp, keeping his right arm outstretched. He had not seen the wall during the descent into Murias, but logically, it had to be there. With this as a guide, just barely touching its welcome solidity, he quickened his pace. When the wall ended, he knew he had almost reached ground level and slowed, moving about ten feet back toward center.

He pictured the stone causeway over which Taliesin had led him—perfectly flat, about twenty feet wide, a half mile in length, without a retaining wall, and open water on either side. Intently, eyes straining, he peered downward. He could not see the surface under his feet—could not see his feet!

MacDougall shrugged. He had no choice. He couldn't remain where he was. One slow step at a time, he started out, testing his footing before completing every stride.

The walk over the causeway seemed to last forever. How closely he skirted disaster he never knew. Whether he was inches from the edge or following a safe course up the middle, there was no way to tell. He only knew that at long, long last he heard and felt the faint crunch of the white sand and pebble road underfoot. It was then that he realized that his jaws were clenched, his fists knotted at his sides, and every nerve as taut as a drumhead. For minutes he stood there, forcing himself to relax, thinking of what lay ahead.

Ahead were the Ch'in!

Slowly he started up the road, aware of the dead silence. The only sound was the faint crunch of his boots on the close-packed pebbles. It was muffled by the fog, but, because it was the only sound in this silent world, it came loudly to his ears. As he recalled it, he had about a half mile to walk before he reached the spot where he had tethered his horse; and that horse was vital to his escape. To walk the many miles to the Gate was not to his liking, though obviously possible; but he needed the food and the supply of water in the saddlebag. So somehow he'd have to get the horse.

At least, if the Ch'in heard him, they couldn't see him. At the thought, he grinned mirthlessly. What advantage was invisibility when nothing could be seen? Right now sound, not sight, must be his sole concern.

He stopped and listened. Certainly a hundred men would not be completely silent. And the horses would be moving, perhaps grazing, certainly restless in the unfamiliar fog. Quite likely, the noises made by the Ch'in would hide his own faint sounds. However, just to be safe, he'd stop and listen frequently. He did so at about every twenty strides.

And his vigilance paid off! Finally, coming through the silence, he heard hushed voices in conversation, even the whinnying of a horse, indicating his close approach to the encampment. He slowed to a near crawl, easing over to the right side of the road until he felt turf underfoot.

He inched along, guided by the voices; finally he knew he was almost among the guards and stood stock-still. He had given no specific thought to how he'd get his horse, except perhaps by stealth, getting the animal untied, then making a run for it. But suddenly there flashed into his mind the obvious method; its very boldness was its assurance of success.

He remembered that their captain had crossed to the opposite side. With any luck he'd still be there. Stealthily, Alan slid back to the road and carefully moved out to the middle; then, with no attempt at silence, he walked toward the quiet voices.

"Curse this fog," he exclaimed hoarsely as he reached the turf. "How can anyone check on anything in this murk?" He groped into the woods, an extended hand finding a tree and holding on. "Ho!" he called out, though not too loudly. "Captain K'ang has sent me to check on the Bard's and Yellow-head's horses. As if they'd wander away in this thick stuff! Can anyone tell me where they are?"

A disdainful grunt came from a dozen feet away. "Farther up the road—there's a big rock in the way just before you reach them. Watch you don't break your neck. It's just big enough to fall over."

"Thanks! I'll be careful. Ever see anything like this fog?"

A noncommittal grunt came in answer.

Slowly, but with no suggestion of stealth, MacDougall groped along the edge of the road and found the rock and the horses beyond it, still safely tied as he and Taliesin had left them. He spoke quietly, as if to himself, even as he untied the mount, coiled the rope, and fastened it behind the saddle.

"Nothing wrong here—hmmm—better retie the knot." And as he swung into the saddle he cursed fervently, crying, "Watch where you're stepping, you clumsy beast!" Simultaneously he kicked the horse in the ribs and slapped its rump. The startled animal leaped ahead, struck the roadway, and, guided solely by instinct, sped into the wall of fog.

For several minutes MacDougall made no attempt to control his mount, knowing that, as long as he heard the familiar sound of hoofs on the pebbled road, there would be no problem. He was sure there would be no pursuit. Certainly the Ch'in would be puzzled, wondering what had really happened, probably calling out to the errant checker; but as long as the fog held, there was no chance that any would attempt to follow him.

At length the animal slowed to a canter and then to a walk. MacDougall let the horse choose its own pace, for they had a long way to go. They must be passing through the rolling farm country by this time, but ahead lay the steep climb, and he wanted his mount to retain energy for the mountain crossing.

Surprising, MacDougall thought, that the horse continued on its course when it could see nothing; though actually this was no different from traveling on a dark night. Night? This was a world without night. But though he could see nothing, he knew the road was straight and as long as he could hear the crunching of hoofs on pebbles, he had to be on course.

He reached an upgrade that grew rapidly steeper until his mount was laboring. MacDougall remembered the rapid descent on the approach to Murias; there was a flat plateau at its top. This was the worst part of the trip. He thought of resting the stallion, but decided against it. He'd have to press on; there was always the possibility of the fog lifting, clearing the way for quick pursuit.

On and on he went into the blind grayness. Gradually the silence became oppressive, a heavy thing, burdensome, almost tangible. Time dragged ponderously and his imagination began to work. He thought of the grotesque Fomorians, picturing them flowing through the round stone tower into his unsuspecting world. Worse would be shape-changers like Morrigu, Balor, or Dalua. What had the spurious Macha called the last? Dalua the Dark King, the Laughing One, shedding darkness wherever he went. And there were others of the Celtic deities about whom he knew nothing.

He reached the crest of the slope and leveled out on the plateau. Again he thought of stopping to rest his mount, but decided instead to walk for a time, leading the animal. After all, as a rider, he was no featherweight.

Strange that there had been no sign of Balor or the others following him. According to Taliesin, they could appear wherever they wished instantly and in any shape they chose. And now he believed it. Certainly by this time they must have decided that he had left Murias. The gate-keepers would not let two apparent false ringings go un-reported. He was grateful for the absence of pursuit, but sooner or later there would have to be *some* action on the part of the unholy trio of gods.

At last it came. He seemed to hear, very faint and far away, an eerie, high-pitched laugh. There was madness in the sound, and it sent a chill coursing through Alan MacDougall. It died in the stillness; as he listened intently for a repetition of the wild laughter, he tried to tell himself it was his imagination. Just as he actually began to believe he had imagined it, the laugh was repeated, closer now. It started on a lower note, mounting higher and higher—and it was laughter without mirth, mindless. Taliesin had called Dalua the Witless One.

Again silence fell, prolonged, dragging, while Mac-Dougall waited, senses tensing involuntarily. It came fi-nally—and it was far ahead across the flat area, as if searching, seeking him out. Then—silence. And now the fog itself seemed to become more oppressive because of what it concealed.

There came another sound, vastly more frightening

than the senseless laughter. Though distant, clear and high out of the silence pealed a mournful howl, strange and utterly wild. It was followed by other cries from other throats—what could only be the howling of a pack of wolves.

But that was impossible!

There were no wolves on this island; at least there had been no mention of them, and certainly the Bard would have spoken about them. It had to be illusion—illusion created by Balor or Morrigu.

The wolf cry died in the fog. Alan felt the trembling of the stallion, steadied him, and swung into the saddle. Illusion? It could also be shape-changing—Balor forming of the Fomorians a pack of actual wolves!

Again came the chorus of howls, now seemingly close by, the more terrifying because of its nearness. He felt the horse start, felt him quiver and toss his head. Then came the laughter, mingling with the howling, moving about them, near and far, ahead and behind, with no apparent pattern.

There came a third source of terror, the flapping of giant wings as if some huge bat were circling overhead. There flashed into MacDougall's mind the Bard's reference to Morrigu assuming the shape of what the Scots called a hoodie, a carrion crow, skimming over battlefields, spurring the warriors on to greater ferocity.

MacDougall felt his usually docile mount burst into frantic speed, as though to outrun the terrors that beset them on every side. At the same moment he realized he could no longer hear the hoofs spurning the pebbles— which could only mean they had left the road, were racing blindly over the thick grass of the meadow, and might encounter forest at any moment!

The panic driving the horse suddenly seized the man. Disaster impended with every stride. Impact with a tree at this pace could mean serious injury, even death! With all his strength, he drew on the reins; but the stallion had the bit in his teeth, and he could not slow the animal.

Instinctively he leaned far over, stretching out against the broad back. On and on they rushed endlessly—and suddenly the howling wolf chorus burst through the fog in their very path!

The stallion shied wildly. MacDougall felt himself flying through the air and instinctively let go of the reins. He felt the crash of impact, a blinding pain amid a flare of light—and oblivion.

MacDougall's return to awareness began with a painful pounding in his skull. Lord, what a headache! The prize headache of all time. What had happened? He had a vague recollection of flying; but how could he think with this infernal pounding? His hands groped upward and pressed against his throbbing temples.

He heard a man's voice, deep and kindly. "He seems to be coming to his senses. He took a hard fall, thrown, it appears, from that racing horse. But I can find no trace of broken bones. Difficult to tell by touch alone."

A woman's voice answered, low-pitched and gentle. "Little wonder that a horse would panic with those mad tricks. Balor and his wolves would be enough to frighten any animal. Not to mention Dalua and Morrigu's flapping wings. It has been a long time since they have been heard—never in this land that I can recall. I wonder who he is."

"What matter? From his dress, he would appear to be a Fomorian, though he has none of their deformities." After a pause, the man added, "I do believe the fog is less dense than it had been."

Memory returned to MacDougall in a flood. He felt himself stiffening and tried to relax, to adjust to this new situation. Who were these people into whose hands he had fallen? He felt the man's hand on his forehead, somehow cool and soothing. He tried to sit up and groaned.

"Easy, my friend," the deep voice admonished. "You've had a bad fall. Here—drink some of this." A canteen was held to MacDougall's lips and he drank deeply. He sank back to the turf. His invisibility? He drew a hand across his half-opened eyes; he saw the spread fingers, no longer transparent. The spell evidently had ended with his fall. Just as well, though he hoped he could call on it again if needed.

The man's voice went on. "What brings you into this area? Few are the travelers who venture this far from the cities and the roads. There is nothing here to attract, only the forests and the rocky highlands. This is the domain of the Outcasts."

The Outcasts! Vividly MacDougall's mind formed a picture of the ambush into which he had fallen during his second meeting with the dwellers of this land. "Are you—?" he began, then halted.

The man laughed quietly. "Yes, we are Outcasts, but not thieves and marauders. We have friends among the farmers and fishermen whom we help on occasion, but we avoid the cities and the caravans." His voice grew bitter. "We displeased Moirfhius, Druid of Falias, and we had to flee to escape his persecution. I was a student at the School for Druids then—but the details are of no interest to you. And who are you?"

MacDougall answered promptly. "Who I am is not important. I, too, am an Outcast, but my difficulty was recent and with Balor and Morrigu and Dalua—which apparently you surmised." Grimly he added, "They have been searching for me in the fog, as you have heard. Balor's wolves frightened my horse and he threw me."

The woman spoke. "We know these woods and we can help you hide. We have no liking for the Unholy Three."

MacDougall sat up, grimacing, then rose painfully to his feet, assisted by the Good Samaritan. The headache was at least bearable, though he'd certainly appreciate a couple of aspirin tablets. He looked around him. What had the man said—the fog was not as dense? It was true; no longer that impervious opaque wall, it now appeared to be a conventional gray fog, obscuring everything, but permitting half-sight of nearby objects.

He looked at the couple, self-proclaimed Outcasts—middle-aged, clad in very ordinary robes that would have appeared normal in Falias, hers a medium green and his a deep blue. Both were smiling in friendly fashion; but thought of the spurious Macha awakened sudden suspicion. He concentrated on his armlet, peering intently at the two, seeking for concealed forms. They were as they appeared. No shape-changing here.

"How do you feel?" the woman inquired. "Well enough to travel? We should get into the shelter of the woods in case the wolves return. They are real, you know, even though they are Balor's creation and are transformed Fomorians."

MacDougall hesitated. "My horse?"

The man shook his head. "I'm afraid it's gone. It would take a miracle for us to find it. Where are you bound?"

"Mainly away from Murias, but in the general direction of Falias."

"A long walk, though not so bad if this unnatural fog lifts." He added an afterthought, "We can find the way even in the fog. And we'll be pleased to guide you."

During the conversation, the manifestations of the three gods had continued, albeit some distance away, possibly in pursuit of the terrified stallion. Now, high overhead, could be heard the flapping of great unseen wings—Morrigu's searching.

"Let's move," MacDougall said.

His rescuers led him toward a dimly seen thicket. In moments the trees closed about them. They moved deeper and deeper into the ghostly forest until in every direction there was nothing but closely growing trees. For MacDougall, all sense of direction was gone.

"We are heading across the plateau," the man said after a time. "At the base of the downslope on the other side, we should find the road."

"How can you determine direction? I have no idea which way we are headed."

The man chuckled. "We just know."

MacDougall had no way of telling how long a time they spent on their course through the forest. There was only light undergrowth, and the gray haze permitted them to see their way, after a fashion, so progress was steady. They were aware of the questing wolves, high-flying hoodie, and occasional eerie laugh, but none came close.

At length they entered a natural clearing, an area of thick grass. Its extent could not be determined, since it vanished into the fog to their left and right and before them. Near its edge they halted, the man speaking to the woman.

"Do you remember this? We appear to have moved somewhat south. I had heard of this clear area but had never seen it."

"Nor had I, of course. As I recall it, and as I feel it now, this is a Forbidden Area. We could stay in the woods and circle to the north—probably should." The woman hesitated, undecided. "I feel it unwise to cross here."

Impatiently, MacDougall spoke. "If we must go to the other side, if that's the right direction, it makes a lot more sense to cross an open space than to stick to the woods. It can't be that wide, and the idea of its being Forbidden isn't logical. Forbidden—by whom?"

"Just—Forbidden," the man answered doggedly.

"Well," MacDougall exclaimed, "I'm crossing here. I've already been in one Forbidden Area; why not another? Are you coming or taking the long way around? If that's your plan, I'll wait for you on the other side."

The two looked at each other, as if silently conferring. The woman finally answered reluctantly. "The feeling isn't very strong—I guess there's no real reason—"

They started across the meadow, MacDougall briskly leading the way. They had gone about fifty feet when his attention was caught by a steady glow in the fog to his right. He turned his head and saw the suggestion of a slim, radiant tower vanishing upward into the mist. He halted, looking more intently, then pointed.

"What's that?"

His companions stopped short and stared in the direction he indicated. There was puzzlement in the woman's voice. "What's what? I see nothing."

Impatiently MacDougall exclaimed, "That tower! It's glowing—if it weren't for the fog, it would be brilliant."

"Tower?" The man was startled; he peered intently into the murk. Even as he gazed, the fog seemed to lift ever so briefly, like a rift in a cloud. MacDougall saw the conical structure stretch high into the momentarily revealed aurora, glowing like a golden pointer. Into his mind flashed the thought of the Tower of Babel reaching unto heaven.

"Are you jesting? There is no tower."

Unbelieving, MacDougall turned to stare at the pair. They seemed completely sincere. Could it be that what he could see so clearly was hidden from their eyes, visible only to his armlet-stimulated gaze? Another of the mysteries of Tartarus?

"I know what I see!" he exclaimed. "It is not an illusion. I see a very tall tower, a pointed cone, now vanishing upward into the fog, glowing with a golden light. In the brief, clear glimpse I had, I saw no windows—unless they're too far above me to be observed—"

A raucous cry, loud and harsh, interrupted him as familiar flapping wings passed directly overhead. The thing hovered above him like an enormous black crow, then circled in a tight spiral, higher and higher until the mist hid it, its hoarse call echoing triumphantly through the fog. There came an instant response.

Wolves! Baying hungrily, a pack of a score or more came charging out of the mist, huge, gray, and shaggy, with black lips curled to reveal great fangs. Instinctively MacDougall whipped out his sword. Though once Fomorians, they were now unmistakably wolves.

"Get behind me!" he cried, even as he realized the unevenness of the conflict. Under his breath he added, "I hope Nuada helps me now!"

"Nuada!" The woman must have heard, and her words came scornfully. "No need for Nuada here!" The voice had changed subtly; now it sounded familiar, holding force and authority. "This time Balor has gone too far!" Her arms flung outward, waving toward the wolf pack.

"Fomorians, change!"

With the words, where wolves had been, one for one, suddenly appeared naked Fomorians, repulsive in their grotesquerie. Just as quickly, they vanished.

One last frustrated cry was heard from the hoodie overhead, and it, too, disappeared. Startling silence fell on the world.

"Enough of this fog," the woman added quietly. With a wave of her hand it was gone, the brilliance of the aurora again flooding the sky.

Everything had happened so rapidly that Alan MacDougall's thoughts had trouble adjusting. He stared from the man to the woman with swiftly growing comprehension. And with understanding came cold anger.

"So you, of course, are Danu, the goddess for whom the *Tuatha De Danann* was named. We have never met, but I have heard you—in dreams. And you, I suppose, are Dagda. And everything that has been happening is a game, centered around me! What an enjoyable pastime for gods! Outcasts indeed. I should have realized, from all your knowledge of Balor and Morrigu.

"I'm sick of it, understand? Fed up! And even if it means I'll never get back to my own world, I'm not taking any of you with me. Is that clear?"

The voice of Danu was calm and undisturbed. "So be it, if you are able to maintain your resolution. But we can be patient. Time means nothing to us. From what you have revealed, fourteen of your centuries have passed since we came to what you choose to call Tartarus. After a century or two, assuming that you do not age, you may change your mind. And we will be watching and waiting. You cannot elude us."

A thought flashed into MacDougall's mind. "No? That may be—but you did not follow when I went into the

Hall of the Dead. What about this tower in another Forbidden Area? Or is that more of your deception?"

He glanced over his shoulder at the structure pointing skyward in all its golden glory, then looked back at the two.

There was consternation on their faces, even a hint of fear.

"There is no tower!"

MacDougall smiled blandly. "So there's something I can see which is hidden from your eyes. And if this is Forbidden, the tower is the reason. I'm going to visit that tower. Are you coming with me?"

Would it work? MacDougall hoped he sounded more confident than he felt. The tower was there; he was going to walk toward it; but would they try to stop him? If they tried, could he resist their powers? He had his sword, but they would attempt no physical attack. He saw the uncertainty on their faces, turned, and walked resolutely across the turf. He fought an impulse to look back, aware of a strange shrinking in the small of his back, like one walking away from a man armed to shoot. But nothing happened.

As he drew nearer the great structure, his thoughts became centered on the startling thing. In the first place, it was much farther away than he had thought. It seemed to recede before him. And it was much larger, truly immense. At first sight, he had gained the impression that it reached into the aurora; closer inspection seemed to verify that impression. It appeared to be a perfect cone, its substance unlike anything he had ever seen, unless it was the glowing material that formed the interior walls of Murias and the Hall of the Dead. But this seemed more metallic, suggesting gold itself, gold with internal fire. And there were no windows that he could see, no detectable openings of any sort, at least on this side, merely an enormous cone of living gold.

When he reached the base of the wall, he leaned back and stared upward, only then realizing its true immensity.

It seemed incredible that a structure of this size could be unknown to Danu and Dagda, to gods and people alike, for that matter. Invisible? Evidently—but why? And why was it visible to him? The fantastic armlet, of course!

Like everything else this must be the creation of Lucifer. Was it for the Daughters of Lilith or for the present inhabitants of this enscorcelled land? MacDougall thought of the Hall of the Dead and of the transparent sleepers in the crystal boxes on the top floor; and suddenly the thought of entry into this place became uninteresting.

He looked back. Surprisingly small and apparently unmoving, the figures of Danu and Dagda remained where he had left them. They hadn't the will—or ability—to follow. It was a strange taboo, this Forbidding.

MacDougall started around the base of the tower, actually hoping he would not find an entrance. Though, of course, there had to be a way in for those who used the structure.

As he circled the wall, he thought of the watchers. For them, he must appear to be describing a great circle, to vanish as he passed the midway point—unless for them it was transparent and they could watch him through its substance. It almost had to be that, or they could see its shape by what it blocked. He continued around, carefully scanning the wall for signs of an entrance, and found its smoothness unbroken. He reached the side where again he saw the distant, motionless figures of Danu and Dagda. Fantastic! There was no door!

A second time and more slowly, he circled the golden tower, examining every inch of its surface from the grass to a foot above his head. There was nothing, no sign of crack or seam, merely polished smoothness. Back where he started, he reached out, touching the surface. He felt the cold of metal. But almost immediately he gained the impression of sudden warmth under his hand!

Involuntarily he drew back, then in doubting wonder again touched the wall; without question, there was warmth and it had intensified. It was accompanied by a faint vibration, almost like a slight electric shock, but without discomfort. He pushed against the wall and felt it suddenly yield, felt his hand and forearm merge with it, then pass through its substance!

With heart-stopping impact, an inmistakable hand gripped his, strongly, firmly—and drew him swiftly forward, off balance. There was a momentary vertigo, an instability, a sense of compression like that of his entry into Tartarus, and he was through.

He was inside the tower!

CHAPTER 7

The Golden Tower

Alan MacDougall's hand sank slowly to his side as it was released; his gaze was held almost hypnotically by the unwinking eyes fixed on him. They were the bluest eyes he had ever seen, gemlike in color and hardness, and they were set in a statuesque ivory face with thin black brows, crowned by lustrous black hair that was full-cut and perfectly groomed. The overly red lips smiled, yet it was a smile without depth, an expression somehow sinister. Alan felt the man should have worn a beard, but the strong, square chin was hairless. The total effect was one of unreality, overdrawn, staged. There was nothing unreal however, about the sharp stab of fear that struck MacDougall, nor about the clammy moisture in the palm of his hands.

The man, taller than MacDougall by a full six inches

and powerfully built, bowed from the waist and spoke in a voice deeply resonant, sonorous.

"Welcome, Alan MacDougall. It was inevitable that we meet in the course of time, if I may use a phrase which actually has no meaning here."

Before responding, MacDougall forced himself to examine the man quite openly while he regained his composure. He saw a figure resplendent in black and gold. The open, black robe was of the finest wool, its entire surface embroidered with delicate, glittering gold threads in an intricate interlocking design. Gold lace fringed the full, Oriental sleeves. Beneath this was a plain black silk vest with a high, tight collar, the latter encrusted with delicate gold filigree. Full-cut, black silk trousers were gathered at the ankles above slippers of gold-embroidered black silk with pointed, upturned tips. All of this formed a setting for a pendant suspended about the man's neck on a massive gold chain—a delicately faceted teardrop of flashing crimson the size of a man's thumb, and with more fire than any ruby ever possessed. It must be, Alan thought, a blood-red diamond.

His gaze returned to the unwavering blue eyes. "Thank you for your help in entering. I fear I couldn't have made it without your assistance; your door is so unconventional. Since you say we were fated to meet, who are you?"

The other ignored his question. "You are an unseen factor, a piece inserted in the game from outside our planning; as such, you present very interesting possibilities. Had you not come to us, we would have come to you." The deep voice became suddenly and exaggeratedly reassuring. "Not that we object to your participation—indeed, we welcome it. We trust your stay with us will be a long one."

The fixed smile seemed to become faintly mocking. MacDougall felt a sudden stab of apprehension.

"Are you—Lucifer?"

The smile vanished. "Lucifer? Your name for the Most

High. No, I am not the Lord of Light. A trusted lieutenant, perhaps, but certainly not the Master."

"You must have a name," MacDougall persisted.

Again the deep bow. "You may call me Ahriman, a name as good as any other."

Ahriman? Wasn't that the Persian god of evil—which would then be the same as Lucifer? "You are a Persian?" Alan asked.

"If you wish." The dark man's gesture could have meant anything. He went on smoothly. "As you can see—" He indicated the room behind them. "—there is no provision here for entertaining guests, so we will ascend to the top of the Tower to more suitable quarters."

Alan glanced past Ahriman into the round chamber, until then unnoticed. There was little to see. Lacy, gold-colored drapes divided the room into sections of different sizes with no visible occupants. A sudden thought came: could he trust his eyes? Taliesin's instruction had been to think into the armlet. He did so and saw the room unchanged, but he was gripped by an impression of something far less tangible, yet frightening. It was the semia-wareness of other forms, of living beings just outside the edge of perception, almost visible but eluding sight; and the near sound of movement just beyond detection.

It was the impression of a fleeting moment, interrupted by Ahriman's voice.

"Will you join me? Your hand, please."

He faced the Persian, who grasped his hand firmly. And in less than a breath, without a trace of motion, they were elsewhere.

They were in a room that was a golden delight. There were thick, gold-colored rugs on the floor, with heavily upholstered chairs to match—and they were in the midst of the aurora, an indescribable spectacle. Involuntarily MacDougall stepped to the wall and watched the play of lights seen from a unique perspective. It was as if the sky were a kaleidoscope of fragmented sunsets, changing at the whim of a restless child, and he were in its heart. The amber tint that the wall imparted served only to enhance the beauty, a wonderland of golden light.

MacDougall turned at the sound of Ahriman's voice. "Few have ever seen this as you see it. What you now behold is certainly a creation worthy of the Lord of Light. Strange, it is not, that those who dwell here want to leave, that they find the prospect of return to their former life of overwhelming interest?" He motioned toward a chair, then seated himself.

"I suppose," MacDougall commented, "a prison, no matter how attractive in some respects, is still a prison. And Tartarus, with its normally endless life, is a prison. The sentence is forever. Forbidden fruit has always been the most enticing, an obvious cliché. And release from monotony is of priceless worth."

The Persian looked intently at MacDougall. "What do you know about this world—which you call Tartarus?"

Alan hesitated. How much should he reveal of what he had learned? "I know only what Taliesin has told me out of Celtic mythology—how this world was created by Lucifer for the Daughters of Lilith. Later, long after it was abandoned, it became the home of those who once had lived in Britain, the old gods and their followers, plus a certain number of Norsemen and Chinese, Trolls and Fomorians. Other bodies were held in reserve to maintain a balanced population."

The blue eyes held MacDougall's. "What about your presence here?"

Alan shrugged. "By sheer accident, I found the link between my world and this one. A Gate. And, being curious, I explored."

Ahriman sounded faintly amused. "You failed to mention the armlet—which, of course, you are wearing, else you could not have seen the Gate, nor this Tower, nor me for that matter. Much is embodied in that pair of golden serpents, far more than you can know." The smile vanished.

"You can return through the Gateway?" he asked suddenly.

MacDougall forced a chuckle. "The universal question, and always the same reply. I *think* I can. But why all these questions? Surely you already know the answers."

The Persian studied MacDougall as if weighing a decision. "As I said earlier, your entry into the affairs of this little world presents interesting possibilities. You see, anything or anyone the Most High introduces is his, under his control. An unknown factor adds zest, a new element of chance. It breaks the very monotony you referred to. It opens new avenues of play."

"You said this was a game," MacDougall commented. "Is that all it is? In a sense, it's like a vast chess game with living pieces. Isn't it hard on the unwilling pawns and knights and queens?"

Ahriman raised quizzical brows. "Not really chess, since that suggests opposing players. Remember, all were dead. They were given what they now value as they never valued it before—a new body. They can always die, and some do; but I know of no suicides during the Island's existence.

"And now you enter the scene, poorly prepared for the part you could play. You have powers at your disposal which would amaze and delight you, were you aware of what they are. And you have one great asset. You have never died." He paused as if awaiting response.

Before MacDougall could speak, his attention was caught by an extraordinary auroral display in the sky behind Ahriman. He watched, unmindful of the other's growing annoyance.

Abruptly he said, "All this, if I am to accept the chronology of the myths, has been going on for thousands of years, as we reckon time. This is a self-sustaining world, existing outside the one I know. And it demands power, tremendous power. That power had to go into its creation, even if Lucifer reshaped already existing matter. What was—what *is* its source?"

For the first time, genuine amusement glinted in Ahriman's eyes and his smile widened.

"Why concern yourself with power? It is everywhere in limitless supply, free for the using. Its focal point here in Tartarus—to use your name—is this Tower. But that is not important.

"Ask, rather, about *powers*. Not power itself, but the powers that control it, the powers that you have seen employed in so simple a fashion as Taliesin's fog. Or in your own invisibility, your entry through my 'unconventional' door, and our recent transport to this room. There are powers beyond any of these, or any you can possibly have imagined. Powers you could claim."

An eager note entered the deep voice. "If you cooperate, I can reveal to you all the properties, the powers, of the armlet, multiplying your abilities. Now the little gods of this place have powers beyond yours; but that need not remain so. Indeed, there are almost no limits to the abilities you could attain. It would be most interesting to see what you would do if you were in control of this world."

For a moment—but only for a moment—MacDougall thought of himself as ruler of Tartarus. Then he laughed aloud.

"And if I were cooperative—and of course I have no idea what that entails—I would then be under your control, and the unknown factors you talk about would no longer be unknown! Sounds to me like going around in a circle." He halted at a sudden thought. "How do I know I am not being controlled right now?"

Ahriman shook his head, sadly, it seemed. "I am disappointed in you, Alan MacDougall. Surely your intelligence should tell you that I do not *want* to control you. Your interest for us lies in your independence of action—though even your doubt introduces a new factor. On consideration, I withdraw my suggestion that I reveal the further powers of the armlet." He added, "For the present."

After a brief pause, he continued. "Your entry into the Tower was not foreseen. The possibility was there because we knew the armlet made sight of it certain. But had you feared, had you failed to touch the wall, we could not have drawn you in. Your natural curiosity enabled us to—invite you."

That, Alan thought, might or might not be true. Only one fact was clear in all of this. He was dealing with a personality and a situation he could not handle. Caution, Alan, caution, he told himself; keep an open mind, but believe nothing.

When it became evident that MacDougall had no intention of contributing anything to the conversation, Ahriman stood up, and his guest stood up with him.

"It is in my mind to show you one other wonder of the Master's creation." Pausing as if weighing the factors involved, Ahriman nodded. "Yes—I think it is knowledge you should possess."

The Persian grasped Alan's hand; then, disconcertingly, they were standing on a narrow catwalk high on the wall of a room far wider than that at the top of the Tower. In a fleeting glance, Alan was aware of a golden rail that prevented their falling, of the opacity of the curving wall behind them; but he had eyes only for what the chamber held. And as he stared, his eyes grew wide in unbelief; he told himself that this was the most amazing creation he had seen since passing through the Gateway.

In gemlike perfection below him, stretching from wall to wall, lay a three-dimensional replica of Tartarus! Brilliant light poured from beneath the catwalk to illuminate the incredible model. It was as if a duplicate of the Island had been compressed by some marvel of magic into infinite smallness with no loss of detail. It was the ultimate in miniaturization.

Sapphire-blue water formed the setting for the Island, with beaches, forests, meadowland, hills, valleys, and craggy mountains providing the natural terrain. Carved, crystalline gem-cities lay at points arbitrarily called north,

east, and south—Falias, Gorias, and Findias, each totally
unlike the others. A white thread of road formed a cross
intersecting the landmass, the left arm of the cross ending
in a minute finger pointing into the sea, beneath which
must lie sunken Murias.

MacDougall gazed in utter enchantment and growing
wonder. Truly this was a creation possible only to god
power.

The voice of Ahriman, bearing more than a hint of
sardonic amusement, brought him back to his surroundings. "You find our toy impressive?"

MacDougall made no attempt to conceal his admira-
tion. "It's fantastic! I've never seen anything to compare
with it. But—why? What is its purpose, assuming it has
a purpose?"

The fixed smile returned to the normally immobile face.
The Persian bowed, then led the way up a narrow ramp
behind them, unnoticed by Alan in his preoccupation with
the miniature Island. It projected from the catwalk in a
slow spiral, suggesting a surrealistic golden ribbon climbing into vacancy, ending in what appeared to be a broad,
round platform of unusual design, suspended above the
center of the model. It was a ten-foot crystalline disk like
a great lens; around it ran a wider continuation of the
catwalk. Like the walk and the ramp, it was edged by a
graceful gold railing.

At the far side Alan saw a combination table and chair,
formed of the ubiquitous golden substance of the Tower
itself. On the table lay what appeared to be a golden tool,
reminding him of an oversized, twin-handled forceps or
tongs, its jaws smoothly padded. Beside it was a domelike
translucent cap with great lenses attached, to cover the
eyes of the wearer.

As MacDougall followed Ahriman onto the platform,
he looked down through the lens of the miniature landscape below and felt a momentary queasiness. He resisted
the impulse to grasp the rail, rejecting the impression that

he was standing at a great height with only the rail between him and destruction.

Again Ahriman's voice brought him back to reality—if indeed this was reality.

"Unfortunately, as is evident, I cannot offer you a seat. Since I plan to demonstrate the uses of our model, you will have to stand. I think, however, you will find it quite interesting. And as you will readily appreciate, your eyes will be the first to behold what I reveal, except, of course, for members of the Master's staff."

As Alan watched the Persian seat himself and don the strange headdress, he thought fleetingly of the suggestion of motion and sound on his entry into the Tower. The staff? The thought vanished as things began to happen.

He felt more than heard a deep humming rising from the crystal disk at his feet. It deepened in intensity momentarily, then faded into near silence. The sound seemed to transfer itself to the substance of the lens, and a vibrant, shimmering film flowed across the surface as if some change were taking place in its very atoms.

The Persian directed his own gaze toward the center of the lens and said, "Watch the wall on your left."

There appeared suddenly, as on a screen, what seemed to be an aerial view of Falias, three dimensional and with lifelike fidelity. Instantly it changed, the image zooming in on the familiar street where Taliesin lived, following a single horseman moving up the white thoroughfare. From somewhere came the normal urban noises, including the sound of the horse's hoofs on the pebbles. The scene vanished, replaced by a view of the banked seats in the Hall of Games in Murias. The clash of swords arose from the steel of two grotesque gladiators in the arena, the hungry growl of the spectators underlying the metallic clangor. This scene just as quickly became the corridor leading to the quarters of Balor, then passed into the apartment where Morrigu was in the midst of a tirade, berating Dalua with shrill abandon. This in turn was replaced by the view and sounds of a caravan of the Ch'in moving along a white roadway. Scene after scene followed, apparently without limit.

The wall cleared. Ahriman removed the helmet and smiled at MacDougall.

"You saw on the wall what I saw through my lenses, the images appearing for your benefit. In actual use, of course, all attention would be centered on the subject desired, and no enlarged image would appear."

With a weak attempt at a laugh, MacDougall protested, "We can gain the same effects in any video or motion-picture editing room."

The Persian shrugged impatiently. "You know this is not the same. I can see and hear at will anything, literally anything, on the Island."

"Can you, for example, view the inside of what I call the Hall of the Dead outside Falias—perhaps the upper floor where the Daughters of Lilith lie?"

"Watch." Ahriman replaced the helmet.

As clearly as Alan had observed it, the spectacle of auroral sky and high-piled crystalline chests with their spectral cadavers appeared on the wall. And vanished.

"But you *did* nothing!" Alan protested. "There seems to be no apparatus—"

Ahriman's smile became supercilious. "Again your vaunted power! I use powers—they are so much more effective. Mental powers, coupled with what you probably would refer to as magic. Genuine magic."

MacDougall tried to express a nonchalance he did not feel. "A very efficient spy system, I'll concede. But why not? A world in which magic works, where you—or your Master—makes the laws—"

"Ah, but you have not seen the greatest use of our toy! We can do more than observe. We can—influence. Watch."

Helmet in place, the Persian grasped the giant forceps, pointing the instrument through the center of their perch. On the wall appeared the crowded stables in Murias. A cream-colored stallion grew large in the view. Out of the corner of his eye MacDougall saw Ahriman manipulate the instrument, and suddenly the horse stood in an expanse of pallid grass; in moments it fell to grazing. As the scene vanished, the deep voice commented:

"That could just as easily have been anyone, god or man, or anything of my choosing. There was no reason for me to transport an individual, nor any object that could cause confusion, so I chose a horse. Where I have placed it, an Outcast will find it—and the discovery will change the course of his life."

He paused, then added, "I never act without a purpose."

"But the gods—can't they—" MacDougall began.

"The gods with their combined powers, or some of them alone, can accomplish this with fair consistency, but incur a percentage of failures. I can do it at will and with far greater accuracy. But we rarely exercise this ability because it is disruptive, and we let the dwellers work out their own affairs without interference, except when matters get out of hand."

Alan stared through the still-shimmering lens at the incredible model. "But—your instrument of transfer—isn't it observed? And how do you find what you seek? You are working with the model, but—"

"What happens in the miniature also happens in Tartarus. They are one. As for the tool, no one can see it any more than he can see the Tower. And no search is necessary. I simply picture the person, object, or place I seek—and instantly I—my sight or influence—am there. But you have seen enough to show you the powers, magic and mental, that could be yours—"

There came an interruption, a faint gonglike sound, barely audible, yet setting up a soundless but penetrating vibration within all of Alan MacDougall. He saw the Persian stiffen and remain immobile, not a muscle moving. The rigidity held for moments; then Ahriman spoke softly, obsequiously. "Yes, Master. At once."

The Persian stood up. "I have been summoned. I should

be gone only a very short time. Remain here. Do not attempt to leave. Indeed, you could not leave without help."

With the last word, he was gone.

Alan MacDougall elevated his eyebrows. "They certainly do things suddenly around here," he said aloud, then stood in momentary indecision, staring at the tabletop. He glanced at the arched ceiling and the walls. There was nothing to indicate surveillance—and why should there be? Visitors must be rare; probably he was the first. And he was alone. The strange shimmering of the lens persisted. He shrugged. Why not?

Seating himself at the table, he picked up the helmet, took a deep breath, and put the golden dome on his head. It was amazingly light, offering no discomfort. He looked straight ahead through the spectacles, his sight blurring in distortion. Then he stared through the great lens at his feet and gasped.

"Fantastic!" he breathed. No known laws of optics could act like this. The detail was incredible—but he could not hold anything in focus. One moment he was part of a throng in Falias, the next he looked down as from a low-flying plane at the Tower itself. Images changed and shifted with bewildering speed. He closed his eyes and tried to remember Ahriman's comments. He recalled the phrase "magic and mental."

He visualized an image of Darthula and had momentary glimpses of the Princess, but none was clear or lasting. There must be a way to control this thing! If he could master it—and the forceps—he might be able to rescue both Darthula and Taliesin! Then sudden hope welled up.

The armlet! Think into the armlet. Think of Darthula. How he did it he could not have told, but now as he stared into the lens, he saw the girl as clearly as if he had been at her side. Taliesin came into the scene.

They were no longer in the City Under the Sea; they rode side by side in the midst of the Bard's Norse guards. Freed, probably, by the gods. They were in animated conversation, and he, Alan MacDougall, was the subject they were discussing. He scowled as he heard Darthula say, "But I find him fascinating—and I want him." He closed his mind to the vision, and it was gone.

He thought of Danu and Dagda, whom he had left at the edge of the meadow, watching as he walked toward the Tower. He saw them still waiting, seated on a convenient boulder. At random he moved about the Island like a child with a new toy. The comparison struck him, and with it the thought that this was a diabolic plaything. Nothing was concealed from its prying eye. There was no privacy in Tartarus.

No rescue was necessary; but information about the gods Morrigu and Balor and whatever deviltry they were planning would be highly interesting and useful. It would be interesting also to observe in complete safety the area he had passed through with such great care.

He pictured the spot on the second floor of the Hall of Games where he had hidden behind the spread of shrubs wrought in gems; from there he moved along the corridor. Again, surprisingly, he saw the Druid Semias in conversation with a pair of Fomorians. He could hear every word they said, but none of it interested MacDougall.

What an opportunity! This was a temptation he could not resist. If only he could control those fantastic forceps, Semias the troublemaker was in for the surprise of his life. As Alan picked up the strange instrument, he wondered how any tool could be manipulated so precisely that such minute motions were possible. It had to be more Tartarian magic.

He pointed the device at the lens, as Ahriman had done, and whistled at the result. The padded arms of the tongs seemed to extend into almost infinite distance, tapering gradually to a fine point. Again he brought into focus the image of Semias. There was no time to try the manipulation elsewhere; the Persian might return at any moment. The latter had said that anything or anyone could be moved. Alan knew the right spot where the Druid should be placed; he saw it in his mind's eye—the flat crystal roof of the Hall of the Dead!

Carefully MacDougall extended that so-distant tip toward the Druid, sensing at one and the same time the weird, contradictory feeling of reaching down into smallness and of being on the scene with the man for whom he reached. Strangely, there was no feeling of delicate movement; somehow he was in complete control. Magic indeed!

He held the forceps poised above Semias until the latter had finished his conversation and walked away; then, with mingled tenseness and gleeful anticipation, he acted. In that instant the Druid stood alone on an expanse of crystal with the wild aurora dancing all around him.

For a moment MacDougall watched the incredulity on the hawklike face change to consternation, then become abject terror as the man evidently grasped where he was. Alan shut off the image. For an instant he hesitated, then decided the Druid was in no real danger. His being in the Forbidden Area must be doing horrendous things to his thoughts, but eventually he'd reach one of the gods, or they'd find him; besides, he deserved what he'd gotten.

Alan thought of Morrigu; recollection of the Macha masquerade made his ears burn. She was next if he could manage it; and suddenly he was completely confident that he could, if Ahriman delayed his return.

MacDougall found her in Balor's quarters, conversing with the Fomorian god and Dalua. At that very moment Balor's puzzled voice interrupted whatever they were discussing.

"Semias is in some sort of trouble. He's trying to reach me. He's completely terrified and he makes no sense whatever."

There was more, but MacDougall had changed the view to an aerial panorama of Gorias. He knew what he wanted, but he didn't know the city. In a short time he found what he sought—a stable where horses were quartered. More specifically, the dungheap behind the stable!

With unholy glee and with utmost care, he placed the tongs around Morrigu; deftly he dropped the old crone on the very apex of the steaming manure pile!

He took no time to gloat over his handiwork, blotting out the scene in the midst of her outraged shriek. He had already decided on Balor's destination and wanted to achieve his purpose before the Evil Eye took evasive action. The bay outside Murias was his objective, and the hold of a fishing boat was his specific goal. He found it after a bit of trouble, then reverted to Balor, now standing and shouting about someone paying with his head. Suddenly Dalua was alone, and Balor of the Fomorians floundered in a wet and slippery heap of flopping fish.

Alan shut off sight of the Evil Eye and, returning to the image of Balor's apartment, he found that it was empty. Dalua had fled.

Well, he couldn't have everything. He decided against pursuit. He had paid back those who had caused him the most grief, and there was no chance that they could blame him. Better quit while he was ahead. Carefully he placed the forceps on the table and was in the act of removing the helmet when he heard a deep voice at his shoulder.

"Have you enjoyed my absence? A fascinating viewer, is it not?"

Startled, MacDougall leaped erect and turned. "Caught in the act!" he exclaimed. "I just couldn't resist—" How long had the Persian been standing there, and what had he seen?

Ahriman raised a reassuring hand. "I would have been disappointed in you if you had not looked around a bit. I wondered if you could master the focusing. Apparently you realized the part your armlet had to play. Or did you?"

MacDougall floundered momentarily, not knowing just what to say.

Impatiently Ahriman shook his head. "No matter. I fear I shall have to terminate our visit. My attention is required in other matters elsewhere. I regret our abrupt parting, but urgency requires it." He took Alan's hand,

and instantly MacDougall found himself on ground level. Somehow with his hand released, he was facing the amber wall; he saw the meadow and beyond it the forest.

He looked back at Lucifer's lieutenant and began to speak uncertainly. "I—I appreciate what you've shown me and—I thank you for your hospitality. Perhaps we'll meet again."

The fixed smile broadened, and there was a mocking glint in the Persian's gem-hard eyes. "It is inevitable. And now farewell. Walk straight ahead. There will be no resistance."

Nor was there. Two strides brought MacDougall through the wall and out onto the turf. He glanced back to see the smoothly glowing, golden surface. Giving no thought to the two gods in the meadow, he strode away. He wanted to put as much distance as possible between himself and the smiling man in the Tower. He could feel those frigid eyes on his back, thought of the mockery they held, and only now realized he was really afraid. Shamelessly he admitted it, and in retrospect he marveled at the boldness he had assumed in his dealings with the one who must surely be the real power in Tartarus.

He reached the woods, walking straight ahead until he felt certain he was hidden by the trees. Only then did he think about direction. He wanted to go east and north to find the road and the Gate, but for all he knew, he might be heading due west—or in any other direction. He had nothing to guide him. The aurora dancing overhead was no help at all. There was nothing for it but to continue on as straight a course as possible. This was an island. If he walked far enough and straight enough, he was bound to reach the sea.

Mentally he reviewed his experience in the Tower, and as he thought of the offer Ahriman had made, he realized its absurdity. Rulership of the Island! It made no sense whatever. He thought also of the Persian's convenient absence, which had resulted in his opportunity to manipulate Balor, Morrigu, and Semias, and he wondered if he had not done precisely what he was intended to do. Now that he thought of it, it seemed so obvious. That uninterrupted shimmering of the platform lens had to be intentional. Ahriman, by his own statement, never acted without a purpose. Alan was to introduce unknown factors into the game and he had done so with a vengeance. He shrugged. What he had done could not be undone.

As he continued through the woods, he became aware of a strangeness, a lack. It was the lifelessness, the absence of bird sounds; there was no rustling of scurrying creatures; no wind stirred the leaves. In any other woods in which he had walked, there had been what he thought of as green-gloom, an atmosphere that went with forests. Here it did not exist. He shrugged off the feeling of eeriness.

He stopped to rest and remembered the scroll he had thrust into a pocket of the Fomorian costume. It was still there. Ridiculous, his wearing this black stuff over the much more practical outfit in which he had entered Tartarus! He removed it, transferring the scroll to his knapsack. He found a smooth spot and, with the cloth rolled into a ball and placed on the knapsack as a pillow, he stretched out for a nap. No question about it—he didn't approve of this world's sleeping schedule.

He awakened refreshed; and as he took a drink from his canteen, he discovered it was his last. He had neglected to refill the vessel at the last stop on the way into Murias, depending on the supply of water carried by his horse. There was nothing to be done about it now but to get moving. He set out at a good pace in what he hoped was the right direction. An uneasy feeling began to disturb him. He might be going in circles. Damn such a place!

He had walked for an extended period when he became aware of a change most unusual for Tartarus. It was growing darker!

There was no mistaking the change. It was like dusk falling in the tropics, a sudden marked fading of the light, and with it an altering of the character of the forest. The trees became stunted and the spaces between them grew ever greater, until the woods abruptly ended. Beyond, barely discernible in the gloom, lay a stretch of sparse and sickly grass whose uncertain sustenance rested in a gray-black soil that merged quickly with black sand where nothing grew. He had reached the black plain in which Findias lay.

What had Taliesin called it? The Desert of Gloom. And the sky overhead—he recalled the Bard's description: "A sky of jet, where even the aurora appears but rarely, and then in timid waves that wax and wane, the Dancing Men never."

MacDougall surveyed the scene with a sinking heart. It was all Taliesin had said it was. The glow of the weak and ghostly aurora just barely dispelled complete darkness, giving off hardly as much light as a moonless sky in the Highlands. Certainly the plain had been well named as the Desert of Gloom.

It was small consolation, but now he knew where he was, at least in part. The road probably lay to his left; and though the city of Trolls did not sound very appealing, he surely could get food and water there. Suddenly remembering, he grimaced with distaste. Findias was the home city of Arias, the Gray Druid, his first enemy on Tartarus.

He had no choice. He had to find the road. He'd follow the edge of the woods, which would mean he was skirting the northern end of the plain. With no great enthusiasm, but with purpose in his stride, he set out.

He was tired when he began this part of his hike, and after a time, with the dry sand dragging at his boots, weariness seemed to strike at his very bones. Then suddenly he burst into a loud guffaw. Out of nowhere had come a picture of Morrigu sprawling on the dungheap. He halted, stood there in the darkness, and roared with laughter. Too bad there was no one to share his mirth. Finally he resumed his walk, his weariness in part forgotten.

Then he came to the road.

The straight, white stretch of pebbles was a most welcome sight, and he headed south with renewed energy. Best of all, he could detect a faint glow in the distance, evidently the torchlighted city. With Findias so close, he began to think about how he would be received.

A faint sound caught his attention and he stopped short. Horses' hoofs on the road behind him—a caravan heading toward Findias! He thought of riding the rest of the way, then remembered his first greeting by a caravan. And this could be Arias returning from Falias. Better to hide until he saw the makeup of the group—except that there was no place to hide.

Decision was taken from him as the first horseman came into view, an indistinct figure in the darkness. MacDougall stood in the center of the road, waving his arms. The lead horseman drew rein, and suddenly a familiar and welcome voice shouted, "Alan MacDougall, by all the gods!"

It was Taliesin, Bard of Bards, and his thirty Norsemen!

CHAPTER 8

The Druid of Findias

Both men were genuinely glad to see each other, for personal reasons as well as for the obvious practical ones. After they had exchanged greetings, MacDougall asked, "May I have a bit of water and a bite to eat? It has been quite a time—"

"Of course! I wager you haven't eaten since our last stop. Svend," Taliesin called out to his captain, "we rest here. Food and drink for the son of Dougall." He turned back to Alan. "Not the best place for a rest, this darkness, but before we go into Findias, we should know what happened to each other."

While MacDougall satisfied his physical needs, the Bard recounted what had taken place in Murias after their separation. The trouble had begun with the Unholy Three in concert blanketing Taliesin's mental communication, with

Danu specifically, but just as effectively with Alan. Semias and a group of Fomorians had imprisoned the Bard under heavy guard. The situation had remained unchanged until he had felt the control weaken—thanks to Morrigu's loss of consciousness, as he later learned—and he had not only reached Alan but had also gotten through to Danu. From then on, either by direct contact with both Taliesin and Darthula or through others around them, the *Tuatha De Danann* had been in control of the situation.

"After it became certain that you had somehow escaped from Murias," Taliesin concluded, "the *Tuatha De Danann*, by combining their powers, were able to transport Darthula and me outside the city. As you are aware, there is no love lost between the Three and the Family, so there was no difficulty in adding more than enough power to make the transfer. My men presented a different problem. I wanted them out of Murias, and again numbers prevailed. Danu and a group of gods kept the Unholy Three occupied until I had communicated with the Norsemen, and they left Murias in the regular way.

"All this took time, of course; and even after we met with the Ch'in, that fog still blanketed everything. Danu decided to leave it there to hamper the spying of Balor and Morrigu, but though it gave us concealment, it was a nuisance." Taliesin chuckled. "When I learned about the 'inspection' of our horses and that yours had run away, apparently with the inspector, I knew you had made it that far. Then the antics of the three began—the wolves, Dalua's cackling, and the hoodie. All in all, it was slow going.

"That ended with the fog suddenly lifting, and from then on we made good time. When we reached the crossroads, Darthula, of course, headed east for Gorias with her Ch'in, and we turned south toward Findias. And here we are. Now it's your turn."

Quickly MacDougall summarized the happenings up to the sighting of the Golden Tower. "I confess I was annoyed when I learned that my rescuers were Danu and

Dagda, but, everything considered, I suppose I should be grateful. What disturbs me most, I think, is this constant surveillance, the meddling I have to expect." He grinned in the darkness with sudden recollection. "Recently I did a bit of it myself."

Taliesin was puzzled. "You mean—?"

"Never mind. I don't think you really want to know." MacDougall hesitated. "You probably know about the Tower already, since Danu saw what happened. That is, she saw me disappear. But because it took place in a Forbidden Area, you'd probably find the details upsetting." MacDougall told of his sighting the golden cone, of its invisibility to Danu and Dagda, and of his approach.

"Since I entered the Tower, I must have vanished from the sight of the two watchers. Inside, I met a man and saw things which could only be disturbing to you. *Very* disturbing! Even I have trouble believing what I saw. So I think the less I say the better."

Hastily Taliesin agreed, adding a puzzled comment. "Somehow anything having to do with the Forbidden things makes me most uncomfortable. I've tried to analyze it and I've decided this must be something built into these new bodies we were given when we entered this life."

"Anyway," MacDougall concluded, "after I left the Tower I started walking, trying to keep a straight course. I hoped I was heading north or east, but apparently I was facing due south. I finally reached the Desert of Gloom, turned left—and that's it."

During his recital, a vague question had been gnawing at the edge of Alan's mind. Now it crystallized.

"By the way," he inquired, "what made you decide to come to Findias? I can't see any logical reason."

There was a long silence, then Taliesin answered with obvious reluctance. "After you disappeared, Danu and Dagda watched for you to reappear. They saw when you suddenly materialized, then entered the woods facing south. They made sure you continued in that general direction and so informed me before they went on toward Murias to keep an eye on the troublemakers."

"I should have known. But now that you've found me, what's the purpose of your continuing into Findias? Why not head north?"

The answer came promptly. "Supplies, especially food. And a sleep in a comfortable bed before we ride back to Falias. After all, we're almost there, and I am sure all of us will appreciate the rest."

In short order they were on their way, MacDougall astride one of the extra horses. Their eyes had grown accustomed to the limited light, so they had no trouble following the white road; rapidly they approached the torchlighted city.

The spectacle was striking, the velvety blackness of the sky framing a rounded, gossamer dome of red and yellow light. Brilliant at the base, it gradually lost its intensity and became tenuous, finally merging with the sable blackness.

As they drew closer, MacDougall could distinguish the torches jutting from a brazen wall, its top serrated, each peak ending in a spearhead point from which flared a fan of flame. Brazen? Incredulously Alan realized that the wall, all of eight feet high, was a curving barrier of solid, polished brass! And the torches were eternally burning gas that must be coming from wells deep beneath Tartarus!

This was startling enough, but nothing compared with that which was to follow.

Without warning, from the heart of Findias leaped a lance of the most intense white radiance, a spear of light impaling the heavens. So concentrated was its brilliance that it seemed a solid, and there was no spreading of this beam. Rather, it appeared to taper like a veritable spear. A laser beam, MacDougall exclaimed to himself.

"The Spear of Findias." Taliesin's voice held a note of awe. "It holds endlessly—or but for a moment. It comes when least expected and goes the same way. It has always been so. The spear from the brazen mouth! You shall see."

They continued toward that brass wall; and there, highlighted by the flare of the torches, was the city gate. At least, MacDougall thought, it should be the gate, since the road led up to it. It was the strangest gate one could imagine—a tremendous brass serpent's head, twice the height of the wall and proportionately wide, glaring down at them!

As if aware of their coming, that fantastic thing opened, the lower jaw dropping ingeniously to form a ramp, the upper jaw rising, with conventional double doors moving aside behind it.

MacDougall heard a chuckle from Taliesin as they rode up the ramp. "Shocking, is it not? There are more surprises in store for you."

The two leaders drew aside and watched as the Norsemen entered Findias; then Alan saw his first Trolls. He had had a vague idea of little, humpbacked elves, half remembered from his childhood reading, and in one respect he was right. They were short. As the door closed behind the caravan, two Trolls came into view, perched high on the gate behind the serpent's eyes. They came scurrying down stairways set against the gate, both about three or three and a half feet tall. Their legs were slightly bowed, their arms and hands were unusually long, and their ears and noses were overly large; otherwise they were well proportioned, and certainly not humpbacked. Their plentiful brown hair was long and straggly, and their rather dark-skinned faces were bewhiskered. They wore sooty gray jackets, knee breeches, and sharp-toed brown sandals.

One approached Taliesin and in a high, nasal tone exclaimed, "Oh, blast! I have made a mistake. I thought you were the Gray Master returning, hence let you in so promptly. Oh, blast!"

Dismounting, Taliesin laughed aloud. "No harm done. Are you not Nurremurre? I am Taliesin, Bard of Bards, and wish to replenish supplies and rest our weary bones before returning to Falias. I was here not so long ago with a cargo of food. Will you attend to our horses?"

"Oh, I remember you. Yes, yes; and welcome. At once, Master." He put fingers to mouth, and a shrill whistle echoed through the quiet. Out of the underground ramp directly opposite the entrance poured ten or fifteen Trolls, each to take the reins of two or three horses and lead them down the broad way. The riders, already dismounted, stood to one side.

Taliesin asked, "Shall we help ourselves to quarters, and can refreshments be brought?"

The brown head bobbed eagerly. "Oh, yes, yes, of course! I am certain there will be no problem. I will report it to the Gray Master's aides, of course; but—yes, yes, no problem, of course." And with that the little figure sped away past the entrance to the underground, followed by his silent companion, moving in the general direction of the spear of light, which still pierced the sky and shed its white radiance all around.

Taliesin turned to MacDougall with a broad grin. "Surprised? There's more." He addressed his men. "Rest well. And stay close together. One bed is the same as another."

At his word, the Norsemen moved leftward along a lateral street lined on both sides by—and Alan could scarcely believe his eyes—what looked like nothing so much as huge, rounded, conical beehives! They butted against one another, evidently connecting, in sets of five. They differed only in color, the first group alternating blue and pink, the second lavender and yellow, and so on. And about each group, as if binding the units together, was coiled an enormous brazen serpent, a masterpiece of the metalcrafter's art.

The Norsemen opened doorways in as many cones, and soon all had disappeared.

MacDougall stared at Taliesin. "The craziest thing I ever saw! Where is everybody? Vacant houses just waiting for us? That's the last thing I'd expect from Arias, if he's the boss here."

"He is in charge, but do not credit the Druid with this. It is the doing of the Trolls. I'll explain everything after we go to our quarters. First I want to show you what is probably the most striking thing on the Island. Follow."

The Bard moved briskly between a group of five houses and its counterpart, then on between two others, going in the direction taken by the Trolls.

"Findias," he explained, "is circular. The streets are concentric circles with no cross streets, but with ample walking space between the groups of houses. Remember, the Four Cities were created for the Daughters of Lilith.

"In the very center of Findias stands what I want you to see. There might not be time for sightseeing after our sleep, since we will want to be on our way before Arias returns, if possible. No point in asking for unpleasantness."

They were approaching the white pillar of light; its brilliance was almost overpowering. They halted past a final row of houses, and Alan MacDougall gazed in awe.

On a black rock base, taller than himself and apparently octagonal, whose breadth he could not estimate, lay a gargantuan serpent of brass, coiled in a vast mound of polished, golden yellow, every one of its scales perfectly wrought, its awesome head at the apex of the heap facing skyward. From its gaping maw poured the five-foot-wide Spear of Findias. The size of the image alone was breathtaking; the perfection of execution and the strangeness of concept boggled the mind.

"The symbol of Findias," Taliesin said in a hushed voice.

And at that moment, with the startling suddenness of a wink, the spear of radiance vanished, its going creating the effect of suddenly falling night. Slowly their eyes adjusted to the yellow-blue of the torches as they turned back toward the city's entrance.

They had almost reached their destination when MacDougall spoke.

"What's the significance of that light and this repetition of the serpent motif?"

Taliesin's reply was delayed. "My guess is no better than yours. I suppose it may have something to do with the initial conflict which led to Lucifer's downfall. This may be a gesture of defiance. But no one knows."

They reached the gateway and the first row of houses. The Bard led the way into a dwelling across the street from those into which the Norsemen had gone. They entered the same sort of little house.

Here, as in Murias, delicately glowing walls provided the interior with a soft, ivory light, pleasant to the eye and ample for any normal need. The room held a single broad bed barely a foot from the floor, two contour chairs, a small table, and a tall, narrow wardrobe. Since they were in an end house, only one wall was flattened, with a door leading into the next chamber. The Bard opened this door and revealed a room duplicating the first. "Yours," he said.

As both men sank into chairs, Taliesin continued, "In a short while we'll be served refreshments. Meantime, an explanation is due you.

"As I keep repeating, this place was designed for the Daughters of Lilith, not for Trolls. When the small people came, they found these quarters strange and not to their liking. Being industrious and resourceful, they very gradually moved underground. It took time, much time, but that is one commodity without limit here. And since they were neat and orderly in their labors, disturbing nothing already built, no one objected.

"They began by cutting a trapdoor in the floors of their own dwellings. There's one in this room, as you'll see. Beneath, they found the black sand, but only a comparatively thin layer, and below that a heavy, compact clay, ideal for their purposes. They began excavating subterranean chambers, always leaving ample supports for everything above. The material they removed they carried on their backs and dumped into the sea—though that's miles from the city wall. And so it was with everything that followed: the shops, their assembly halls, and later, when they began metalworking, their smelters and forges. They got ore from the hills around Gorias, exchanging finished products for food.

"On the surface, except for the few buildings occupied by Arias and his staff of a dozen or so, Findias is vacant, neatly kept in order by the Trolls—and of all the dwellers in Tartarus, the Trolls alone seem happy."

There came a tapping from beneath the floor, and a hinged trapdoor swung up to reveal a female of the Troll-people. There was little to distinguish her from her male counterparts, except that she had a few more curves and no beard, and her plaited hair was coiled on top of her head. She displayed a warm smile as she carried in a tray of steaming barley and fish soup and some small barley loaves.

"Thank you, Skyndie," Taliesin said, "and will you bring a second portion for my friend, who will be sleeping in the next room?"

The smile broadened. "At once, Master. But I am not Skyndie—I am Ulva."

In a short time she returned with MacDougall's portion, placing it on the opposite side of the little table. Alan had removed his knapsack, and now he recalled to mind the scroll. He drew it out and gave it to Taliesin.

"I found that in Balor's room, and I hope the script makes sense to you."

The Bard grasped it eagerly and secreted it in one of his pockets. "Finding it where you did, with the armlet—and Caermarthen's saying it was there when he came—makes me certain that it must have importance. After we've eaten, you get to sleep. I want to arrange to have supplies put into the saddlebags before I go to bed so we can leave promptly after we break fast."

About to crawl into bed a short time later, and wondering how the Trolls had known which room they had taken, Alan heard a tapping under his floor. At his call the trapdoor rose, and a Troll came up the stairs with a pitcher of hot water and a towel, then bowed his way out. Alan marveled at the unexpected service and took advantage of the luxury. Finally he got under the covers and closed his eyes. He was becoming accustomed to sleeping in perpetual light, and the comfort of the bed had him yawning in moments. But sleep evaded him as the events of the recent past kept crowding into his mind.

After the first confused blending of memory and dream had deadened his senses, he became aware of a bedlam of furious words pouring into his brain. It was the bellowing of Balor, followed by the harsh, cackling tirade of Morrigu.

"*I answered this summons to find out whom to kill!*" Balor was beside himself with wrath. "*Never—never in my long life have I been treated like this! Never has anyone dared to subject me—me, Balor, god of the Fomorians—to such indignity. Someone will die for this! Who—who was so—so—*"

"*You suffered indignity?*" Morrigu interrupted. "*Let me find out who—who cast me— Oh, I cannot repeat it! There will be war! It must have been one of you—probably you, Danu, you oily-mouthed, smooth-talking bitch. No man would dare! It was you, Danu, I vow it—and when I meet you in person, I'll claw your eyes out!*"

"*Shut up, both of you!*" Nuada's voice, by sheer power alone, rose above the others. "*What is this all about? I know nothing about whatever has happened. Will someone explain?*"

"*I also am in the dark,*" Danu said quietly. "*What happened?*"

Morrigu answered. "*Balor, Dalua, and I were having a quiet conversation in Balor's apartment when suddenly I found myself—oh, someone will pay—on a dungheap in Gorias!*" She halted, suddenly startled. "*Balor, could you have—?*"

"Don't be a fool! You disappeared, and moments later I found myself half buried in fish in the hold of a boat in the Murias bay. And poor Semias—someone dropped him on the roof of the replacement center outside Falias, and you know what that means! He's still shaking; I don't think he will ever recover his sanity. He keeps raving about ghostly bodies and he's been in bed ever since."

Danu said indignantly, "Well, I'm certainly not responsible for any such childish pranks. And I can vouch for Dagda; we've been together since Taliesin brought the fog, with my help."

Nuada suppressed a chuckle. "It sounds funny; but, of course, you didn't find it amusing. I don't blame you for being angry, but no harm has been done, except perhaps to Semias. Certainly it wasn't my doing."

Balor ranted with unabated fury. "It had to be one or more of you! No mere mortal could have done it! And it certainly wasn't any of the other gods who have been sitting on their butts for the last thousand years! So, no matter what you say, I have decided. I am mobilizing the Fomor and we're marching on Falias and Gorias. A good war will settle things. This time we will win; no trickery will prevent it. And when we've won, we will also have that Alan MacDougall and his precious Gate. We'll go through; and you, you jokers, will stay behind. If you live! And remember, Nuada," he added scornfully, "the Fomor killed you in another battle a long time ago."

Suddenly MacDougall felt that Balor and Morrigu were no longer present at the conference. There was a cessation of the flow of thoughts so prolonged that he had about decided everyone had gone.

Then Nuada spoke angrily. "He would mention that! We all know it was an accident." A note of anticipation entered his next words. "War with the Fomorians? I welcome it. It has been a long time. It will break the monotony."

Danu added, "We defeated them then and we'll do it again."

Dagda made his first comment. *"The manure pile!"*

The three gods burst into laughter, which gradually faded into silence.

And Alan MacDougall, chuckling to himself, though a bit ruefully, drifted toward slumber. Among his last waking thoughts was an image of Ahramin and his mocking smile when they parted. Now he understood that smile. He *had* done just what the Persian wanted. He'd been a dupe!

How long he slept before a commotion outside partially awakened him, he had no way of determining. Half asleep, but aware of some distant goings-on, he listened but could make nothing of the sounds. Finally he went back to sleep, to be awakened eventually by a sharp rapping on the door leading to Taliesin's room.

"Everybody out!" the Bard called. "You're the last. Breakfast is already here—for two."

Quickly MacDougall dressed, strapped on his knapsack, and joined the Bard at the table. "Sorry; I had trouble getting to sleep, and some noise disturbed my rest. But as you can see, I'm ready to go."

"Go ahead with your breakfast. I've just finished." The Bard was not his usual cheery self; he seemed somewhat downcast. "I heard the same disturbance," he said, "and I think I know what caused it. Probably bad news." He looked at Alan, frowning. "That will wait, I hope. I have what I suppose is good news for you and bad news for everyone else on the Island. I worked on your scroll before I went to bed and I had some success in deciphering it. It is a most unusual script—but enough of that.

"The scroll records the full history of Lucifer's jest— his use of the Island as a prison for the souls of a select body of those who are his. It is a full verification of all I have told you. It includes the story of the Four Gates, the guard who was Caermarthen, and the serpent armlet and its powers. It tells of a Tower, doubtless the one you visited, and of the inevitable desire of everyone impris-

oned here to escape from eternal boredom. Then it adds
the final ironic conclusion to the jest.

"Alan, if my reading is correct, you may leave Tartarus
at will with no interference from anyone." He paused and
yawned prodigiously. "Sorry; I didn't get much sleep. I
want to spend more time..." He yawned again. "No one
will want...to go...with you..."

MacDougall yawned and blinked. His eyes were suddenly unbearably heavy. "This is...contagious."

The Bard's eyelids drooped and his head sank to his
chest, then snapped erect. "Alan...we've been drugged!"

That was all MacDougall heard, except for the faintly
muttered word "Danu..." Then his own eyes closed, and
he felt himself slump to the floor.

The world was gyrating sickeningly when Alan Mac-
Dougall came to his senses. He was lying on his side in
a most awkward position, his hands tightly bound behind
his back. His upper right arm throbbed painfully in the
vicinity of the gold armlet, as if someone had been trying
to remove it. He turned slightly, then became aware that
his ankles also were tightly secured with cord that cut
into his flesh. In his position he could see nothing but a
bare, pale green wall.

At his slight movement, four Trolls surrounded him,
grasping his arms and legs and lifting him roughly erect.
They carried him a few feet and set him on a backless
stool, holding him for a moment to be sure he remained
erect; then, while two continued holding him, the other
pair dexterously wound heavy cord around his legs and
the legs of the stool, anchoring him there. During all of
this, not a word had been spoken.

Turning man and stool away from the wall, the Trolls
stepped back. MacDougall looked around. Instantly his
eyes fell on a figure facing him from a dozen feet away.
The figure was seated and trussed as he was, tied to a
stool as he was, and in addition, efficiently gagged.

"Darthula!" he cried.

Unbelievably, it was the Princess from Gorias. Their eyes met, and there was a mixture of mute appeal and cold anger in her gaze. How in the name of all the gods of Tartarus had she come to be there? he wondered. A harsh, well-remembered voice supplied the evident answer.

"Darthula indeed!" Arias, Druid of Findias, stalked through a doorway and halted midway between the two prisoners. There was triumph and gloating in every line of his gray and bony face as he glanced from one to the other, unholy anticipation gleaming in his bloodshot eyes. "And I have you just where I want you! Enough of this absurd dallying in the matter of the Gate. The gods themselves seem unable to make you supply its location. I have no need of the gods."

He stepped to Darthula's side and ripped off her gag. "If you have any powers of persuasion, exert them now! I have no patience left!"

The girl compressed her lips and stared disdainfully at Arias, but said nothing.

The Druid laughed unpleasantly, then turned to Mac-Dougall. "I am a merciful man. I have no wish to cause pain—" His very expression belied his words. "—but I'll hack off your arm if that's what it will take to find that Gate. I *know* that serpent armlet is the answer! *Talk!*" The last word was a bellow. Arias whipped out a sword— *his* sword, Alan realized, its sheath now hanging from the Druid's waist.

"The armlet is part of the answer, but only part," MacDougall said calmly. "Even with it, I can barely see the faintest impression of the Gate. Everything rests on my memory of where it is and the landmarks around it. Without these, you could not find it in a thousand lifetimes." His words must have carried conviction, for Arias viciously sheathed the blade.

"Then you will show me!"

"Surely you can't expect to get away with this,"

MacDougall exclaimed, stalling for time. "Taliesin and the gods—"

"Taliesin! Pah!" The harsh voice exuded triumph. "I've outwitted the bloated fool at every turn! When his caravan and Darthula's separated, my own was concealed in the woods undetected. I had heard their approach—we had stopped for rest—I was on my way home from Falias with two hundred horsemen. With Taliesin safely out of sight, we followed the Ch'in and, eventually catching up with them, joined them while I talked with her Highness, the Princess. Then at my signal my Norsemen turned on the yellow men. It was beautiful! They put up a good battle, but they were outnumbered two to one, and at close range their lances had no chance against our swords. It was a lovely slaughter. We had losses—but here is the Princess." He bowed mockingly.

"As for Taliesin, he is in that room of his, heavily drugged and under Troll guard. And don't count on the Trolls failing. They are a gentle people, a kindly people—but they are *mine*! They do *my* bidding. And the Bard will remain as he is until I say the word. So look for no help from the fat Bard."

"But," MacDougall protested, "eventually you'll have to deal with the gods. Even Morrigu won't approve of your independent action. And Danu—"

"Danu be cursed! When I control the Gate, they will answer to me." As Arias spat out the words, he drew from under his cloak a coiled, many-thonged whip, which he flicked open. There was a sadistic light in his slitted eyes. "Enough of talk! Will you show me the Gate?"

"You wouldn't dare!" MacDougall cried.

"No?" Arias turned to the two nearest Trolls. "Krogbe and Gurus, turn the stool," he said, pointing to Darthula. Promptly they did so, then retreated.

Swiftly Arias hooked his long fingers into the collar of the girl's filmy bodice and with a single movement ripped the cloth from her back, exposing the fair expanse of skin. With the other hand he raised the whip high and brought it down in a powerful sweep. Nine red welts sprang into angry relief as a single piercing scream was torn from Darthula's lips. Her head sank forward and she began to sob.

"You damned sadistic bastard!" MacDougall grated, red fury consuming him.

With the words, the lash cut across his face, burning like fire, by sheer good fortune missing his eyes.

A second time the Druid raised the lash over the girl's back. "Shall I give her more—or have you learned who is the master?"

"You win," MacDougall ground out hoarsely. "I'll show you the Gate."

The whip hovered threateningly. "No tricks?"

"No tricks. I'm not an idiot."

As he coiled the thongs, the Druid said regretfully, "I expected more resistance, more spirit, than this." Then he ordered the Trolls, "You have your instructions." And with his head cocked proudly in obvious self-satisfaction, he swaggered from the room.

The four Trolls set to work with businesslike dispatch, Darthula receiving first attention. The cords binding her to the stool were removed, followed by those around her ankles. They got her to her feet and, though she had trouble walking, hustled her across the room, raised a trapdoor, and led her slowly down the stairs.

Watching this, Alan MacDougall was the epitome of misery. Why had he ever come into this crazy world? Darthula's loveliness had brought him here, and he had given her nothing but grief. How she must hate him! As for Arias—his thoughts seethed. If ever a man deserved killing, the Druid did. Right now he seemed to be having his own way. But one thing was sure—the gray man would never get a crack at the Gate. Alan had said, "No tricks." That applied, of course, only if he didn't get a chance to play one. And he could be certain Arias would be on guard.

In general, MacDougall knew what he'd do. He'd lead

the way to the vicinity of the Gate—assuming none of the gods got involved before that happened—and then go invisible. Alone, he'd get back to where he belonged. He hoped it would be that simple.

The four Trolls returned for MacDougall, freeing his feet and leading him down to the tunnels under Findias. There was little light in these underground passageways; candles set in niches in the walls provided a minimum of illumination and cast grotesque shadows. But the light seemed ample for the little men who conducted Alan through a complex maze to the corral, which was crowded with horses and Trolls. He had made one attempt at conversation during the walk, but had elicited no response whatever.

They led him to a horse and helped him mount. Then they looped a rope around one stirruped foot, brought it under the horse's belly, and tied it about the other foot. MacDougall scowled. They weren't taking any chances.

"But," he asked one of the Trolls, "how am I to control this beast unless you free my hands?"

The Troll glanced about, then said quickly, "That is my task." And with the help of the other three, he climbed up in front of MacDougall and grasped the reins.

The caravan was forming, all appearing in readiness. Alan caught a glimpse of Darthula with a Troll in the saddle with her; but he and she were far apart. There was no chance for conversation, assuming she *would* talk to him, which was not at all certain. He saw that something like a shawl had been draped over her shoulders and fastened under her chin. He lost sight of her as the caravan started up the broad ramp, the Trolls astride perhaps a hundred horses. They looked odd—and then MacDougall realized they were riding bareback! Something else seemed strange to him, though perhaps it wasn't: each Troll was armed with a sword scaled to his height.

The unusual caravan began emerging onto the surface. The Gray Druid, Arias, led the way; Alan's mount was only a few horses behind that of the leader. Except for

the Trolls manning the serpent gate, the streets of Findias
were deserted. There were no Norsemen, and that was
really strange—probably a sign of the Druid's supreme
authority. The caravan passed through the brazen mouth
and was on its way.

How great a difference, MacDougall thought, between
the approach to Findias and his departure. He'd been
treated royally on his arrival and was leaving as a prisoner. Before, he'd thought of Darthula safely on her way
home; now her future was uncertain. He had had some
vague misgivings because of Arias, and they had been
justified. The welts across his face attested to the fact
and reminded him of the girl's obviously more painful
stripes. He became conscious of numbness in his hands;
he flexed his fingers repeatedly to restore circulation and
felt the needle-pricks of flowing blood. The damned Druid
wouldn't care if checked circulation caused permanent
damage! Alan wondered about Taliesin, hoping he was
unharmed.

Thought of the Bard reminded him of Taliesin's last
statement before he had lapsed into drugged sleep. He
had said that Alan would be able to leave Tartarus at will
with no one interfering. "No one will want to go with
you—" What had the scroll revealed?

In due course they passed out of the darkness into the
light of the aurora, their northward journey continuing
without incident. They maintained a steady pace, and at
last the crossroads lay in sight.

MacDougall kept his attention fixed on this landmark,
wondering when Arias would ask for directions and when
if ever they'd stop for rest. Then it happened. One moment the roads were empty; the next, four figures with
upraised, waving arms stood side by side in the center of
the crossroads only a few feet away from the caravan.
The lead horse reared up in fright, almost unseating Arias;
and for confused moments a chain reaction spread through
the caravan until it came to a halt.

The four were Danu, Dagda, Taliesin, and another man,

tall and handsome, whom MacDougall assumed must be Nuada.

A shriek of fury burst from Arias and he shouted, "Ride them down!"

Yet strangely even his own horse made no move forward, merely turning and twisting under the Druid's apparent spurring. Alan, sensing an aura of power radiating from the four, realized why no Troll had responded.

Nuada spoke, loudly enough to be heard by the rearmost Troll, in a voice MacDougall recognized.

"Well, Arias, this time you appear to have ventured a bit beyond your depth. You have invited trouble. It has come. Dismount!"

The Druid attempted a show of defiance. "I have done only what all of you have tried—"

"Dismount!" The volume in the god's voice was not greatly changed, but there was power in the word that brooked no disobedience. Alan saw the gray of the Druid's face assume a greenish hue. Hastily he slid from the saddle.

"Now release your captives! And do it carefully!"

Not a word or a sound came from any of the Trolls as Arias moved back through the standing horses to the one bearing Darthula. MacDougall saw Danu follow him; and though he could not see what happened, he could picture the Druid's untying the ankle cords and those about her wrists. At length the Princess came walking unsteadily alongside the caravan, supported by the Mother Goddess. Arias made his way to MacDougall. With trembling fingers he set to work on Alan's bonds.

It was a strange scene. Overhead danced the restless beams of the aurora, in counterpoint to the utter quiet of the hundred Trolls watching the humiliation of the one whose word had been their law. The three motionless observers stood as if frozen. Especially impressive was the figure of Nuada, who was as tall as MacDougall and broad of shoulder, clad all in white except for a bright blue cape, his fabled sword at his side, suspended from a broad belt of gold links. His shoulder-length hair was almost as white as his garments.

Ankles freed, MacDougall got off his horse with the Druid's help. His eyes met those of Arias and he smiled. "How the mighty have fallen," he said softly. The Druid glared venomously but said nothing, struggling with the wrist cords. At last Alan was free; awkwardly he chafed his wrists, walking toward Nuada and the others with Arias at his heels.

"Help him!" Nuada commanded the Druid.

"I want no further help from him," MacDougall rasped.

The King of the *Tuatha De Danann* addressed the Trolls. "Return to Findias. Restore the horses to the Norsemen and tell them they are to go back to Falias under command of their captain. Tell the Druid's assistants that he will not be coming back. They are to choose one among them to supervise. The one whom they choose will answer to me. Now go!"

There was no hesitation on the part of the small men. As one, they turned their horses and headed south.

Alan had been watching Arias while Nuada spoke. At his concluding statement, stark terror had crossed the Druid's face. Now all eyes turned toward the retreating riders, and silence held until they vanished in the distance. Then, as if by agreement, all moved back save Arias and Nuada.

Arias finally broke the silence, and panic was evident in the shrillness of his voice. "Surely you would not—I admit I was foolish to think—to think I could—" The words began to stumble over each other, his voice becoming a high-pitched whine. "It must have been madness! It was only what all of you—I ask mercy—Darthula, Princess, I beg—"

"Shut up!" Nuada snapped. "And you a Druid! At least be a man. Who knows, perhaps Lucifer has a third body reserved for you!"

Arias sank to his knees out of weakness induced by his terror. He reached out imploringly.

Nuada ignored the gesture. "I see you bear a sword. Interesting. It suggests a way for you to die with honor—or perhaps you might even defeat me. But no; my sword is invincible, an enchanted blade that cannot lose. And Druids are not skilled at swordplay." A bantering note entered his voice. "A better idea! A fascinating experiment! We shall duel—and I'll control your blade! Something which I vow has never before been done—a duel with myself! I appreciate your bringing it to my mind." His manner changed abruptly. "Druid, stand and draw your sword!"

At the words Arias sagged flaccidly, all strength seeming to leave his body. No strutting now, MacDougall thought. Impatiently Nuada exclaimed, "I see you need help!" And like a puppet animated by strings, the Druid leaped erect, whipping out his weapon.

Thus began the most amazing display of swordmanship one could imagine. Arias rushed in and poured a storm of steel at the King of the *Tuatha De Danann*, sweeping cuts and rapid lunges alternating in an attack that it seemed must bear the god off his feet by sheer force. The Druid fought as one possessed—as he really was. Yet Nuada did not go down. With his left arm thrust idly behind him and his right kept extended, he picked off the onslaught of the other, clicking the cuts sharply away, making them slide harmlessly off his steel.

For a time the god did nothing but defend; and to MacDougall, at least, the reason was obvious. Nuada was concentrating on controlling the attack of the Druid. Only Alan, who had experienced what it was like to have his offensive moves made for him, could fully appreciate the wonder of what he saw. The others, perhaps more than he, were aware of the difficulty of what Nuada was attempting.

As time passed, the fury of the Druid's attack increased. Nuada barely parried several high thrusts that hissed past his face, then attacked in turn, his point leaping out like a dart of light. They circled about each other, and the harsh breathing of Arias sounded loudly amid the clashing of the swords. It became evident that the Druid's body could not long be driven in this manner.

There came a diversion. Overhead a black shadow passed, and the watchers heard the flapping of great wings. They looked up to see the huge hoodie-crow swoop by. Evidently, MacDougall thought, Arias in his extremity had been calling for help. He looked back at the duelers as he heard Nuada exclaim, "Morrigu to the rescue!" The god's eyes turned skyward momentarily.

At that instant Arias darted in in wild desperation, sword braced before him in his own attack. The point pierced the fullness of cloth under Nuada's left arm as he escaped death by a breath. Seemingly by instinct, his own weapon plunged into the Druid's breast, and blood spurted.

Dropping Alan's blade and clutching at his chest, Arias sank to the road, the death weapon pulling loose and his life's blood staining the white pebbles a bright red.

"It had to be," Nuada said grimly, wiping his blade clean on the Druid's robe and thrusting the weapon into its sheath. None of the others stirred as he picked up Alan's sword, removed the sword belt from the dying man, and fastened it about MacDougall's waist.

Ignoring the black figure flapping overhead, Nuada looked from Danu to Dagda to Taliesin. "Shall we go?"

They nodded. The four of them encircled Darthula and Alan, their clasped hands forming a chain—there was an impression of blurred flight—and they were standing in a room obviously feminine.

"My home!" Darthula cried and, flinging her arms around Alan's neck, she kissed him.

CHAPTER 9

The Jest of Jests

Beyond the polished silver latticework of the long fence, the rock wall dropped sheerly away to the sapphire waters hundreds of feet below. Another of the scenic spectacles of Tartarus, Alan MacDougall thought as he looked out over the sea, calm as a vast mirror and, like a mirror, reflecting the capers and sarabands of the Dancing Men, the flares, fans, and waves of the aurora overhead. The lights below, in reverse image, differed from those above only in the blue tinge of the reflection. It was beautiful!

At last he turned away, gazing with appreciation at the unusual home of Princess Darthula. Difficult to categorize in modern architectural terms, it suggested a cross between a Swiss chalet and a rather squat, white pagoda. On the sides near the top were dainty little roofed balconies, set on the gracefully curving and uniformly receding tiers of a pagoda. Each tier led back to a wall of sheer crystal, the means of providing light for the interior.

Surrounded by an expanse of the ever-present pale green lawn, the building was set off by carefully placed picture trees like those he had seen during his first glimpse of Tartarus, dwarf trees seemingly inspired by blue willow plates.

Beyond them and to the left and right lay Gorias, a city situated on five peaks. On each of the other four summits were pastel-colored, pagodalike homes; dotting every hillside, randomly placed, with narrow roads winding about between them, were other chalet-pagodas, ranging from two tiers to as many as six. Every color of the spectrum was there, but only in the lighter tones.

Those winding streets, incredibly, were crowded with the Ch'in, both men and women, all in pastel robes, the women distinguishable by their ornately bejeweled mounds of hair. MacDougall could not recall having seen so many people busily doing nothing—unless it was a mass of bargain hunters on a sale day in a shopping mall.

Time to go inside, he thought. Curiosity had prompted his inspecting the grounds, strongly encouraged by a fifth-wheel feeling. After their sudden arrival at Darthula's home, the Princess had gone immediately to have soothing ointments applied to her back. The three gods had found closely arranged chairs and had seated themselves to stare blankly into space. And Taliesin had buried himself in the all-important scroll.

MacDougall reentered through an arched door, opened at his approach by a waiting Ch'in who ushered him into the room in which they had materialized. The three gods, Taliesin, and Darthula were engaged in earnest conversation.

"I don't see how conflict can be avoided," Danu was saying. "Balor is assembling an army of Fomorians, almost the whole male population of Murias, and arming them with lances, swords, and shields. He has succeeded in whipping the grotesques into a near frenzy. They are a savage bunch at best, always ready for a fight." She turned her attention to Alan MacDougall.

"We were doing a bit of observing—" She smiled faintly. "I suppose spying would be a more honest term. As far as we can tell, they haven't located you, though they probably assume all of us are here in Gorias because of Darthula. Of course, it is only a question of *when* they find you, for they can locate us without much difficulty.

"Just before we severed contact, Morrigu left, her destination Findias, where she intends to recruit the Trolls. How successful she'll be only time will tell."

"I am sure she will fail," Nuada said firmly. "I know the small people, and they have no stomach for fighting. But the Fomorians alone will be formidable foemen, make no mistake about that." He paused. "I think we can come to but one conclusion. We will have to meet force with force, and with as strong an army as we can muster. We should mobilize the Norsemen in Falias and the Ch'in in Gorias. Certainly there is no point in waiting for the Fomorians to attack. We can't have the war in the cities. There will be horsemen and foot soldiers, with shields for everyone. If only there were time to train archers—but that would take too long. The Trolls would have to make the bows and arrows for us. That is out of the question."

"May I say a word?" Taliesin interjected solemnly. "I think what I have to report may alter your thinking materially."

All eyes turned toward the Bard, his statement raising questioning brows.

"Of course, my son," Danu said.

Taliesin held up the open scroll, revealing the fine, closely written hieroglyphics. "Our friend Alan found this in the stone tower in the Other World. Later he questioned the Druid Caermarthen about it, and he in turn said it was already in the tower when Lucifer condemned him to endless duty there, guarding the Gates. Over the centuries, he studied it often but could never find the key. Balor stole it from Alan, who recovered it, and gave it to me in Findias; I have been considering it ever since. As you know, I have no small skill in such matters. My first reading led me to a certain distressing conclusion, but because of its nature, I withheld revealing my findings until I could confirm them. I have now done so."

There was deep solemnity on Taliesin's round face and in his voice; not a sound came from the others.

"It is a message written almost certainly by the One variously called the Lord of Light, the Prince of Darkness, and Lucifer—or written at his behest. It verifies what the myths have told us about the Island—his creating this place, its Four Cities, the eternal light of the Dancing Men—everything about what MacDougall calls Tartarus, a world accursed. And all for the Daughters of Lilith. It tells of the winged sons of God, Lucifer's minions, coming to visit.

"Then when men came, with Adam being placed in the beautiful garden, the visitors no longer appeared, and the soulless Dwellers in the Four Cities faded and died. MacDougall tells me they lie as transparent shells in the Hall of the Dead.

"For millennia Lucifer gave no thought to the beautiful world he had made—the proof of his ability to create like God—until he thought of the Great Jest." Taliesin sounded bitter. "And this is the Hell to which we were condemned, a place of eternal monotony, a timeless land where the countless hours drag endlessly. We have new bodies, but with them an inborn terror of death because there might not be another.

"Yet in the minds of all who are leaders was planted a memory, a knowledge, of a Gate! A way back to the old life, where things change, where there is novelty and zest and adventure. This was always an undying hope.

"In the scroll it was foretold that one day a Messenger would come through the Gate wearing the two-headed serpent and knowing the way back. This would be our opportunity! Through the Messenger we would return, full of hope. And then would follow the Jest of Jests.

"Within hours after entering the Other World, these bodies—designed and made for Tartarus—would melt into nothingness! Only a wraith would be left, a spirit condemned to wander, to seek and seek endlessly for it knew not what—but never finding. There would be no worship for the gods, no power, no recognition from those in the Other World, nor even the bare realization of our very existence. We would be ghosts of ghosts, not even capable of haunting dwellings gone and forgotten for a thousand years.

"From one Hell into another would we go—and that one worse—and eternally hopeless!"

A dead silence held unbroken for timeless moments.

"But can we," Nuada finally began, "can we take the message of the scroll as truth? Can we believe anything coming from the One who has been called the Father of Lies?" Then he added weakly, his eyes fixed on Alan MacDougall, "There's proof enough, I suppose."

"So we can't ever leave?" Darthula's question seemed that of a disappointed child. She fingered a gorgeous sapphire pendant.

Danu said gently, "Only if you wish to leave that lovely body."

"Then I suppose," Dagda commented, "there's nothing to prevent MacDougall's departure when he wishes, with none to interfere."

Taliesin laughed shortly. "None except Balor, Morrigu, Dalua, a horde of Fomorians, and a few assorted Druids who know nothing about this scroll!"

"But if we get word to them—"

Nuada shook his head. "You know they have closed their minds to us and will receive no communications from us. And even if they heard, would they believe? They would consider it a trick," he added wisely, "a trick to catch them off guard so we could get out with Mac-Dougall."

Alan had remained silent throughout. The most startling part of the revelation, for him, was the prediction concerning the Messenger wearing the two-headed serpent. It felt odd, his being the fulfillment of a Luciferean prophecy. Why had he been chosen—if he had been, indeed?

In the momentary silence, he spoke.

"I think I have a solution to all of this, simple and direct. With the help of friend Taliesin, I have learned how to become invisible—through the armlet, of course. So we'll have you transport me, invisible, to a point on the Falias road about midway between the crossroads and the City of the North and leave me there. Still invisible, I'll find the Gate, return to my own world, and close the way. Then if need be, I can find some means of destroying this armlet so none may ever again see the Gate—certainly never again open it."

Silence greeted this, to Alan, thoroughly practical suggestion. Then Nuada raised objection.

"It's uncertain. How do we know that the Unholy Three aren't spying on us at this very moment and would be alert to—"

"If they were, I would know," Taliesin interrupted. "But if they were, they know already what we have learned and will have lost interest in Alan. If they believed all this—an uncertain conclusion."

"Even if your plan succeeded, Alan," Danu said, "it still would not prevent the fighting. You forget they are intent on avenging the insults of the dungheap and the fish."

MacDougall exclaimed ruefully, "And that's all my fault!"

At the mixed chorus of "What? You! How?" from four of the five, MacDougall wondered why he had said that. Childish boasting, probably. Only Taliesin had said nothing, eyeing Alan quizzically.

A strange expression appeared on Danu's face, one of suspicion and awakening comprehension.

"Young man, what happened after you vanished from before our eyes? You walked halfway around a circle, disappeared, and reappeared quite a while later. What really happened in the Forbidden zone?"

Alan looked at Taliesin, seeking guidance. The Bard nodded. "We might as well hear it all, even if it is Forbidden. Another shock or two cannot make matters worse."

So MacDougall told them, beginning with his passing through the wall of the Golden Tower, assisted by Ahriman, to his exit, skipping nothing, even including the fear he had experienced in the Tower and as he walked away. His audience seemed to be holding its collective breath. There was no sound, only a change of expression on the face of each, a growing distress, almost consternation.

Darthula was the first to speak. Her cheeks had reddened and her beautiful eyes flashed. "You mean we have *no* privacy—that that monster can see *everything*?"

MacDougall shrugged. "I guess that's what it adds up to. There's nothing hidden from his eyes—if he wants to see."

Suddenly Taliesin's laugh broke the tension, and he sounded genuinely amused. "Danu, Dagda, Nuada—you can do almost as well as that! Oh, maybe not as efficiently, but the spying of you gods leaves little privacy." He faced Alan. "And according to the Christian priests in Scotia, your God sees all and everything is recorded."

Nuada sounded almost cheerful. "Really, nothing has changed. Only now we know about it. What concerns me is their ability to manipulate, even, let us say, to change the course of a battle, to give victory to whom they choose, to take decisions out of our hands."

Danu said hopefully, "I think Alan said they only interfere to prevent catastrophe; normally they let us work out our own problems and play our game our way. In spite of all this, I think we should be making plans to counter the attack of the Fomorians."

"What about my suggestion?" MacDougall persisted. "Why can't I get out of this? Maybe with me gone, if you tell Balor and Morrigu that it was I who insulted them, they'll forget this stupid battle."

Nuada frowned. "I suggest we give it more thought before we come to a decision." With that he spoke to Dagda, making reference to Erus, Druid of Gorias, and the part, if any, he should play in the coming conflict.

Alan turned away in disgust to come face to face with the approaching Darthula. She was smiling warmly. For the first time he was fully aware of her bejeweled adornments. Delicate gold and silver chains, gem-spangled, were laced through her carefully groomed and high-piled hair. Bracelets circled her wrists, ten or more on each, and her fingers flashed with many rings, each a work of art.

"Alan, let me show you something of Gorias. It is a lovely city, so different from the others." At his polite acceptance, she continued. "You'll have to change to something more appropriate; as you are now, you would attract too much attention."

"Sorry," MacDougall protested stubbornly, "but I'm not changing clothes. Perhaps a loose robe over what I'm wearing—it has been done before—but not a complete change."

Darthula bit her lip and began to pout, then changed her mind. "I guess that will do. Just a moment while I find something." She tripped lightly from the room.

"*Alan, Alan, can't you see?*" It was Taliesin's thought touching his brain. "*The reason they are not agreeing to your very sensible suggestion is simple. They want this battle to be fought! They can't leave Tartarus, so that particular change is barred. This is the most interesting thing to happen in an eternity. They hate the Fomorians, always have—and Balor and Morrigu—and they want you to remain as a possible excuse for conflict. Maybe if you were gone and they got through to Balor with the facts, he might quit; though I doubt that would stop Morrigu, who loves gore. But they want war! Have no fear, during the conflict we'll find a way for you to get out.*"

Alan's eyes met those of the Bard and he gave a faint

nod. At that moment Darthula reappeared with a heavy, full-cut, pale blue robe. Long-sleeved, it slipped over his head, after he bowed to the need of parting with his ever-present knapsack. He thought it looked like an old-fashioned baby's nightgown, but it effectively covered his clothes.

Darthula regarded him approvingly. "You are so *tall*, Alan. I had trouble finding something suitable. Shall we go?" She slipped her arm under his and led him out, light and meaningless words flowing from her lovely lips. He listened with half an ear, making noncommittal sounds at appropriate moments; but as they started down the steep and winding street, his mind was busy with a puzzle.

Who could understand women? He had expected her to hate him for that burning lash of Arias, for all the trouble he had brought her—yet she had kissed him resoundingly. He had thought her interest in him hinged totally on her wish, like that of all the others, to leave Tartarus, perhaps aided by the novelty of his background; and now that she knew leaving was impossible, she clung to him like a long-lost lover. Anyway, she was lovely and pleasant to be with. He began to pay attention to what she was saying and to watch the passing scene.

They had gone some distance, winding in and out among a wide range of pagoda sizes, when MacDougall noticed there was a group of perhaps six or eight Ch'in ahead of them and an equal number behind them.

"Don't look now," he said quietly, "but I think we're being followed. And there's a group of men ahead. We are boxed in."

The Princess glanced back quickly and laughed her delight. "Those are my guards, of course. I never go anywhere in Gorias without them." She snuggled up closer to Alan, her left arm clinging more tightly and her right hand closing on his forearm. She looked up at him trustingly. "I feel so safe with you. I think I would feel that way even without the guard. But as I was saying, I think it was just too wonderful that you came to the Island because of me and that you followed me to Murias when Balor had taken me there. Oh, I know all about it. Taliesin told me. And in Findias—oh, I know you couldn't do anything to help me—but we were in it together—" Her girlish chatter went on and on.

Damn Taliesin, MacDougall thought. Anyway, this explained her attitude. And, fool that he was, he liked it!

They had entered an area that differed from anything he had seen in the Four Cities, a small section of what appeared to be shops. He was genuinely interested, wondering what kind of exchange system worked in Tartarus. People ate, wore clothing—even gems, as Darthula amply proved—and had servants. How were all these things paid for?

"A question, Darthula?"

Her gaze met his expectantly. "Yes?"

"How do you buy food and pay your guards? I have seen no sign of money or any other medium of exchange."

She looked disappointed, then puzzled. "Food is provided, of course. And I don't pay my guards or the servants. It is a privilege to be chosen to serve. There are so many of the Ch'in—the Norsemen and Fomorians, too, for that matter—who have nothing to do. Think of it! Nothing to do forever."

MacDougall nodded. That would be awful. "But you say the food is provided. How?"

She looked at MacDougall quizzically. "You are interested in the strangest things. Each city has several food centers, and we take what we need." She pointed toward a shop ahead of them, if shop it could be called. No walls barred entrance to a wide interior. Tables and bins bore quantities of the staple foods of Tartarus—dried and fresh fruit, barley and coarsely milled flour, dried and salted fish. Several of the Ch'in were in attendance; and others, bearing vessels of different kinds, were selecting what they needed.

MacDougall frowned. "But the workers here—Oh, I

know—it's a privilege to be able to work. But why don't the people take more than they really need?"

Darthula was genuinely puzzled. "Why should they? And if they do, what matter? It has been done, of course— but the hoarded food spoils; and even greed dies with endless centuries. After all, there is always enough."

"People farm and trade in grains," Alan objected. "I've seen that. And there are outlaws who rob for a living."

"Food is distributed through central warehouses, and those are in the cities," Darthula explained. "People who choose or are forced to live far from such places must get their food as they can. Besides, farming is a popular way to find occupation. And many believe that the produce gained thus is better than what is distributed."

"But your jewels—surely they have value."

"That is a bit different. For jewels, we barter with each other. Actually, they have no real value, but some of us enjoy them. One gets weary of the same things, so one exchanges with someone else."

"But where did they come from in the first place? Someone had to make them, to cut the gems, to fashion the gold."

Darthula shook her head. "No one asks about that. They were in Gorias, the City of Gems, when we came." She frowned thoughtfully, then added, "I suppose they came from the Daughters of Lilith, whom the Bard speaks about. Some of the Trolls," she concluded, "have begun fashioning gems and fine gold, but the older jewels are finer. The Troll women do our weaving and they, too, are skilled in needlecraft."

Conversation ceased for a time as they moved on into the winding maze of Gorias, through the flow and ebb of the crowds. MacDougall studied the passing faces, seeing a blankness there, a lack of purpose, a bored resignation. He thought of the Fomorians moving stolidly through their zigzag streets, of the Norsemen walking or riding, always moving, and understanding came. They had nothing to do. The Trolls worked, had *made* work. The farmers and fishermen worked. There was purpose to their existence. They had a reason for living. The servants and guards, understandably, were happy to serve. Nothing to do forever—what a *hell* of an existence! No wonder his coming had created so much interest. It broke the boredom. No wonder this beautiful woman wanted him to stay.

"What did you do in the Other World?" the Princess asked in an obvious attempt to make the conversation more personal. "And," she added shyly, "is it proper for me to ask—do you have a mate—back there?"

They had just started on an upgrade when she broached this question, and at that instant MacDougall was startled to see a familiar and unmistakable head rising well above the crowd. Ahriman! The being he had met in the Golden Tower, the "trusted lieutenant" of Lucifer! Mentally he scoffed. He must be mistaken. What would the Persian be doing in Gorias? The head turned, displaying a profile—and it was Ahriman!

"What did you say? I'm sorry. My attention was distracted by that tall man ahead of us. It's the man I met in the Tower. You said—"

Darthula pouted. "You certainly are attentive!" She was annoyed and didn't try to hide it. "I was asking about your life in the Other World. I wondered—" She stopped short. "*What* tall man?"

MacDougall pointed. "The only really tall man in sight. He stands at least a head above everyone else."

Comprehension came slowly to Darthula. "You met him—you mean that monster who spies on everyone?" Suddenly she was interested. "But I don't see a tall man."

"Of course; I'm the only one who can see him. The power of the armlet, remember? The Tower and everything in it were invisible to Danu and Dagda. But what can be his purpose in coming here? It seems so out of character, so pointless." Abruptly he made up his mind; he quickly released his arm, placed his hands on her cheeks, and kissed her forehead.

"I'm going to follow him, try to see what he's up to. I'll find my way back to your home."

Briskly he stepped forward, stretching his long legs. Ahriman had already lengthened the space between them, and the density of the pedestrians made rapid progress difficult. Alan managed to keep the Persian in sight, but could get no closer. Then his quarry turned one of the sharp corners that characterized these streets and Alan thought he had lost him. He tried vainly to pick up speed and reached the corner, to see Ahriman still visible up ahead.

The chase seemed to go on and on, and since most of the way was up steep inclines he began to mind the effects in his legs and lungs. At last, to his relief, the Persian turned toward a large pagoda, probably the most pretentious Alan had yet seen, and vanished from sight.

MacDougall slowed down, satisfied that his persistence had paid off. Undoubtedly Ahramin had entered the place. He approached cautiously, trying to slide inconspicuously into the grounds, which, like Darthula's, were dotted with the distorted trees. He moved behind the dubious screening of one of these and looked back at the passing pedestrians. No one appeared to have noticed him. Moving from tree to tree, he started circling the pagoda.

He came upon a rear door, crept up to it, and heard from behind him a sharp command:

"Don't move!"

Despite the words, MacDougall spun around to face four Ch'in with fixed lances, the points uncomfortably close. Behind them stood a fifth man; and as Alan caught a full view of his face, he started. He knew him!

At the same instant he, too, was recognized, and the man burst out, "Alan MacDougall, by all that is sacred! And you've come to call, though in a most unconventional way. How convenient!" It was Erus, Druid of Gorias.

"That was not my intent," MacDougall said. "That is, I was following—" He broke off, knowing how lame his story would sound, his following a man no one else could see. "Never mind. You wouldn't believe me anyway."

"No doubt I wouldn't," Erus said sardonically. "But welcome. Wang Chou!" he called out.

The door was opened by another of the Ch'in, who stood aside and bowed. As MacDougall stepped forward, Erus checked him. "After some precautions. Chishan and Hsinglan first." Two of the warriors slid past, lances ready, entered, and took their places facing the doorway. Erus bowed. "Your turn, my friend."

With a grin, MacDougall looked at the Druid. "You certainly are cautious enough."

"Somehow," Erus answered, "you have escaped or eluded several of my associates, so I am taking no chances. Enter."

Inside, the Druid addressed the servitor. "A strong cord, Wang Chou, as an added precaution."

"At once, Master." The man left the room.

Alan exclaimed angrily, "Tying me up is ridiculous. And you'll regret it, as did Arias. I hope you don't end up the way he did. I am a guest of Princess Darthula. Fellow guests are members of the *Tuatha De Danann*— the Mother Goddess Danu, Dagda, and Nuada—as well as the Bard Taliesin. They will not view this kindly."

Erus raised jeweled hands in mock consternation. "I fear for my life, but I will brave their wrath! And you expect me to believe such nonsense! After you are securely bound, we will manage, I think, to pry some truth out of you. Will Balor be pleased when he learns about this! The Gate—"

The Druid stopped short as there came a sudden, loud knocking on both front and back doors. In the shocked silence, the clear voice of Darthula cried, "Alan, are you in there?"

"Yes, Darthula," he answered as loudly.

Both doors swung inward to admit what seemed a flood of Ch'in guards, swords in hand. At their heels came the Princess, who rushed up to Alan and clasped his hands.

"You walk *so* rapidly, my dear, I thought we'd never catch up to you. Did you deliver the message to Druid Erus?"

"I—no, not yet. I didn't really have an opportunity." MacDougall checked an admiring grin. "Suppose you tell him."

Darthula faced Erus, who was trying valiantly to hide his combined reactions of shock, chagrin, doubt, and confusion. "He—he arrived just moments ago—and I—I had some questions—" The usually suave Druid groped for words, floundering.

"There is a council of war being held in my home," Darthula said smoothly. "Nuada has called it. Balor is preparing to lead an army of Fomorians against Gorias and Falias. You are to assist Nuada in calling to arms the men of our city to join with the Norsemen of Falias in repelling the attack."

Erus was dumbfounded. His pallid blue eyes stared unbelievingly at Darthula while he tried to grasp the significance of her statement. "Surely you jest. All this for—for—" He glanced toward MacDougall. "For him and the Gate?"

"Of course not. Not for him, but to avenge a fancied wrong. I am sure Nuada will tell you all about it. Will you come with us?"

"Yes—oh, yes. But I can't believe—" He pulled himself together and spoke to MacDougall, silent appeal in his eyes. "I guess I jumped to conclusions, perhaps said things unthinkingly—"

Alan stared steadily at the Druid, then said with an icy smile, "Think nothing of it. A natural mistake."

For the first time, Darthula seemed to notice the men with the lances. "What are these—"

"It is all right," Alan interrupted. "I'll explain later."

Within a short time the Druid was ready to leave; and the group, with its single addition, began retracing its way to Darthula's home. Erus had suggested the desirability of having his own guard, but the Princess had smoothly overruled, saying her men would be more than adequate and would escort him on his return.

Except for the light and cheery monologue of the Princess, to which the two men answered only when they had to, it was a quiet trip. MacDougall was thoroughly annoyed with himself. What a hero he'd turned out to be! He had walked into an ambush, a trap; and if it hadn't been for Darthula and her Ch'in, he'd still be in trouble. Rescued by the damsel in his distress! Damn!

And the actions of Ahriman—what had really brought him out of his Tower? It didn't seem logical to think that his sole purpose lay in leading Alan into the hands of the Druid Erus. Was it perhaps to get the Druid involved in the war? Unlikely. That would have happened in any event. Or maybe the Persian had set in motion plans that would lead to future developments. Who knew? Maybe it was something entirely unrelated to MacDougall's following him. Time would tell—Alan hoped. Time? In this world? *Pah!*

When Erus was brought into the company of the three gods and the Bard, there was a brief moment of questioning surprise. MacDougall covered what could have been an awkward moment with a quick comment.

"Surprised that he came so quickly? He was eager to come. We delivered your message after a bit of difficulty, and here is the Druid to help in raising an army among the Ch'in."

"Fine," Taliesin responded. "I suppose, Erus, we should give you all the details behind this development."

The next several days—assuming that sleeps terminated time periods, though that provided a very irregular calendar—were busy ones for all but Darthula and MacDougall. They concentrated on getting to know each other better.

Nuada and Erus worked together in reaching the Ch'in and preparing them for the conflict. In addition to the lance that every man possessed, they were issued swords and shields. Because these were in short supply, Danu and Taliesin made a quick trip to Findias for additional weapons, at the same time circumventing the attempt by Morrigu to draw the Trolls into the war. Dagda went to Falias, where ancient Moirfhius was pressed into reluctant service.

Surprisingly—or perhaps it wasn't really surprising—both Ch'in and Norsemen welcomed the coming conflict. There was keen excitement in the air, almost a feeling of anticipation, as if some major athletic event were planned between ancient rivals. The fact that death would come to many seemed to be ignored; it was as if only others were threatened. But above all was the release from eternal boredom, already realized and with more change to come.

MacDougall, Nuada, and Erus remained as guests of the Princess during this period, the Druid staying at Nuada's insistence. As time passed, Alan noticed a troubled, haunted expression appear fleetingly on Erus' face. Something was obviously disturbing him.

MacDougall kept his eyes on the man during their moments together, which occurred largely at mealtimes and shortly before seeking sleep. These came at roughly fixed intervals, since both hunger and weariness manifested themselves after comparable exertion. At the same time he made efforts to be cordial, thinking perhaps, since he was the only outsider, Erus might venture to confide in him.

He was busy in another quite extraordinary way after he went to bed. He had succeeded in becoming invisible during his escape from Balor and he hadn't abandoned the idea of escape through invisibility. He needed practice, and his procedure was simple. He concentrated on that indispensable armlet—thinking invisibility, light passing through or around him—then held a hand over his eyes to check. And it worked. The return to normal opacity was simple.

What he wanted was speed. The time might come when

his successful disappearance would depend on near-instant action. Practice produced proficiency; necessary time length shortened; and control approached perfection. At last he was satisfied. To remove all doubt, he found a moment when Darthula's bedroom was empty and, standing before the polished silver sheet that was her mirror, he tried it. He vanished as quickly as thought.

Unfortunately, the Princess selected that inopportune time to return; and when he appeared, he saw her reflection behind him, her eyes wide with astonishment.

"Alan, what are you doing?" She came up to him and caught his hands in hers.

MacDougall tried to make light of the situation. "Oh—excuse my intrusion. I needed a mirror. I was practicing my magic disappearing act. I may be a real asset someday when Morrigu tries to grab me with her talons."

Tears appeared in Darthula's sapphire-blue eyes, and her lips quivered. She was not deceived. "*Must* you leave? We could be happy here together. And the Gate would always be open since only you know the way, should you grow weary of—of Tartarus. Is there someone—?"

Alan knew Tartarus had not been her original thought. Gently he put his arms around her and held her close. "There is no one. And you are very lovely and desirable. But I've grown weary of perpetual dawn. I'm homesick for my own world, for day and night, for storm and calm, for cold and warm and hot—for *change*! And when I've gone, at least one source of conflict will have gone with me. Oh, I can't explain—"

"You have explained." Her voice was muffled against his shoulder. "And I understand."

She turned her tear-lined face up to his. "But, Alan—must it be now? I could make you happy—so happy—I know I could!" Suddenly she pressed her lips against his with a fierce hunger, her arms tightening about him savagely, and he felt her form molding itself to his.

Instinctively he responded to her embrace, his heart racing. Why now, indeed? He opened his eyes to gaze into the violet ones so close to his own. What was the urgency? She was so beautiful—

She drew her mouth away and whispered fervently, "Please, Alan—there is no haste. Time is forever. The years, the centuries—they will be ours."

The years—the centuries! A sudden chill coursed through Alan MacDougall. Fourteen centuries had passed since Darthula had awakened in this perfect body, given life by Lucifer. That knowledge was there and would always be there, to arise like a specter between them.

The Princess sensed the change in him, and simultaneously their clasps relaxed. Gently Alan drew back, grasped her hands and held them.

"You are so lovely, my darling," he said huskily. "I have never met anyone like you and I know I never shall. But there is an instinct within me that tells me I should return to the place whence I came—for the good of your world and mine—and that if I weaken now I shall never be strong enough to go. But I'll never—never forget you."

He kissed her quickly, released her hands, and moved swiftly from the room.

Preparations were complete at last. Danu reported that Balor's Fomorians were moving after the next sleep; and at Nuada's word the horse units of both Norsemen and Ch'in would leave the two cities at about the same time. The gods Nuada and Dagda, both experienced men of war, armed with enchanted weapons, their abilities made well-nigh invincible, would be in the van. The horsemen would adjust their pace to that of the foot soldiers marching behind them.

MacDougall thought this planned encounter at a fixed battlefield quite amusing but he made no comment.

The sleep period ended. With the day of battle at hand, Taliesin, Erus, Nuada, and Alan MacDougall joined in a hearty if somewhat forced breakfast. Little was said, each apparently occupied with his own thoughts. Several times Erus attempted vainly to make conversation, his nervousness quite apparent despite his effort at concealment. Alan ate mechanically, his gaze wandering again and again to the doorway leading to the sleeping area. There was no sign of Darthula.

Breakfast completed, the four mounted their waiting horses and rode to the staging area west of Gorias, a scene of mingled order and confusion. The mounted Ch'in were already in position and were waiting for Nuada, who would ride at their head. Behind them, hundreds upon hundreds of footmen milled about in rough formation. Many, MacDougall observed, bore expressions of eager anticipation; and from them arose occasional loud bursts of laughter.

According to plan, Taliesin would ride at the rear of the cavalry and Erus and MacDougall would march with the infantry, the latter as observers. As the Druid and Alan dismounted, two foot soldiers were ordered into the saddles, joining the mounted ranks. Taliesin hesitated, then he, too, slid to the turf, retaining his hold on his reins.

Erus could no longer hide the terror that had been lurking so close to the surface. His face was pale and shone with perspiration. He could not stand still, and his gaze kept darting around as if he were seeking escape. Nuada, about to ride away, stared down at the Druid and spoke harshly, making no effort to hide his scorn.

"Why are you afraid? You are not required to fight. You can turn and run at any time. But just to be sure you attempt no treachery, consider this. Arias decided on independent action with regard to MacDougall and, unfortunately, he attempted to best me with the sword. I confess I may have had something to do with, shall we say, coercing him into the contest. He was no swordsman, as we know, but I helped him, guiding his sword arm. Alas, my help was not enough. He died. It might be well for you to remember this." Turning his mount, he sped away.

Head down, face hidden, Erus moved slowly through the pale grass to the strip of woodland some twenty feet from the road. MacDougall and Taliesin, standing side by side, watched him go. As the Druid found a seat on a rock, head still bent, the Bard said grimly, "I have long wondered about Erus and the constant hiding of his thoughts. I hope he conceals only his fears." He paused, then added, "Truly it has been said that a coward dies unnumbered deaths."

At that moment the Ch'in began to move along the white road, hoofs and sandals crunching on the pebbles. In moments the foot soldiers fell into a brisk cadence, becoming a marching army.

Abruptly Taliesin put an arm around MacDougall and forced a smile. "Alan, my son, I must leave. But I must tell you first—I understand. You seek an opportunity to return to your own world. And of course if it presents itself, you must take it. Unseen, you will have the means. Go with my blessings. This is not your realm, not your war, and not your problem. Memory of the son of Dougall will remain with me forever—if my existence lasts that long."

Soberly Alan nodded. "What can I say? You have become my friend—like a father or a brother. I regret having to leave you and Darthula, you two among all the thousands of Tartarus. But I feel my being here multiplies your difficulties. I should never have come—"

"Not so," Taliesin interrupted. "Your coming has brought blessed relief from boredom. You cannot conceive how monotonous life in Tartarus has been through the endless dragging times. And you have set in motion events that will have interesting developments for who can know how long in the times ahead. Even the revelation of the scroll—and Darthula's caring...No, my friend, we have gained greatly through your visit."

Taliesin's grip tightened, then his arm released its grip. He looked deeply into MacDougall's eyes.

"Perhaps the wish fathers the thought—but you may return." The Bard's voice sank almost to a whisper as he turned away. "You may return." Mounting his horse, he galloped along beside the marching Ch'in.

Standing motionless, MacDougall thought, Now—go invisible and be on your way. He hesitated, then glanced at Erus. The Druid was watching; Alan decided he'd better not vanish while being observed. He looked back toward Gorias and saw the approaching end of the marchers. Be honest, Mac, he told himself; you know why you're delaying. You don't want to leave without a final word with Darthula.

Then he saw her—or rather, saw three white horses swiftly approaching from the City of the East, the central mount noticeably larger than the others. As the trio drew near, MacDougall's heart leaped. There was Darthula as he had first seen her riding toward Falias at the head of the caravan! With the ornate silver and white harness on the animal, the same regal air as she rode sidesaddle, the palely glittering gems in her fine-spun platinum hair, and her flowing white garments, she was every inch a Princess.

The three left the pebbled road and approached over the turf. Now Alan heard the tiny silver bells, the sound almost lost in the fading cadence of marching men.

Darthula gestured, and her pastel-robed escorts halted. Riding up to MacDougall, she drew rein. She looked beyond him, frowning, and Alan glanced over his shoulder to see the Druid Erus abruptly face the woods. Darthula looked down, removing one white glove, and held out her hand. As Alan grasped it firmly with both of his, she spoke, barely controlling the tremor in her voice.

"I could not let you leave without wishing you farewell. And I do wish you well," she added fervently, "no matter what takes place. And as once you left—and returned— so perhaps you will return—again!" Tears suddenly filled her blue eyes, beading her lashes; her lips trembled. "You will find me—waiting."

Alan tried to speak, but no words came. Darthula began leaning toward him, then swiftly withdrew her hand, wheeled her horse about, and sped back toward Gorias. Torn by mixed desires, his thoughts in turmoil, Alan MacDougall watched until the three white horses merged with the hills of Gorias, silhouetted against the aurora.

He spun around, startled, as a sudden convulsive hand grasped his arm. He met the wild stare of Erus.

"They are mad—all mad! You heard Nuada. He threatened to kill me! That's what he did. And don't you see—the Fomorians can't be beaten. It's Balor! When he bares his Eye—and he will—it is death for all he looks at. And he can look at hundreds, at thousands. He cannot lose!"

The Druid stepped closer to MacDougall and spoke through trembling lips. "I—I prefer to be on the winning side! I have been in touch with Balor—constantly in touch. He knows all I know. All about everything. He helped me close my mind. Now I join him! And you go with me!"

He flung his arms savagely around Alan, then cried shrilly, "Balor! Now is the time! I have him! Take us!"

With the cry in his ears, Alan felt himself lifted and suddenly no longer where he had been. The world seemed to flash about him. He had barely time to work his invisibility magic before the seeming motion stopped.

Erus loosened his arms; and as the Druid relaxed, MacDougall, with all his strength, brought his knee up into the Druid's groin. Erus dropped like a pole-axed steer, doubling in agony, gasping for breath, writhing on the grass. MacDougall, free and invisible, leaped warily to one side.

Balor roared, "What's wrong with you? And where's the man?"

Alan heard the gasping moan of the Druid and his vain attempt to answer, but his attention was directed toward his surroundings. Where was he? Recognition came almost instantly—the plateau east of Murias, just before the descent to the undersea city. He saw Balor astride a great black horse at the head of the mounted Fomorians, behind them the motley mass of the malformed stretching back and back, down the slope. Involuntarily MacDougall marveled at the god's power to transport the two men almost instantly across the miles.

Then he heard Erus whisper, "I had him! I tell you I had him—but now he's gone!"

CHAPTER 10

The Gate Between the Worlds

Balor leaped from his horse, caught the front of the Druid's tunic, and wrenched him erect.

"You *had* him!" The god's face was livid, his black beard bristling. "You *had* him! And yet he escaped. Bunglers, every one of you Druids. I have had enough of failure."

Flinging Erus aside, he reached up, fingering his golden eye patch. Hastily MacDougall moved away from the glowering giant. Erus, still gasping, groveled at Balor's feet.

"No, Master! No!" he screamed shrilly. "Another chance, I beg you!"

The god hesitated, then lowered his hand. "I grow weak in this tiresome world." He signaled to an aide. "Give him weapons. He takes his chances with the foot soldiers. In the front. See to it . . . My horse! We move."

MacDougall heard the beginning of a whimper from the Druid, which was quickly checked as he followed the aide. Putting the traitor from his mind, Alan moved stealthily over the stretch of grass, well toward the front but away from the army of Murias. No need for stealth, of course. Any sound he might make would be lost in the general hubbub. It was difficult to adjust to the idea that he could not be seen. There was only one danger he could think of. He looked back and saw slight marks in the pale grass where he had stepped. If one were watching, it would be a puzzling sight. Fortunately, the grass was wiry and resilient, and the track vanished in moments. And who would be watching?

Still at a substantial distance from Balor's army, he halted and looked back again. The Fomorians were on their way, the god leading, astride his powerful black mount. It was a strange army, Alan thought—"the lame, the halt, the blind" suggested itself—but he knew better. Despite their varied deformities, from all he had heard they were fierce, deadly fighters—heading for a ridiculous battle in a world where an Evil Eye could actually kill! It should have seemed absurd, but it didn't.

Enough! What was *he* going to do? This change in his fortunes, this opportunity, had come so suddenly that he had no plans except to get to the Gate. His first move was simply to proceed with the Fomorians. He had to reach the crossroads, and that was their destination. Since they had to meet the armies approaching from both north and east, it was the only logical place for contact.

He remained on the turf, well away from the road and close to the front of the marchers. As he set out beside the latter, he became aware that the pace was being set by Balor and that to keep up almost required jogging. Indeed, MacDougall quickly found an easy jog more comfortable than the rapid march. After a time, his breathing became somewhat labored and he considered dropping back, but decided against it. He didn't want to reach the crossroads with the fighting already under way. At this speed he should be headed northward before the battle began. A lot different, this, from groping through the fog!

Where, he wondered, were Morrigu and Dalua? Somewhere planning or working mischief, no doubt. Perhaps spying on the forces of Gorias and Falias.

The course was an undulating downgrade for most of the way, recalling to Alan's mind the uphill ride toward Murias. On foot, of course, the distance seemed far greater. But the miles passed rapidly, and at last, ahead, he saw the woods that must mark the crossroads, the woods in which Arias and his caravan had concealed themselves to spy on Taliesin and Darthula.

Balor's great voice called a halt. "We will reach the crossroads before either the Ch'in or the Norsemen. Now you know the reason for the rapid march. You footmen will move into the woods on all sides and hide; when the enemy appears, you will attack from ambush. Get behind as many horses as possible and hack their legs. Engage their footmen and break up their ranks. Forward!"

A simple, obvious stratagem, thought MacDougall, and one that could spell disaster for the forces of the *Tuatha De Danann*. If only there were some way he could warn them. Taliesin had communicated mentally with him; perhaps he could reverse the procedure. If so, it must be through the armlet.

"*Taliesin!*" He concentrated his thoughts on the twin-headed serpent, at the same time visualizing the Bard.

"*Alan!*" MacDougall caught the other's surprised response. Surprise became pleasure as Taliesin continued. "*At last you begin to learn to use the power of your golden snake. Are you all right?*"

"*Quite all right—and on my way to the Gate, unseen. Traveling with the Fomorians at the moment, without their knowledge, of course. We are already at the cross-*

roads. I've just learned that Balor is planning an ambush, foot soldiers attacking from the woods on all sides, their main aim to disable the horses. That includes the north road, so you'd better warn Dagda to be on the lookout. Thought I'd let you know. Couldn't avoid this last bit of meddling."

He hesitated. "There's one other piece of information which may or may not be important. In spite of Nuada's warning, Erus has turned traitor. In fact, he has been communicating with Balor from his first involvement, and now he's joined the Fomorians. No time to explain, but things haven't worked out as he planned. He'll be fighting with the foot soldiers. If you see him, he's one of the enemy."

Alan sensed the Bard's incredulity. "Erus—fighting? But no matter. We, too, are almost at battle point. Thanks indeed for your help; and may good fortune attend you."

MacDougall broke contact. Neither the Ch'in nor the Norsemen were yet in sight; and as instructed, the Fomorian infantry was fanning out, fading into the forest.

Alan veered to the left, setting course at an angle across the woods. It might be interesting to watch the battle, but in fact the whole idea repelled him. Let them have their silly war—just to break the monotony. Though he had played a part in precipitating it, he had no desire to be a spectator. He wanted out—the quicker the better!

A vision of the caskets in the Hall of the Dead flashed into his mind. Three restoration machines would have a busy time very shortly, assuming that the bodies would find their way into the underground system.

He made good progress, keeping the sounds of the Fomorians to his right, letting this aid him in maintaining his direction. He had covered a considerable distance and could see the cleared area of the road to Falias just ahead when he heard shouts and the metallic clangor of weapons. The fighting had begun between the Fomor and the Ch'in, since the Norsemen had not yet arrived. In moments the bedlam of voices, the screams of horses in agony, rose in dreadful volume.

Then above all this rose another sound—hideous, revolting, lacerating—the shrieking of Morrigu, the hoodie, the carrion crow, flapping and fluttering over the conflict, inciting the warriors to greater carnage.

MacDougall came out of the woods to the meadow beyond, the white road stretching away to the north. He looked back and saw above the treetops, not one, but five great black figures, soaring and dipping and screaming in ever-greater frenzy. Dredging into his memory, he recalled Taliesin's mentioning other war goddesses—Fea the Hateful, Nemon the Venomous, Badb the Fury, and Macha, Queen of Battle. Hags of horror.

They were fascinating to watch and nauseating to contemplate. He could not avoid picturing men falling, blood spurting, dying voices screaming. He turned resolutely away and stalked northward through the grass beside the white road.

He reached a rise in the roadway and descended the slope on the other side. The bedlam of sound faded somewhat; he could more easily shut it from his consciousness. He centered his thoughts on his goal, not too far away now. He felt a mounting excitement at the prospect of returning to his own sane world.

Sane? Perhaps that wasn't the right term. He grimaced as he pictured the conflict between nations, no more rational than the one behind him; predators stalking victims through nighttime city streets; children by the thousands starving, while uncounted tons of edibles went into garbage dumps every day; and miserable refugees fleeing war-ravaged lands. Anyway, it was *his* world.

He kept his eyes fixed ahead, expecting momentarily to see the oncoming army of Norsemen. They had to be near. It was true that Falias was farther from the crossroads than Gorias, but not that much farther.

He became aware of an uneasy feeling, a sixth sense telling him he was being followed. He glanced back. There was nothing but empty road and meadow. In sudden concern he looked down at himself—and saw the grass bent beneath invisible feet. He halted, then looked more carefully behind him as the feeling persisted. He fixed his eyes on the turf, following his track until all trace of it vanished. Then his heart leaped.

Where his tracks had been, other footprints appeared, smaller, closer together!

He was being followed by someone who, like him, could not be seen. His thoughts raced as he resumed walking, quickening his pace. Dalua, by all that was holy! Well, there still was some distance to go, which would give him time to decide what action to take.

He thought of his armlet. It had revealed Morrigu in her true form, concealed by the seductive Macha; could it also make the invisible appear? It was worth a try. He walked even faster to put more distance between him and the one following, then turned and stared across the meadow, concentrating on—thinking into—the golden serpent.

There, clearly visible, dark head bent forward, eyes fixed intently on the turf, was Dalua—Dalua, thin shoulders hunched, black-clad, seeming to exude darkness, moving without laughter now, in complete silence. The god was following, of course, to learn the location of the Gate.

Momentarily Alan was tempted to remain where he was and, when the Witless One came close enough, run his sword through him. Good riddance—but that was something he simply couldn't do. He went on.

He heard the approaching army of Falias, then saw the Norsemen appear over the crest of a rise, Dagda stiffly erect on the lead horse. Their coming suggested a possible tactic to throw Dalua off his trail. The horsemen, about two hundred strong, were keeping to the road; but the marchers behind them were spread out, many walking on the grass on both sides. Breath quickening, MacDougall waited until the noise of their approach rose to what he felt was ample volume to conceal his own sounds, then sprang onto the pebble surface and sprinted toward the Norsemen.

Moments before collision, he dashed back onto the grass, continuing to run with all speed just at the edge of the marchers, close enough to touch them. After a time he slowed for lack of breath; but at last he reached the end of the army from the North. Ahead of him lay a long swath of grass flattened by tramping feet; as he trotted along on the beaten area, he thought with satisfaction, "Follow that if you can!"

He looked around and saw only the retreating backs of the marchers; there was no sign of Dalua.

He began watching for the telltale landmarks. He should be getting close. At last he saw the first one, the rock by the roadside. His heartbeat quickened with anticipation. But he must be certain; he could not afford to waste time in fruitless hunting and give his shadow the chance to catch up.

He had made no mistake. There was that lone tree standing apart from a group of others that grew in a tight clump—then the long slope beyond it—and above him, the boulder with graduated stones stretching away from it. This was the place!

He wanted to shout. He was so close to freedom! Exuberantly he dashed toward the huge rock, then halted as if he had hit a stone wall.

The dancing lights had gone out! Suddenly there was no aurora, only blackness—complete, utter, unbroken blackness!

MacDougall froze. It was the most shocking experience of his lifetime. Nothing could have been more unexpected, nor more inexplicable.

Inexplicable! How could he forget Ahriman in the Golden Tower! With the model of Tartarus and that all-seeing eye! And the Tower was the source of all power!

Staring into the blackness, alone in the complete silence, only his own breathing and the thudding of his heart audible, Alan MacDougall began to put the pieces together.

In his memory he saw Ahriman and heard him say, "We welcome your participation; we trust your stay will be a long one." He thought of the outrageous offer the Persian had made—limitless power, rulership of this little world—and of the offer withdrawn "for the present."

Again he heard Taliesin telling of the reading of the scroll and the prophecy regarding the Messenger "wearing the two-headed serpent and knowing the way back." He tried to recall the Bard's precise statement:

"This would be opportunity! Through the Messenger we would return, full of hope. And then would follow the Jest of Jests. Within hours after entering the Other World, these bodies ... would melt into nothingness! Only a wraith would be left ... ghosts of ghosts."

The prophecy said they would return. Not could, not might, but *would*. It had been predicted by Lucifer that others would go with Alan through the Gate.

If he went alone and closed the Gate as he intended, the Jest of Jests could never happen. The prophecy of Lucifer would not be fulfilled!

But he had never been meant to return alone.

Now the appearance of Ahriman in Gorias made sense. He had deliberately been leading MacDougall into a trap that was supposed ultimately to deliver him into the hands of Balor. Alan's escape, however, had not been foreseen. He could not verify it, but he was certain that somehow Dalua had been set on his trail by the Persian. And his eluding Dalua had led to this ultimate drastic step—shutting off the aurora.

Drastic? That was a weak word.

He thought of the consternation that must have struck into thousands of hearts. It must have been a tremendous shock even to Balor, Nuada, Danu—all the gods, in fact—though perhaps not as great for those who knew about the Golden Tower. He tried to visualize Morrigu and her other crows in midflight. Imagination failed.

Only the Trolls in their underground warrens would have escaped the terror. Others must think their world was coming to an end. Maybe the Fomorians left in Murias—but what if the radiance in the glowing walls and the aurora linked, with even that light gone? It was pointless to conjecture. The significant fact remained that this was a step with only one purpose—

To prevent his leaving Tartarus!

He had not moved since blackness had fallen. He pictured his position, visualizing himself with relationship to the boulder toward which he had started. He began to move ahead, step by careful step, crouching, arms extended, groping. The fog had been bad; this was far worse. After each step he paused, feet planted, arms moving about as far as he could reach on every side. The rock—if he could reach the rock—

Its roughness grazed his fingertips. He grasped it and clung to it. Blessed anchor!

Strange, how alien everything seemed in this blackness. Never had he felt so helpless, so disoriented. His one consolation was that everyone else on the surface of Tartarus must feel the same, or worse. He stood unmoving, trying vainly to pierce the dark. He looked intently in the direction where he thought the Gate must lie.

Out of the corner of his eye he caught a faint wink of light! It came and went so quickly he decided it must have been his imagination, or a trick of an ocular nerve.

It happened again!

He stared fixedly at the spot; and when the light repeated a third time, hope flared. What could it be? It was like the flicker of a match behind a one-way mirror. As quick as a lightning flash—and that was what it was! he thought jubilantly. Lightning had struck outside the doorway of the stone tower, and he was seeing a flicker of light that would have been as nothing in less than this utter darkness.

Could he be sure? Sure enough to venture away from the anchor-rock? He waited, holding his breath. The flash came again, brighter, gone instantly but leaving a momentary afterimage that was definitely a disk. It had to be the Gate.

Fixing the position in his mind, he stepped out into the silent blackness. Every muscle was taut, every nerve stretched to snapping. If only the flashes continued... There came another, directly ahead. More confidently, he lengthened his stride. His only concern was to avoid the rocks of his own placing. Another faint flash—

With bone-chilling suddenness, there burst through the silence a shrill, triumphant peal of wild laughter. Dalua—close at hand!

MacDougall froze, straining to hear sounds of motion, to sense the position of the Dark One. The laugh—did it mean that his location had been detected, or that Dalua had seen the flashes of light beyond the Gate? And had he realized what they meant? If the latter was true, only speed mattered.

Another flash—another burst of laughter—and MacDougall, casting aside all caution, sprinted toward the Gate. At that instant, with a blinding impact, the aurora reappeared. Ahriman had turned on the lights.

MacDougall, seeing his own arms flailing, knew invisibility was gone. There was no concealment now, only escape. The Gate was so close. He heard running feet at his heels, heard the bellow of Balor, the shrill cackle of Morrigu, and other, rapacious female voices. The gods had arrived through instant transfer, summoned by Dalua.

There was the last small rock—and MacDougall flung himself head first into the unseen opening, landing hard, arms braced, on a flagstone floor. Was he hurt? No time to check. He rolled over, leaped erect—and saw between himself and the round opening, outlined against the aurora, a group of small men with flashing swords and raised shields. They laughed joyously as they wove a curtain of bronze before the Gate, barring entry to the hulking figure silhouetted against the undulating light.

With sudden hope, MacDougall realized that the gods

of the Fomorians had none of his foreknowledge; for them to leap into the unknown as he had done required an abnormal degree of abandon. So they hesitated—and that infinitesmal hesitation had given the little men time to act. Little men? They were that—smaller even than the Trolls. But they were there—and they were on his side.

Blades met glancingly in the dark, and Alan thought of the bell-like chiming that had led him up the hillside that morning ages ago.

Repeated flashes of lightning outside the stone tower made visible a blackly bearded face peering through the opening; a brighter flash clearly revealed a gold band and eyepatch, the patch raised. Obliquely MacDougall saw the balefully glaring eye—which vanished as a bronze blade darted out like an adder's tongue and buried itself in the staring orb.

A maddened scream of agony rang through the tower, shrill and high as a woman's, clear above the roar of thunder. Balor fell away from the opening, knocking over someone behind him.

Another head appeared in the Gateway—the angular, wrinkled visage of the crone Morrigu, sharply revealed by a lightning flash. Again a bronze blade darted out. Alan heard an agonized shriek ending in a choking cough and a burst of blood; at the same instant, several other female heads and shoulders crowded into the aperture, one still encumbered by a pair of great batlike wings. And from them came a chorus of savage, eager cries as they tried to claw their way past the others.

The cries turned to screams of pain and rage as the blades darted among them. Their sheer weight, it seemed, must force entry; indeed, one black-clad torso with two wildly waving arms and, above it, a great membranous wing joint were halfway through when the scramble for exodus began. The merciless rain of thrusting blades cleared the Gateway in moments. In that instant, even as a burst of eerie laughter from the other side of the opening vied with a crash of thunder, MacDougall sprang to the wall and flung shut the dimly seen bronze Gate.

A sudden hush fell, broken only by the sounds of heavy breathing and the steady rush of wind-driven rain pelting the Highland oaks. Momentarily the lightning and the attendant thunder had subsided.

A tangible feeling of relief swept over Alan MacDougall. Reaction sent him reeling against the wall and he began to laugh boisterously. He thought of Dalua and checked the outburst. Jubilantly he shouted, "I made it! In spite of hell and high water, I made it!" Then he sobered. There had been no high water, but he had been closer to the other part of the figure of speech than he ever wanted to be—perhaps even in it!

His surroundings began to register on his senses. The storm outside had renewed its fury, muffled slightly by the stone walls, but coming through the tunneled doorway with little frenzy lost.

He stood listening to the shrilling of wild winds ripping through the forest. The crackle and roar and rumble of nature's big guns blasted from mountain to valley, to rebound and reecho from slope to crag in a mad contest between cosmic gunners. The lightning flashes followed one another so closely as to be an almost continuous flare. Alan was glad he was sheltered from that fiery electrical nightmare; he was also glad to sense all of it.

The radiance funneling through the doorway set his attention on the others in the round chamber. The place was full of little swordsmen! It was strange that his mind had been so slow to recall their presence. Startled, Alan glanced around a half circle of short, green-clad men ranged around the wall, facing him. Each bore a leaf-shaped sword and a circular bronze shield.

"Who—who are you?" he asked, speaking English, he realized, instead of the strange tongue that had been his in the other world.

A small figure stepped forward and spoke, his voice not what Alan had expected; it was strong and of medium pitch. His words came slowly, as if they were unfamiliar, long unused.

"We are the Sidhe. There are others to whom men have given the name—but we are the Sidhe. Not many of us are left in the Highland forests. I was your brother Malcolm. I cannot tell you how the change took place, the enchantment that bound me in—your form; but I was your brother Malcolm. Now I am Cinel Loarn.

"I knew you when you came searching. I helped lead you to this tower. I knew about the Gates. We were here unseen when you went into the other world. And we have been on guard ever since to prevent entry of those who should not return. Now that you are back, the Gate should remain closed.

"Alan, do not grieve for me. I am happy. I am here, and here I belong. I would not return, were I able. And now we leave. Farewell."

Mentally groping, trying to grasp the incredible, MacDougall said inanely, "In—in this storm?"

"We are of the woods. We revel in storm." Then he and his companions were not there anymore; they had vanished.

Alan thought he heard faint sounds of movement and felt a feather touch on his hand. Then he was truly alone.

He moved over to the heavy oak table and half sat on it, trying to bring order to his chaotic thoughts. Little Mac, now actually one of the little people—how could that be? He saw again in memory the parchmentlike cadaver he had buried under the cairn and heard the words uttered only moments before: "I was your brother Malcolm. Now I am Cinel Loarn." Without his exposure to all he had experienced in Tartarus, this last revelation would have had him doubting his sanity. How explain it? A changeling—

He cringed suddenly as the thunderbolt of all thunderbolts burst about him. A searing lance of the most intense brilliance exploded in a vast gout of light in the room itself, and Alan MacDougall felt himself swept aside as if by a giant fist.

Blackness of another kind closed on his consciousness.

Alan MacDougall opened his eyes to stare into gray shadows. Mental blankness in moments gave way to a vivid recollection of his last conscious instant—that monstrous lightning blast. He stirred in discomfort, rolling over on his back. He must be lying on the stone floor of the tower. He listened for sounds of the storm, but heard instead the rustle of leaves stirring in a gentle breeze. Tentatively he moved his arms and legs; except for some stiffness, he seemed to have suffered no damage. He looked around; subdued sunlight was entering the doorway. To one side and above him, he saw heavy splintered planks that had been the tabletop on which he had been seated.

Lucky I'm alive, he thought.

Carefully he stood up, his eyes instinctively seeking the bronze disk that had given him entry into the other world. He saw only the rough wall. Quickly he scanned the room; of the Gateways there was no trace. He thought of the armlet and concentrated on the serpent, but there was no change. Unconsciously he grasped the golden spiral, which turned easily about his arm, no longer clinging. Its strange power was gone.

He moved closer to the wall, then suddenly crouched, staring intently at darker shadows on the rough rock. He swung his knapsack around and found his flashlight. As he trained the bright beam on the wall, MacDougall caught his breath and felt a sudden chill.

Crimson stains colored the rock—blood, unmistakably. There was a splattering on wall and floor—but more startling than the presence of the blood was the shape of the main spot. Extending upward from a small puddle on the floor, it was an irregular blotch twelve to fifteen inches wide—uneven except for its upper edge. That was a perfect inverted arc, outlining what must have been the bottom of the Gateway! Almost reluctantly, he touched the wall above the curve and felt only cold stone.

Abruptly Alan turned away and strode to the tunnel exit, crouched, then moved out into the morning sunlight filtering through the forest. He found the boulder that once before had proved a seat for his meditation. For moments he sat there motionless, trying not to think, absorbing the sensations awakened by his surroundings. There was a fresh smell of woodland after rain, a cool breeze stirring the oak leaves high above, and the faint sound of a distant bird.

Finally, somewhat relaxed, he started with that fateful morning when the singing blades had awakened him to lure him to the mountainside. He began to relive his fantastic experience. He glanced at the cairn marking Malcolm's remains; he thought of Cinel Loarn, who had spoken for the Sidhe, the swordsmen with their dancing blades guarding the Gateway in the lightning glare. He saw again the intruding Fomorian gods repulsed and the bloody wall that was proof of the encounter.

A question occurred to him. Why hadn't the little men passed through the Gateway and entered Tartarus? He was certain they could have done so—and perhaps they had. But why should they? *They* wouldn't have been drawn by a beautiful face; and strange as it seemed, they were part of this world, his world, and not the land created by Lucifer.

Alan thought of that creation and its beautiful cities—crystalline Falias, quaintly Oriental Gorias, Murias Under the Sea, and Findias of the White Spear. Strange, torch-lighted Findias, set in the Desert of Gloom, was a city of which he had seen so little. He recalled the Hall of the Dead with its endless rows of cadavers and the transparent chests that enclosed pellucid female occupants.

He thought of the Gateway—no, Gateways, for there had been four bronze disks on the wall. Were all of them entries into Tartarus? Or did the other three lead into other lands of Lucifer's design? Suddenly he shook himself. He never wanted to know.

Inevitably his thoughts turned to the dwellers in the Land of the Dancing Men: Taliesin, the Bard of Bards, who had been friend of friends to him; the Princess Darthula with her Dresden-doll loveliness; Ahriman, self-styled—and probably—lieutenant of Lucifer, with his chilling powers; the sundry gods of that strange island; the Norsemen, the Ch'in, the Fomorians, and the Trolls—and he had left them in the midst of a war whose outcome he would never know.

But could well surmise! With both Balor and Morrigu out of the fight, victory would be assured for the *Tuatha De Danann*. And it could well be that with those two gone, Tartarus might be a better place for its dwellers. Certainly it could be no worse. Alan brightened and grinned faintly. In any event, it certainly would be different, and that in itself was an improvement. This, at least, his visit had accomplished.

Alan MacDougall's stomach brought him back to an awareness of his surroundings. The joyous chuckle of the mountain stream rushing down its rocky channel made him realize his thirst. He stood and headed toward what had been a rivulet, now triple its breadth from the downpour of the night before, and drank deeply of the icy water. As for his hunger, there was nothing he could do about breakfast until he found people, and that meant making his way off this mountaintop.

Flashlight in hand, he returned to the interior of the tower. He had left a large part of his gear there when he entered Tartarus; he'd need all of it now. Everything was just as he had left it. He made a sweep of his torch for a last look at the place where he had found Malcolm, the place that had led him into an unparalleled adventure—and for a last glance at the crimson blotch on the wall—

The blood was gone!

Doubting his senses, Alan MacDougall crossed the

flagstone for a closer look. The bloodstains had vanished! Had he imagined seeing them? He knew he hadn't. He groped for an explanation, then suddenly found it. Here was the fulfillment of the Jest of Jests, as foretold in the vellum scroll:

Within hours after entering the Other World, the bodies of the Tartarians, made for Tartarus, would melt into nothingness. Only a wraith would be left . . .

Even this shed Tartarian blood had faded into nothingness!

MacDougall had had enough of this place!

Outside, he went immediately to the big boulder, placing all his belongings on the flat-topped surface. He put his sword beside the sleeping bag, then slid the armlet off, examining it in a bright beam of sunlight. Beautiful workmanship—but now only so much gold, the eye gems four unusual, polished oval cabochons, the crimson tongues carved rubies. Nothing more. He placed it with the sword.

He stripped, took a rapid, breathtaking ice-water bath, put on his spare outfit, and combed his hair and beard. He filled his canteen, then repacked knapsack and backpack, stowing away the armlet and, as best he could, strapping the sword to the outside of the pack. He found his watch, again ticking, and put it on his wrist, setting it by sun and guesswork.

All set for travel, he paused for a silent moment before the cairn, then headed for the eastern slope of the mountain, following the way opposite that of his ascent. He was hungry, and food was two days away by the route he had used to get here. Certainly this course could take no longer for him to reach a meal; it might even be shorter. He cast a final glance at the tower; then, with eyes fixed steadfastly ahead, he began his hike.

There was no path to follow other than the natural aisles between the trees; but since the way led downward and there was no heavy undergrowth, he made good progress. The stand of oak ended, to be followed by a forest of pine. He was about to enter the evergreens when a faint, familiar sound brought him to a halt. He listened intently.

There it was—the high, clear chiming of the singing blades, as if Malcolm and his fellow Sidhe were bidding him farewell. The bell notes faded into silence. For minutes he stood there listening, but the sound was not repeated.

He entered the pines, the sharp tang of resin immediately assailing his nostrils, the soft carpet of fallen needles strange underfoot. A hush veiled the world; and now Alan was aware of the green-gloom he had missed in Tartarus. Somewhere a bird sang, and bright sunbeams filled the gaps between the trees. Overhead, through the green branches, he saw patches of vivid blue.

The pines merged into white-barked birches, their clean green leaves fluttering in an intermittent breeze, freighted with the fragrance of an unseen meadow. Below lay an expanse of moorland, the approaching slopes golden with mounds of gorse. He saw a bright blossom detach itself from a thorny bush—or so it seemed—to dart across his line of sight. He knew he had seen a yellowhammer in flight. He lost sight of it, but heard its cheery *sweet, sweet, sweet* rising from a clump of gorse. Nearby a thrush burst into its flutelike song, exuberant, full of the joy of living. Another answered in kind.

As if it were a tangible thing, Alan MacDougall felt a burden rise from his shoulders. This world, despite all its shortcomings, all its conflicts, all its unrighted wrongs, was a wonderful place. For here was a world of hope and purpose where a man could *do* things, where there were always new things under the sun!

How differently he saw things now! He'd always considered himself a practical, hard-headed Scot; he knew now that there was a lot—a tremendous lot—that he didn't know. There was much outside the mundane, much that he could learn, much for him to think about.

Whistling cheerily and walking with quickened stride, Alan MacDougall continued through the gorse and across a stretch of budding heather to a narrow country road leading into the world of men.

ABOUT THE AUTHOR

Lloyd Arthur Eshbach was born on a farm in southeastern Pennsylvania on June 20, 1910. He still lives in Pennsylvania and has spent most of his years in the same area. He began reading science fiction and fantasy in 1919 with the fanciful tales of Edgar Rice Burroughs, A. Merritt, and their contemporaries in the pages of the Munsey magazines. He wrote his first salable SF story in 1929 and in the 1930s became a "big-name" writer. He began publishing SF books as Fantasy Press in 1947. Although he was not the first specialist publisher in the field, he was the first to present a full line of science fiction titles. His own writing, always a spare-time effort, included, in addition to SF, tales of fantasy and the supernatural, mystery stories, adventures, romances, and juveniles, some published under pseudonyms. With his entry into publishing, his writing became quite sporadic, and his last story appeared in 1957.

After the failure of his publishing venture—a fate met by all of the SF specialist houses—he became an advertising copywriter, a religious publisher, advertising manager of a major religious publishing house, and a publisher's sales representative.

In 1978, in retirement, Eshbach began writing again, his first effort being *Over My Shoulder: Reflections on a Science Fiction Era*, a memoir of his life in SF, concentrating on the history of the fan hardback book publishers of the 1930s, 40s, and 50s. This was issued in a limited edition in 1983. He completed E. E. "Doc" Smith's last novel, *Subspace Encounter*, left unfinished at Doc's death in 1965, which was also published in 1983. Now he is engaged in writing a four-novel fantasy, the first volume of which is *The Land Beyond the Gate*.

Piers Anthony's
THE MAGIC OF
XANTH

For those who like their fantasy adventures
laced with humor.